HANDFUL

OF

Also by Janie Franz

The Bowdancer Saga

The Bowdancer

The Wayfarer's Road

Warrior Women

The Lost Song Trilogy

Verses

Refrain

Coda

The Premier

Sugar Magnolia

Ruins Discovery

Ruins Artifacts

Ruins Legacy

HANDFUL

OF

DiRT

JANIE FRANZ

Per Bastet

Handful of Dirt

Published by Per Bastet Publications LLC, P.O. Box 3023 Corydon, IN 47112

Cover by T. Lee Harris
ISBN 978-1-942166-78-8

Available in trade paperback and DRM-free ebook formats

HANDFUL

OF

DiRT

DEDICATION

To Gen Olivas. The world will miss your snarky wit and your caring heart. Soar with the angels, my friend.

ACKNOWLEDGMENTS

My special thanks and utmost respect go out to:

Lt. Gen Olivas, a corrections officer at the Dona Ana County Corrections Facility, Las Cruces NM, who gave me deep insights into the dangerous job she faced every single day and often offered up a story or two that I snatched and amended here.

M.G. Barreras, retired Lieutenant, Albuquerque Police Department and currently assigned to the UNM Police Department, who opened a door into the life of law enforcement families and into the day-to-day experiences of officers from uniforms, Kevlar, and utility gear to paperwork and patrols. Also, Lt. Barreras gave me a tour of the Santa Fe Police Academy where she once taught and allowed me to ride in a police car to attend an officer's funeral. In addition, Lt. Barreras provided me with insights into the workings of private investigators, since she also works as one.

KB Bynon, a field deputy medical investigator for the Office of Medical Investigation (OMI) in Albuquerque, NM, and a 40+-year first-responder, paramedic, and educator, who offered special expertise in conducting field investigations and in the duties of paramedics and EMTs.

Dr. Stephanie Lucero, Home Town Doc, Santa Fe NM, for her medical expertise in consultation and tracking down vital information needed to provide authenticity for this work.

Judy Rosenstein, a retired Albuquerque and Chicago public defender, who allowed me to pick her brain about all of the nuances of practicing law in another state and how that can be done.

Musician Chris Arellano for showing me the breadth of Nortano music and first introducing me to *Puno de Tierra* at the Music on the Mesa Festival in Taos NM. Check him out at: http://www.chrisjarellano.com. There are clips of that song there and on YouTube.

Writers Matt Leyshan and Stuart Clark for showing me the beauty of creating small scenes, each from a different point of view, and how those can still keep the plot moving. Thank you, Matt, for encouraging me to try it and to work with an outline for the very first time.

And finally, Rebecca Gowlan, Tim Thompson, and Tina Jakob, instructors, of the Forensic Archaeology and Anthropology at Durham University in the UK and Graham Pik and Zoe Walkington instructors in Forensic Psychology at the Open University in the UK. These online courses were especially helpful, as well as my previous experience at archaeological digs in Nevada and South Carolina.

Caveat: I wanted to acknowledge the real geographical places used as locations in this work of fiction (Payson AZ, Chama NM, Dulce NM, Abiquiu NM, and Espanola NM), as well as offices (the OMI, the forensics lab in Santa Fe, the Rio Arriba County Sheriff's Office, and the Jicarilla Apache Tribal Police Department). Their use in this work is done with respect and should not reflect in any way on the people who live and work there or on the critical work of law enforcement that is done within those offices. The configurations of some of the offices in this book are fiction.

The stories of aliens and animal mutilations around Dulce, however, have been embedded in local lore for generations, just as the sightings and stories told around Roswell, NM.

Chapter One

Day 1: Sunday, past midnight, near Dulce, NM

The old man raised his face to look at the night sky, only dimly illuminated by a partial moon. Studded with clusters of tiny sparkling gems, the sky made the old man smile. Those twinkling lights were spread out like the many presents on his great-great-granddaughter's name day quilt that night. She had gotten a good haul to start her journey of life. He tipped the bottle of tequila in his right hand to his mouth, taking a long swig, letting the top-shelf liquor burn his gullet on its way to join the rest of the bottle in his aching stomach. Though the old ulcer rebelled, he released a satisfied sigh, pleasure mixed with pain. His great-granddaughter's husband, Alphonso, had spared no expense for the celebration, stocking in four cases to supply all of the extended relatives.

The old man chuckled, remembering how he'd avoided the bar during the party so the Old Woman wouldn't yell at him there and all the way home. He'd expertly swiped one bottle, stuffing it under his jean jacket as everyone made their goodbyes on the porch. That always took forever as blessings and forgotten news were shared. He'd slipped out the back door and took the path into the bush, stumbling through the landscaping of Alphonso's massive four-bedroom adobe home just outside the tribal boundary. It was supposed to be a shortcut to the trailer he shared with the Old Woman beside the garden she'd have him hoeing when the sun came up. He chuckled again. It was good to be fortified and alone all morning, working outside where the Old Woman's complaints would drift off onto the wind.

Staring up at the night sky once more, the old man realized he'd gotten turned around a bit. The sky was wrong. He blinked a few times, reorienting himself, turning his body as he stared, his mind taking in the starry expanse and feeling small. He grunted and began to sing. The words were old and from a culture not his own, though he understood the language. He'd learned to speak Spanish long ago to win the Old Woman's heart. He grinned, remembering that sweet smile she once had and her buxom charms she soon showed to him. It made him bellow the words louder. He'd heard the song on the radio sung by a *Norteno* musician from a northern New Mexico family that should have had as much press as the Al Hurricane clan. Those songs moved the old man, even the *ranchera* and country ones that the Old Woman liked to dance to on the kitchen floor as he pulled her fleshy body close to his. But on this night, the words hit him in the gut like the tequila. *No mas un puno de tierra.*

The old man's feet tripped over the uneven ground as he sang to the heavens, spinning his body with arms wide, belting the words through his raspy, aging throat. He landed hard near a boulder hidden by bushes, smashing the bottle over a booted foot. As he raised his hand, bloodied now, he stared at it, nearly blind in the dark, as the tequila soaked into the dry earth. The old man patted the boot that was not his.

"Well, my friend, I can't offer you a last drink."

The old man pushed himself up and leaned back against the hard rock. He offered his bloody hand to the figure with the worn Stetson covering his face. When there was no response, the old man patted the man's chest. "No matter. You sleep it off." He sang out that fateful last line of the song and added, "We're just a handful of dirt, my friend. Just a handful of dirt."

The old man's head began to droop as his eyes closed, sleep letting his body slide against the figure in the darkness.

Chapter Two

Day 1: Sunday, morning, near Payson, AZ

Kate stared vacantly out the window over the sink in the farmhouse as her hands absently rubbed years of cooking oils off a ceramic chicken. The detergent in the warm water did more work than her efforts, though she gave it a good measure.

"You're going to wash the paint right off that rooster," Toni said, coming up behind her.

Kate jumped at her wife's presence, startled out of her own reverie and not having noticed Toni's ever-soft footfalls. Only when Toni rested a hand on the smaller woman's hip did Kate let out the breath she'd been holding. She looked up at the blue eyes in the brown face she still found so startlingly incongruous but had grown to love over the years. "I know," she admitted. Turning back to the brick-a-brac she was washing, she withdrew the ornamental rooster and placed it on the drainer. "Dutch loved those chickens so much. They're all antiques now."

Toni turned her wife to look at the smaller woman's face. "He'll be here. You don't have to wash the entire contents of this kitchen."

"I thought Allen would be here first thing."

"His plane came in late last night. I checked. It was delayed. He probably had a late breakfast with his father. You know it takes a while to drive up from Phoenix, and that old truck I left him isn't a stallion anymore. You can't push that engine."

Kate nodded, placing her damp hands on the worn suede vest Toni wore over her blue plaid shirt. "I know. I just want him here finally and for always, teaching in the fall and no more flying back East for college."

Toni twisted her head to look at her. "That's right. So, let the boy savor the city for a while yet before becoming a part of the landscape here."

Kate grunted out a laugh and looked up. "You're right. And, well, this may just be a pause before he flies off to somewhere else to follow whatever dreams he has."

"Our son's dream has always been to come back here and teach. He's desert-born. He'll stay."

"You're so confident about that. You certainly didn't stay where you were born."

"And neither did you. This country drew us here."

Kate nodded. "And Dutch's generosity helped us stay. I have no idea why she willed this ranch to us. We weren't her kin."

"Allen was special to her."

"Allen was — is — special. Period."

Toni smiled. "He'll be here soon. Then you can spoil him for ten minutes before he slips into that ancient wisdom of his. He must have driven his professors crazy. My grandmother was sure impressed with him back home in New York state."

"But she rode him hard."

"You bet she did. She didn't want him to turn out like me."

Kate put her arms around Toni's neck and rose on tiptoes to kiss her. "You aren't so bad, big boy."

Chapter Three

The ranch pickup sped along the two-lane blacktop into a landscape of gently rolling hills and forgotten roadside buildings. Allen leaned back into the worn leather seat, his left arm resting on the open window, as he took it all in. Home. At last. Or near enough to it.

His plane had come in later than he had expected so he headed up I-17 to stay the night at a motel near Camp Verde. It was an extra expense, and he'd even had a late breakfast before getting on the road, but he didn't want to deal with his father's family just yet on his final homecoming. It was a blessing the plane had been delayed by a storm before his last leg there. Besides, there was a particular smile he wanted to see in Payson first. Unlike himself, she was totally into her career with big ambitions and would soon outgrow the law office she worked in. Sweet Caroline had just been promoted to partner at Sandra Lopez' modest law firm that served the Apache nation, and she longed for that big-profile case that would make her name.

Though he grinned, Allen shook his head. The last thing he needed or wanted was high-profile anything. His whole life had been a study in how to remain under the radar. He'd taken the job as a private investigator the summer he came home from his freshman year at college because Sandy needed someone with his particular abilities on her team. She'd helped him get his license, and it provided a better income than working at a summer camp or being a teaching paraprofessional for summer school kids. Though he would teach history at the local high school in the fall, he still wanted to do more with his abilities than know when a teenager was lying about why he hadn't turned in his report. Sandy made sure his hands were in things that kept his abilities honed; though most of those things were cases that dealt with land deeds, domestic violence, and property damage, usually involving women who felt powerless. They weren't high-profile, but important. He felt useful.

Allen flipped on the radio. Toni always left it set on a *Norteno* station. He missed the music of this land, though his college roommate called it circus music, with the accordions and ompahs. Allen had tried to educate him that it was a mix of all sorts of influences like Cajun and Zydeco and that the ompah really was the beat of *cumbia* that had origins in South America and the Afro-Caribbean region, particularly Cuba, that had gotten all mixed in Mexico to form what is danced to today. His roomie had thrown a towel at him to shut him up after an extensive musical lecture. Allen had written his honors thesis on the use of cultural music in the classroom to reach at-risk kids. He wondered if Caroline liked to dance.

The town of Payson crept up on him in his musings. It wasn't like him to lose track of his surroundings, but sweet Caroline was a pleasant distraction. He swung through some side streets and finally ended up in the parking lot of a strip mall where the law offices were located. Parking well away from the office door as a courtesy to customers, though there never were very many at once, Allen got out, slammed the old truck door, and headed for the office.

"You're back," the young Apache woman in her early thirties, her mane of dark hair, carefully tamed into a tight, scrupulously neat French twist, spat out. Dressed in a crisp, navy business suit, she abruptly left the room with several folders and a slight swing of her hips.

Once more, Allen shook his head. The epitome of cool. Uh-huh. He remembered one steamy embrace the night before he flew out last August for his final semesters of school. It had almost led to something both of them would have had trouble explaining to family or themselves.

"What are you doing here?" Sandy Lopez said as she entered, looking him up and down. She was as elegant as sweet Caroline, both with that native beauty, but she had found her personal style and herself probably at a much earlier age. Dressed in a denim skirt, a red embroidered Western blouse, and suede boots, she looked more like a model than a lawyer. But underneath that comfortable exterior was a cunning mind that often shut the mouths of arrogant, important men.

"And a good morning to you, too."

"Your mama's gonna have your hide if you don't get out to the ranch. What are you doing here, anyway?"

"I wanted to check in and tell you I would be available for work this summer as usual."

"Don't you have prep to do for school in the fall?"

"Lordy, Sandy, it's June. I have all summer to get my ducks in a row. I can still work for you if you need me."

"It's Ms. Lopez to you," she snapped and then grinned, opening her arms out to him.

Allen only hesitated a moment to make sure he was shielded and gave her a hug. It had gotten easier to be spontaneous, but he still had to be careful. Being too close to women always tested the skills Toni and her Seneca clan had taught him. It had made for a very unusual talk about the birds and the bees with her.

Stepping back, he admitted, "It's good to be home."

"It's good to have you home. It's been slow here, so I don't know how much I'll use you. But what work there is, I'll toss your way." She paused. "I thought I saw your dad in town today. Did he leave Phoenix before you did?"

Allen glanced away and took a deep breath. "I didn't stay there. I wanted to get out of the city as fast as I could. Traffic was light in the wee hours when I came in so I went up to Camp Verde."

7

"Boy, you're going to have both your parents on the war path, and they'll be bringing that to my doorstep!"

"I'm sorry, Sandy. I just couldn't deal with all that right now. And I'll keep them away from you."

She harrumphed and then turned her head toward the inner office, raising an eyebrow. "There's a dance Saturday night with a local band. Mixed *ranchera* and country."

Allen grinned and stuck his head through the doorway. "Caroline, it looks like we'll be working together again. All year long this time."

She looked up from the filing cabinet she had open. "We haven't had much need for a PI." She returned to stuffing files behind tabbed dividers.

"Well. . . ." His voice trailed off. Why did this woman always make his mouth go dry and his tongue stop working? He never could figure her out, and he refused to open up and read her.

She shot him another cool glance. "Was there something else?"

Allen cleared his throat. "Yeah." He paused as she held that cool, indifferent look. Allen took a deep breath. "There's a dance. Saturday."

Caroline returned to her filing. "Oh?"

"It's *ranchera* and country. A live band." He swallowed. "Do you dance?"

A faint smile passed over Caroline's lips as she stuffed in the last couple of files and slammed the drawer closed. Facing him she said, "We'll give it some deliberation."

Allen grinned. "I'll pick you up here at seven."

Chapter Four

The sound of retching penetrated the quiet bustle of the officials who were swarming the pastureland, dotted with boulders, that stretched out beside a shallow stream.

"Oh, give it a rest," Sheriff Manuel Mendoza grumbled, stuffing a cigarette between his lips and lighting it. He blew out the fragrant smoke from paunchy cheeks, not bothering to remove the cigarette from his mouth.

"Don't be hard on him," Lieutenant Mark Lucero of the Jicarillo Apache Tribal Police said. "He's young and inexperienced. I've been to Afghanistan, but I've never seen anything like this before. Even the EMT looked a little green."

Jerking the cigarette from his lips, Mendoza spat, "He needs to get over it. We'll be working this case." He stepped closer to Lucero. "Why'd they call you, anyway? This isn't tribal land."

Lucero picked up a stone from the ground and flung it into the stream only a few yards away from the blood-stained boulder and the body where the field deputy medical investigator was taking photographs. "But that is," he announced.

"Who found this mess?"

"A local rancher spotted the crows overhead, and he rode out to look."

"Rode? I didn't see any tire tracks out here but ours."

"Horseback." Lucero jerked his head behind them. "You can see the hoof prints. Fresh. He didn't want to get any closer than necessary. We're all leery of the dead, especially when there might be two bodies."

Mendoza squinted at him and harrumphed. He took another drag off his cigarette and tossed it on the ground.

Lucero stooped, rubbed the still burning end into the dry earth, broke off the filter, and then scattered the unburned tobacco into the wind. He stood, stuffing the filter into his uniform shirt pocket.

"Takin' my DNA?"

"Habit." Lucero looked over at the investigator, who had put a jeaned knee on the ground and angled the digital camera at the victim's open shirt. It exposed a bloody slit across the blue-painted torso, just below the ribcage, cleanly cut, with no intestines bulging out. Blood was everywhere, though: over the top of the granite boulder, all over the ground, all over the victim, Miguel Valencia, and all over the old man they had found passed out nearly on top of him.

"Do you think the old man did it?" Mendoza asked but didn't wait for the other officer to answer. "I remember this old guy. Must have been 80 if a day, wiry old coot. Brought him in for a DUI. Found him next to his car that he'd smashed into a tree. A young rookie was taking his prints and asked how fast he'd been driving when he'd been pulled over. The old man answered in Spanish that he hadn't been driving. The rookie asked him who else was in the car. The old man said no one was. Then the rookie asked him again if he'd been driving. This went on for a while until finally the old man got mad and said that he hadn't been driving the car when the patrol officer found him after he hit the tree. The young officer laughed so hard. Made the old man even madder. He hauled off and slugged the rookie. It took me and two other officers to get him into a cell to sleep it off." He looked over at Lucero. "It wouldn't surprise me one bit. Didn't one of your guys say he'd had a fight with the dead guy?"

Lucero winced, remembering his own rookie blurting that out just as the sheriff's department arrived. Miguel Valencia was a relative. He was the rookie's great-great-uncle. Lucero's own kinship to him was more complicated, more recent, and more diluted. "I heard. The deceased was the old man's son-in-law and his great-great-granddaughter's grandfather. He didn't want him at her baptism."

"Why the hell not?"

Lucero sighed. "Long history. Divorce. Abuse."

"Seems like the old man had a good reason to do him in."

The tribal officer frowned. He'd said too much. Still, that kind of bad blood was no reason to do what had been done to the man.

Mendoza hitched up his pants. "Guess I better see if the investigator found the murder weapon. It could just be the old man's broken bottle."

Chapter Five

Day 1: Sunday, noon, Payson, AZ

The double thumps against the truck's rear quarter panel drew Allen's attention to the mirror hanging over his windshield. No one there. His engine idled still in the strip mall parking lot as he moved the gear shift back into park.

"We missed you last night." The voice from the driver's side open window was pleasant but hid an edge of displeasure.

Allen stretched his arms out, bracing his hands on the steering wheel. He wanted his father to see where his hands were. One of his inner-city teaching cohorts ribbed him about being a brother in disguise because he did that every single time anyone confronted him, especially when he was driving. Though Allen had learned control over the years, it had become a habit that reminded him to never react in anger. The young man looked at his father. "The plane got in very late, and I didn't want to disturb your family."

Paul Rodriguez held his son's gaze for longer than was necessary. Finally, he glanced away and then back. "Logan missed you." The action and words were meant to produce guilt.

Allen didn't take the bait. "I'll come down and take him fishing once I get settled."

"He won't have any time. You know that." Paul countered. "Not till later."

Narrowing his eyes, Allen asked, "What are you doing up here? It isn't time yet, is it?"

Paul stepped back from the car door in a dismissive move. "It's very soon. I thought you'd have kept track of such an important time in your brother's life."

"It's important to him," Allen admitted. "And to you."

"You have a part to play, too."

Allen reached down to the bench seat and picked up a pair of sunglasses. "I abdicated, remember?"

Paul ignored the dismissal. "I'll be up at the ranch at the end of the week to take you to the site."

Shoving the glasses over his nose, Allen put the car in reverse. "Can't. I've got a hot date." He backed the truck out of the parking spot, and then paused as he shifted into first, sizing up his father. The older man's short stocky build and graying hair hid power, but a very different kind than his own. For a split second, Allen pitied the man. Swinging the steering wheel hard, he gunned the truck and headed for the road leading out of town to the horse ranch.

Chapter Six

"Damnedest thing I've ever seen," Ben Castiano, the field deputy medical investigator, said as he stood up to answer the sheriff's general question about what he had found. He jotted a few notes on forms on a clipboard.

"What do you mean?" Sheriff Mendoza grunted, looking down at the gaping hole just under the dead man's rib cage. "You've seen knifings before."

"Sure. But they're not clean like this."

"Clean? There's blood everywhere. One of my deputies was puking his head off. Even all over the boulder."

Ben eyed the boulder, only noticing a bit of vomit on the backside of the rock. "I mean the wound," he said, bringing Mendoza back to the matter at hand. "It's a thin line, almost surgical, right across the torso and . . ." He bent down again. "It looks like it went right over the diaphragm, cutting it cleanly, sort of like an attempt at field dressing." He straightened again. "You know, like for a deer."

"Field dressing? You mean the guts are gone?"

"No, the intestines weren't touched, as far as I can see. That's all lower. It's an odd wound."

"How could the old man do that the way his hands were shaking?"

"Were they?" The field investigator carefully stepped around the body to point to the top of the boulder. "Look here."

Mendoza didn't move. His 6'4" frame allowed him to just rise on his toes to see further.

"There's a void," Ben said. "See. Here and here." He pointed a gloved hand at each side of the top. An area about the width of a man's body was untouched by the blood that covered the top as if spray painted there by some ghoulish graffiti artist. The blood spray was marred by random drops of blue.

"Think he was knifed there?"

"Most likely. There's a lot of blood here. But I expected more, really."

"More? How much blood can one man have?"

"And the blood didn't flow as in a bleed out as you'd expect from a gutting. There is some spray, mostly over the very top, as if he were bent over backwards."

Coming back to Mendoza, Ben said, "I'll arrange for transport of the body to Albuquerque, but it'll take some time. I'll need to contact the funeral home in Espanola to see if they can keep the body until then. We'll know more when we do an MRI and a full postmortem. We'll run a tox screen to see if he had any alcohol or drugs in his system. That had to be painful." Looking down at the body at his feet, he shook his head. "I have an odd feeling about this one." Raising his eyes to cast about the isolated area, he added, "Seems a long way to come, just to knife somebody in anger. It reminds me of something."

"What?"

"Don't remember. But it'll come to me."

"Any defensive wounds?"

"None that I can tell offhand."

"That old man could've snuck up on him and stuck him."

"Hmm. Might have taken more than one."

"But the old geezer was here with blood all over him. He had to have done it. He had a major beef with this guy."

Ben bent again. With a gloved hand, he took the Stetson from the man's head to reveal a blue-painted face on the bowed head. "Well, I'll be." Squatting with the hat still in his hands, he twisted his own head first to one side then the other, viewing it from different angles. Carefully, he pulled the plaid shirt away from the victim's chest, first on the right and then on the

16

left. The entire torso was painted blue, along with the neck and face.

Ben stood, picked up a large plastic bag from a small stack on the open lid of his kit, and stuffed the hat into it. He sealed it, took a marker from his shirt pocket, and wrote on the label. Placing the bag on the ground, the investigator picked up his digital camera next to his kit and took another round of pictures of the body before setting it down again. He then carefully pulled the body away from the boulder, grunting as he moved the dead weight onto its side. There was no way to lay the body flat with the man's rounded back. It was a cartoon-like image of a man frozen in time as if by a giant ice machine out in this high country. "Full rigor," Ben announced.

"So, time of death?"

Looking at his watch, the field investigator said, "About midnight or before. Around moonrise."

"That fits. I heard the old man was at a baptism or something until late."

Ben lifted up the man's shirt in the back, noticing that the blue coloring had not been applied to that area. He could clearly see the slight purpling on the skin below the waist. Pulling the man's pants back with a gloved finger, Ben noticed the discoloration deepening further down the man's body. "Body was moved into this position." He stood, nodding. "Killed over the boulder and positioned here." The investigator picked up his digital camera again and scrolled back a few images. Offering Mendoza a quick look, he added. "Yeah. The body was neatly placed. He didn't just slump down here after being knifed."

Interrupting this exchange, a young man dressed in full-body, plastic personal protection gear came nearly running over and shouted, "Hold on there."

Ben frowned, taking a step toward the figure, making him stop abruptly about six feet from the body.

"We have to get more photographs," the plastic-clad man said, craning his head around the investigator to get a better look at the blue man on the ground.

"You got enough until I can get out of here. I need to bag the body. Wanna give me a hand?"

The young man paled as he stared up at the field investigator. Quickly, he recovered to state rather cavalierly, "We don't touch. You do." Slowly, he let his gaze slide back down to the body.

Ben grunted. "Gotta get a bag and a gurney," he announced, leaning down to pack up his field kit.

"Ever see a body before, boy?" Mendoza asked roughly.

There was a pause before the young man answered as he tilted his head to study the position of the body. "Yeah, in training," he muttered, stepping a little closer and squatting, his forensic curiosity taking over. After a moment, he rose and announced, "Reminds me of the animal mutilations we looked at back then."

"Animal mutilations? You mean aliens?" Mendoza laughed and pulled out another cigarette from his shirt pocket. Sticking it into his mouth, he reached into his pants for his lighter.

The young man stepped closer to the sheriff. "Don't light that up around my crime scene."

Taking the cigarette out of his mouth, he blustered, "*Your* crime scene?" Mendoza let out a belly laugh.

"Yes. After the coroner's office gets done, it's mine and my team's. We still haven't found a murder weapon. We need to. . . ."

Ben tuned out the jurisdictional argument as he walked to his truck to get the body bag and the gurney. *Animal mutilation?* Then he shook his head. *No, it's something else. Something more sinister.*

Chapter Seven

Before Allen had even slammed the truck door and stepped away, Toni and his mother spilled out of the sprawling, log ranch house, down the low porch steps, and rushed toward him. Coming home was always like stepping into a feel-good, depression-era movie. But his mother, Kate, was no Mother Joad, though she was strong and wise. She was a modern professional woman, an archaeology professor, who had taught in Arizona before moving to New York with Toni while he grew into his abilities and got his own basics in learning to control them from Toni's grandmother. Still the petite, quiet force in their lives, his mother had aged well over the years. Her auburn hair had faded to a dull chestnut with only a tiny bit of white at her temples. She still looked younger than his friends' mothers back at school.

Though his mother and Toni had nearly run toward him, they stopped, as they always did, about a yard away. Toni stood behind Kate, waiting, ever protective. Her own shoulder-length black hair, perpetually kept back with a silver band, showed little signs of age, though she was well past 60. Toni had reluctantly returned to education in New York but not at the university level she once had in the past. That was something the tall native woman never talked about and Allen never asked. Toni had preferred to excite younger minds, making history come alive, and that enthusiasm had sparked Allen's own interest in the subject. But he was more interested in social reform and modern culture after the industrial age. Allen avoided anything earlier than that. There were just too many ghosts in his head that he didn't want to stir with an immersion in those eras. He left that to his mother and Toni.

Allen stepped closer, and all three embraced. Everyone's shields were up and active, allowing them all to feel the warmth of their family connection like regular people.

Toni stepped aside, raising an arm to point toward the house, urging them inside. "Are you hungry?"

"Are you grilling?" Allen asked, stepping to the bed of the truck for his two bags, hauling them out.

Toni flashed a smile. "I have some fresh mutton."

"Where did you get that from?"

They mounted the steps and entered the foyer with its pine interior and wide staircase to the bedrooms upstairs. "Your stepmother has become quite a horse trader," his mother said.

Allen chucked. "Well, weren't you always a horse trader?"

"We gentled wild mustangs and sold them to the Apache reservation," Toni corrected. "We never traded for anything."

"Until now?" Allen finished, depositing his bags at the foot of the stairs.

"It seems somebody's maverick cousin is a Navajo," Kate explained, leading them into the kitchen where she opened the fridge to pull out a pitcher of fresh-squeezed lemonade.

"And?" Allen prompted.

Toni got glasses from a cupboard and put them on the table, covered with an old-fashioned embroidered cloth. This one had faded red poppies and sheaves of wheat. Allen always was afraid of spilling something on these little masterpieces every summer when they had returned to visit Dutch at the ranch. His mother had always gifted one to the aging owner of the horse ranch every year. Usually, they had a rooster or a chicken placed on it somewhere because the old woman had liked them so much. But this fine one, Allen remembered, had come from his Aunt Delores when her daughter took her first communion. She wasn't really his aunt, but his father considered her husband his brother, so he had always considered him and

20

his family kin. It had seemed odd to receive a present when the little girl should have been given many. And his father had set up a generous college fund for her.

When Dutch's health failed as he finished high school, his mother and Toni had moved back to help out, and Allen stayed on to go to college in New York. Dutch had passed two months ago. He hadn't been able to fly back for the funeral because he was in the middle of preparing for finals and finishing up his honors thesis.

He had lingered a couple of weeks longer to have closure with friends and with the land. He had visited Great-Grandmother's grave on the Seneca land that had been her family's home forever, it seemed, and offered her a final farewell. She and Toni had been crucial for his training so that he could make sense of his abilities, though the woman instructed in riddles and stories that he had to sift through before he found his own answers. When he'd return to tell her what he'd discovered, she'd cackle from her toothless mouth, ever refusing to wear her dentures, except to eat a meal. She'd tell him, "Almost, my son. Almost."

Allen sat at the end of the table and ran his hand over the fine embroidery. It was excellent work, done in impossibly small stitches, far more expert than his mother's work. He looked up at his parents who were pouring lemonade and distributing glasses. Toni had been the perfect choice for his mom. He'd known that from the beginning. There was love and respect there, and it just felt right, even though that relationship had taken a little explaining at school. The kids — high school and college — understood divorce and having two sets of parents. It was just a little odd, when one set was of the same gender. The high schoolers took more convincing that his collegemates.

"This house is full," Allen said.

Kate stopped pouring and stared at him. A moment passed until she understood his meaning. "Memories, yes." she said.

"And love," he added.

Toni moved behind Allen to sit down on his right. "One day it will come to you."

Allen smiled and looked down.

"Or maybe it already has."

Kate sat down opposite Toni. "Oh? Details."

"Don't badger the boy," Toni defended. "He'll tell us in his own good time."

A loud pounding came at the front door and a familiar voice echoed in the foyer as the door slammed. "*Holla.* I saw the truck."

Allen jerked his head around to see a huge Apache/Mexican looming behind him. Isaiah was 6'4", if he was an inch, and stocky, his arms muscled from working a hammer against the anvil at the horse camp, deep in the back country. He flashed a bright smile, rimmed by a mustache that trickled down the sides of his mouth.

"You home for good?" he said.

Suddenly, the sound of feet and pushing and shoving erupted into the foyer. Two energetic boys stumbled into the kitchen. One was around six and the other was a couple of years younger. They bore remarkable copies of the big man's face, without the mustache.

"I thought I told you two to stay outside. You reek of horses." He chuckled. "And I guess I do, too."

"We wanted to see Allen," the older one said.

"Me, too," his brother echoed.

Allen turned his chair and reached out to the boys. They rushed into his arms like squirming puppies.

"Can we go fishing?" the younger asked.

"Are you going to ride with us?" the older one queried.

"Just you. Not Logan," the younger said.

Allen pushed them back. "What's wrong with Logan? He likes to do all those things, too."

22

"He's no fun," the younger said. "He's too serious. You laugh a lot."

"Logan has some serious work to do this summer. He's been preparing for it all his life. He has a right to be serious."

"But we want to have fun," the younger whined.

Allen looked at them sternly. "We'll do some things with Logan, too. But I'll go riding and fishing with you boys alone."

"Promise?"

"I promise." Allen crossed his heart.

"Come along, boys," Isaiah said, pulling each one away from Allen. "We need to clean you both up before the barbecue." He looked at Toni. "I have the mutton in the back of the ATV. I had one of my guys at the camp butcher it for you into steaks and chops. I hope it's not too tough. If it is, my *tia* has a good recipe for mutton stew, cooked for hours."

Toni rose from the table to follow Isaiah. Before the big man left, though, he reached a giant hand down for Allen to shake. "Good to have you home for good. And one day you'll be teaching these wild ones in school."

"My pleasure, Isaiah."

Chapter Eight

Day 1: Sunday, afternoon, Espanola, NM

The old man's hands shook as he raised the Styrofoam cup to his mouth. The action rattled the chains attached to the cuffs around his hands and sent a ripple through the links hanging between the legs of his orange jumpsuit to his ankles. The hot liquid burned the old man's tongue, but it was welcome. His mouth was as dry as the Chihuahuan Desert his ancestors had trekked north from. His head was giving him fits. Everything was all scrambled in there, more than usual. It had been six months since he'd been on a bender, and not one with top-shelf tequila. His gut ached.

"Do you know why you're here?" Deputy George Quintana asked, sitting across from the table from him in the interrogation room. His own complexion was pale from the morning's discovery.

Raising his head, the old man tried to focus on the youngster who didn't seem old enough to be wearing that star on his khaki shirt. "*Que?*"

The deputy repeated the question in Spanish, but the old man stared at him through bleary eyes. "*Que?*" he repeated.

"Of course, he knows why he's here," Sheriff Mendoza said, pacing the small room.

Ignoring the outburst, the deputy asked, "How much did you drink?"

The old man grinned, finding clarity in the memory, savoring it. "The good stuff. Top shelf." He took another gulp of coffee. Realizing it wasn't tequila, he grimaced and put the cup down on the metal table. "The best Alphonso could buy. He's a big man. With money."

Mendoza leaned menacing across the desk. "Why did you kill Miguel Valencia?"

The old man blinked as the fog around his brain closed in again. The expensive aftershave the sheriff wore made him nauseous. "Miguel?" As he voiced the name, the old venom returned. The old man spat on the concrete floor. "May he rot in hell! Hell's too good for that *puto*!"

Mendoza gave his deputy a smug look and straightened his body.

The old man continued to rant. "He abandoned my Lucia, chasing after every *mujer* he could find, leaving her with a *bebe. Abuelo*? Ha! He's just a *donador de esperma*! The *pendejo* better not come near *mi binieta!*" The rant morphed into complete Spanish mixed with Apache as pain built up in the old man's head. He clutched at it and bent over the table, moaning.

"He's in no condition to talk," Deputy Quintana said. "He's still drunk."

"Well, we just heard motive, didn't we?"

The old man gulped air, trying to get enough into his lungs to calm the throbbing in his head and the pain in his gut. He vaguely heard the door open and two strong arms grabbed his own and hoisted him to his feet. He opened his eyes to see a stocky woman, older than the deputy, in a dark blue uniform on his left.

"My head," he grunted out. "Worst hangover."

As the woman and the other deputy hauled the old man through the door, Mendoza warned, "He better not stroke out. I want to take this to trial."

Chapter Nine

Dave Archuleta strained his eyes, searching the bustling restaurant at the Wild Horse Casino before spying Adam Llano stuffing an Indian taco in his mouth. He hurried over and slapped his buddy on the back, nearly making the other man choke. Dave sat down opposite him. "I've been looking all over for you."

Swallowing and reaching for his Mountain Dew, Adam asked, "What for?"

"Ma got a call from your great-gran saying she couldn't find Harley. He didn't come home from the party. She was frantic. Said she'd had a dream he was dead next to a boulder covered in blood."

"The old man's just on a bender. Again. He knows he shouldn't drink with that ulcer."

"What do you expect with all that liquor Alphonso brought? He knows better than to bring it out of here. The casino has strict rules about personal consumption," Dave said.

"Stop complaining. He gets a discount. And besides, it was at his big, new house off reservation land. He was showing off to all his in-laws." Grinning, Adam added, "It was a good party."

"Still." Dave leaned back in his chair. "He should know how Harley gets. He's part of the family now. He's had to have heard all the stories."

A waitress came over and put a menu in front of Dave. "Coffee?"

He shook his head. "Just Pepsi."

The waitress jerked her head toward the casino floor. "You can get that out there for free."

He shrugged. "Could you get me one of those?" he said, and pointed to Adam's plate.

"Red or green?"

"Christmas."

"Did you hear about the murder last night?" the waitress asked, writing the order on a piece of paper.

"What murder?" Adam blurted, stopping the big taco midway to his mouth.

"Some old guy. Blood everywhere according to the EMT, who was called out with Lieutenant Lucero. Wasn't much use there by the time he got out on the scene. He came in just as I came on this morning. Pretty shook up. He bypassed us and went directly to the bar." She took the menu and sauntered away.

Dave stared at Adam. "You don't think?" He stood.

"Nah," Adam said, before taking a big bite of his food. "He's just sleeping it off somewhere," he continued through a full mouth. "Nobody hates him that much. Except maybe Great-Gran." He shook his head. "Nah. She loves him in spite of himself."

Dave wasn't so sure as he stood up. He called after the waitress, "Never mind." Turning to Adam, he said, "I'm heading to the police station."

Chapter Ten

Six tiny, dark green beads slid into place, snug against their mates on the front leg of the stylized lizard motif. Their colors contrasted against the medium green beads along the back of the reptile, giving more realism to the creature on the pure white of the doe skin vest. Logan smiled. Brother Lizard was a friend. He always seemed to pause to raise his head at the boy back home when the reptile played around the precise landscaping of his front yard. Though Logan made no sound when he watched the creature among the smooth tan pebbles, Brother Lizard always knew he was there and would stop and look his way as if to bid him farewell before darting into the shade of an agave spine.

Logan filled his needle tip with another row of dark beads, slid them to the end of the thread, and carefully snugged the needle into the top layer of the thin leather. A small stitch secured them. The boy was pleased with his craft. Soon the ceremonial vest would be finished, and he would begin other preparations. He enjoyed communing with Brother Lizard as he worked. His father had insisted he put snakes on this vest, but Logan found no kinship with them. Brother Lizard had as much power as those other creatures but also liked to play. Logan envied him.

The electronic click at the hotel room door caused Logan to raise his head from his work. His father entered. Logan read the features on the man's face and how his shoulders were slightly hunched. His father wasn't pleased. As his mother rushed to meet him, the man quickly straightened, stiffening something inside him as he closed the door.

"What did he say?" his mother asked in eagerness, oblivious to any change in her husband's demeanor.

Logan secured his needle into the doe skin and waited, stiffening his own back against the pillow pushed against the headboard of the bed. There would be instructions.

"He'll come around."

"But the test begins soon. How can he not—"

His father reached his hands to his mother's upper arms as Logan watched her calm. Logan had seen it before and felt that unspoken power.

"He will." The man turned from her toward Logan. A forced smile crossed his lips. "Logan, I arranged for the sweat preparations on the ceremony grounds. It's not too far from here. We'll ride in like our ancestors did."

Logan's face brightened. "Are we going to the ranch? Can we see Allen?"

"Tomorrow. We'll select the horses and the tack we'll need. But first we must make ourselves worthy. We can meditate in the sauna here to prepare us."

Disappointed, Logan put aside his handwork and went to his suitcase to retrieve his swim trunks and flipflops. He hated saunas. The smell of the treated wood seemed wrong. But he would enjoy the swim in the big pool afterwards. As he meditated, he would think of cool streams as he fished under the trees with his big brother.

Chapter Eleven

Lieutenant Lucero looked up from his reports as Dave Archuleta entered the Dulce Tribal Police Office. The younger man jerked his own head in greeting, propelling him from his seat toward the counter.

"*Ha annsi?*" The officer asked how the other man was in the traditional Jicarillo Apache greeting.

"*Do ansi.*" Dave answered. "It's not me I'm worried about though. I heard there was a killing here last night."

The lieutenant grimaced.

Dave leaned on the counter, moving his face closer to the officer's. "Ma got a frantic call from Graciela Manwell this morning after Harley went missing from the christening party last night. Tell me he was just on a bender."

Lucero sighed and studied the counter's white surface. "It wasn't him we found."

Dave straightened, relieved. Studying the other man, though, caused his features to morph back into a frown. "What aren't you telling me?"

Lucero gave the other man a hard stare. "I can't give you details."

"If he isn't dead, is he in the hospital or—" Dave looked toward the side door that led to the holding cells. "You got him here sleeping it off." Returning his attention to Lucero he said, "Look, you got to let me see him. I have to give Ma something to tell Graciela." He paused, reading something on the deputy's face. "Wait. You haven't called her."

The space between Lucero's eyes furrowed further before he admitted. "Harley's not here."

"Then where is he?"

"He's in Espanola."

"Espanola? For being on a bender? He doesn't even drive. You pulled his license ten years ago. He walked out into the bush."

Lucero took a deep breath. "Go talk to Sheriff Mendoza. It's not in my jurisdiction."

Dave clinched his jaw as his anger built. He realized, though, there were no answers to be found here. As he turned, he felt Lucero's hand grip his arm. When Dave finally looked at him, the deputy said, "Get him a big city lawyer."

Chapter Twelve

Ben had caught a signal when he finally got back onto blacktop on his way toward Chama. Now he punched his phone, wedged into its carrier on the dashboard of his white Ford 150, to end his call to the funeral home in Espanola. He frowned. It would still take two hours to get to the body and then another two to get it into cold storage. Luckily, he lived in Abiquiu. That had cut his time getting to the crime scene. Still, that body had been out in the summer heat for way too long. He had to remind himself, though, that it could have not been found so soon if it hadn't been for an eagle-eyed rancher.

Shifting in his seat, he tried to get comfortable. His AC was finally blowing some decent air, but it didn't settle him down. Something about this case. He shook his head. *What was it? Who guts a guy and takes most of the blood? And why?* He chewed on the side of his bottom lip. *Animal mutilations!* He grunted out a laugh. *Alien abductions! Dulce always attracted the crackpots. It's sacred land, for God's sake! Still. . . .*

Ben commanded his phone. "Google, call Jim Baxter." The phone dutifully located the number and dialed. Soon, a West Texas drawl filled the cab of the truck. "FBI. Baxter."

"Jim, this is Ben Castiano."

"Ben! Well, it sure has been an age since I heard from you. How the hell are you?"

After a chuckle, Ben replied, "I'm doing great. We need to catch up sometime."

"Sure do! It's been — what? — ten years since we hoisted a few together . . . Or rather, I did. You were always the choirboy. How the hell can anyone keep to one drink?"

Ben cleared his throat. Nobody knew what ghosts he had grown up with. "Jim, I need a little bit of help on a case."

"Sure, what can I do?"

"Do you remember that conference in New Orleans we had to go to?"

"Lordy, that was 15 years ago!"

"The one where they had all those strange crime scenes? And had a shitload of weird speakers?"

"Oh, that one! The voodoo guy and that witch lady!"

"Yeah. Wasn't there some kind of Satanist who talked?" Ben asked.

"Real queer, that was. 'Bout freaked out all the churchgoing folks in the conference room! Suddenly, that space got really small and claustrophobic."

"Yeah. Do you have any materials from that conference? Any contact numbers, maybe?"

"What kind of case you dealing with, son? Think some witch done hexed somebody?"

"Don't mock that. Native people here thoroughly believe in witches but not the kind that conference lady talked about, though. Even my people believe in our own witches. Shoot, there are taboos all over the place about everything here, including the dead. Or maybe especially the dead. I think we only got one native guy working as a field investigator, and I wonder about him. I think he does ceremony after every case . . . But, Jim, can you help me out?"

"Geez, I don't know. I probably tossed all that shit out. Then again, it was so odd, I might just have put it all in a file and put it somewhere. But finding that could be a trick. I'm coming to an age where you put something in a safe place, then you forget where that safe place was or what you put there."

Ben released a welcome laugh. "You aren't that old yet. You aren't thinking about retirement, are you?"

"Naw, Margery wants me to, though. I sure can't chase bad guys like I used to. That's why I been working a desk. But, hey, I'll do some digging and get back to you right quick."

"Thanks, Jim. I do appreciate it."

"Anytime, buddy."

As the call ended, Ben smiled and then released a sigh. Jim was good people, but like a lot of people he worked with, Jim still didn't quite get this part of the country or the people here. Ben harrumphed. *Shoot, even I don't understand, and I was born here.*

Chapter Thirteen

Day 1: Sunday, late afternoon, Espanola

"What do you mean, I can't see him?" Dave Archuleta was beginning to heat up due to the stonewalling he felt he was experiencing at the sheriff's office in Espanola.

"Look, you're not a relative and you're not his lawyer. He's in there with him now," Deputy George Quintana said, showing signs of weariness from this morning's early start and what he'd witnessed.

"Then can you tell me why he's here? You can't just drag him all this way to jail for public intoxication. That's nothing."

"Sir, I assure you that this is not a trivial matter."

"Then what's the charge?"

"I can't—" An electronic buzz in the back along a hall to the right of the counter drew the deputy's attention. A door opened and closed to reveal a young man, who shifted his briefcase from his right to his left so he could straighten his tie before walking crisply down the corridor. He stopped at the front counter.

"I'll be back tomorrow morning. I don't think he's fit for an arraignment tomorrow," the young man said, showing obvious disgust.

Dave stepped toward the man. "Are you Harley Manwell's lawyer?"

The young man squinted at him. "Are you a relative?"

"No. But I'm trying to get some information for his family."

The lawyer reached into a pocket inside his jacket and retrieved a card. He handed it to Dave. "Have them call me."

The card read: Richard Mason, Public Defender.

"I have to tell them something more. What's he here for?"

"Murder."

"Murder! For God's sake, why? Who?"

"Miguel Valencia." The lawyer took a deep breath. "It doesn't look good. He was found this morning next to the body with blood all over him. And there was a rumor there was a long-standing feud between them. He was drunk. He still is, though he claims he's suffering from a hangover. I've seen my share of alcoholics among your kind. He's still drunk. He can't stand for arraignment until he's sober. That's usually done within 48 hours." He shifted his body toward the door. "Have his family call me. And only one person. I don't want to have to deal with the entire tribe."

Dave's jaw clinched as he watched the arrogant Anglo lawyer exit the building. He took one more glance at the card in his hand and tossed it on the floor. Dave reached for his phone and headed out the door as he searched through his contacts.

Chapter Fourteen

Allen stretched out his legs and eased back into the lawn chair in the backyard of the ranch house. In the dying light, the evening had grown quiet after the bustle of the barbecue that had been punctuated by Isaiah's booming laugh and the shrieks of his boys as they chased each other among the tables that had been set up in front of the long, stone barbecue pit that was still smoldering. The necessary *Norteno* music the big man always brought was a loud soundtrack to the evening. The quiet now was most welcome, reinforcing how much he missed these homecomings on the ranch.

A tap against his shoulder gently nudged the young man out of his reverie. He turned his head to find a small glass, a third full of amber liquid, almost under his nose, the rich aroma of Irish whiskey, rising like invisible incense. Allen raised his eyes in question to Toni, whose hand grasped the glass.

"You're legal," Toni said as Allen took the glass into his own hand. Pulling up a chair, she added, "It's about time we shared a drink together."

Allen hesitated. "You always said liquor clouds the mind."

Settling into her chair, she said, "It does." She took a small sip. "Especially if you need to keep your abilities in check."

Allen finally took a small sip himself, allowing the flavors to evaporate on his tongue. "And I don't need to do that now?"

Toni smiled. "Not tonight, at least." She reached her glass across to Allen's for him to clink with his own. "Welcome home, son."

They both watched a few glowing embers in the barbecue spark their last before slowly fading to darkness.

Turning to Allen, she asked quietly, "Did you hear from your father? Was he unhappy about you not staying last night?"

"Yep. He showed up in Payson this morning, telling me that Logan's testing was coming up, as if I didn't know." He took another sip of whiskey. "He thinks I'll participate."

"You don't have to."

"I know."

"He wants you to support Logan."

Allen turned to face Toni. "It was a nightmare for me. No child should ever have to endure what I did. How can he do that to Logan and expect me to support it? If it only were just a vision quest. What does he want me to do, anyway? Vision quests are supposed to be solitary. I can't even intrude with my— His abilities just aren't— How could I even reach him?" He settled back into his chair in a sulk. "I don't need to be there, if that's all that's required of me." Allen downed his glass of whiskey, hoping the burn would eradicate his anger.

Toni reached a browned hand to take the glass from Allen, causing the young man to look at her. "Nothing is required of you," she said gently, taking the glass. "You're finding your own path."

A silence enfolded both of them for a bit. Then Toni said, "Remember Turtle."

Allen chuckled, looking at his step-mom. "Are you becoming the inscrutable Indian? You sound like Great-Grandmother."

Toni smiled, finishing her glass. "She did teach in riddles."

"So. Turtle means I need to shield."

"Uh-huh. And be content wherever you are."

Allen smiled genuinely, nodding.

The sound of the telephone reached out into the quiet

40

evening. Hearing the ring reminded Allen that the rest of the world was still out there somewhere, insistent, intruding.

Kate appeared at the back door with the landline phone in her hand. "Allen, it's for you. It's Sandy Lopez."

Allen rose from his chair and crossed the distance to his mother. He noticed a worry line across her forehead, wondering what had brought that on. Allen smiled at her as he took the phone and stepped away from the door.

"Allen, I'm sorry to disturb you," Sandy Lopez began.

Reading more in those few words and Sandy's tone than she was willing to reveal, he said immediately, "How can I help?"

Sandy laughed. "You always know, don't you?" She paused only a few seconds. "I got a call from a distant cousin in New Mexico. His friend's great-grandfather is being charged with murder. He's ninety-five years old! How could he possibly kill somebody?"

"You'd be surprised what people can do, given the reason and the available weaponry."

"I have a feeling about this one." She paused. "It doesn't feel right. I might need you for more than your PI skills."

"What are you going to do?"

"From what my cousin said, the old man has a young racist for a lawyer. You don't get the cream of the crop from the Public Defender's Office. Though sometimes, you do get lucky with somebody who's there because of conscience, not just to fill a quota of pro bono work."

"Are you thinking of defending him? In New Mexico? You don't have jurisdiction there."

"I'm working on that. I need to get the support of a prominent lawyer there to invite me in. I've had Caroline researching Arizona/New Mexico co-operation and New Mexico law all evening. Her head is already spinning, and it'll get worse before this is over. I'm going to need both of you if this goes in the direction my gut is telling me."

"She'll be coming, too?"

"Of course. You both are a matching set. But we're going to have to hurry."

"When are you leaving?"

"I don't know yet. It depends on when the lawyer gets back to me."

"Okay. I'll help as I can."

"Thanks. Pack a bag. Be ready to go." On those words, she hung up.

Allen frowned, then handed his mother the phone.

"Trouble?"

"We'll see," he said and returned to flop into his chair next to Toni.

"How soon will you be leaving?"

Allen opened his mouth in surprise, then smiled. "I need to shield better," he said.

"No, it's just good ears."

Allen looked back at the ranch house, seeing that his mother had returned inside. "Mom won't like it."

"Let me worry about your mother. I have ways to soothe her."

Allen swung his eyes to look at Toni's blue ones, reading a private admission, one that revealed a hint of the intimacy between his parents.

Toni smiled. "You'll find out yourself one day. Very soon, I think."

Chapter Fifteen

Day 2: Monday, sunrise, near Payson

The young warrior stood on the edge of the mesa. His outspread raven feather cloak absorbed the morning light as it creeped over the horizon, more appropriate for a sunset than a sunrise. He chanted in a tongue he had become accustomed to but was not his own — or might have been, somewhere in his long line of mixed heritage.

"I am the strength of the world. I am the strength of life. I am the one who comes forth. I am jaguar. I am snake. I am—" And on and on, a litany of animals and powers, he chanted.

Mala, his mother and Paul Rodriquez' twin sister, mouthed the words of the chant as her son spoke. Pride filled her eyes as she watched.

When the young man turned, arms still outspread, she glanced over his naked body, covered only by a white breechclout trimmed in red. Black ink tattoos covered his chest and muscular legs, protecting and marking the gods' favor. A large snake twined upward on the outside of each leg from ankle to below the groin. A menacing owl stared out from the front of each thigh. Across the solar plexus, the head of a fierce spotted jaguar bore warning not to approach, while over the heart, a bat spread its dark wings. On each shoulder blade flew a humming bird, each beak pointed to the other, protective of the multiple piercing scars below them.

Mala spread her own arms out wide, beckoning the young man to come to her. "You are invincible, Cesar!"

"I am indeed," he boasted, his hands now on his hips as he swaggered to his mother, avoiding her arms. "Huitzilopochtli should be pleased. I embrace both night and sun now."

She placed a hand over some of the Sun Dance scars on her son's chest. "You were so young when we began, with wild energy. It took time to shape that energy into power." She stepped back to state, "We have done all that we can to ensure your protection and your victory."

"I am the rightful shaman," Cesar stated. "It was taken from me before. You are the elder twin. It should have been mine without trial."

"True, my son. But women are not valued. We have never been."

"You will be by my side, Mother."

She smiled, thrilled at the anticipation of ruling through her son. "You will find a bride later who will bear you a son, and he will never have to prove his right to his place as shaman. You are young. Enjoy your rule first before you have to train your successor. You have waited far too long for this."

"Soon, Mother, on the longest day of the year. Soon."

Chapter Sixteen

Day 2: Monday, mid-morning, near Gallup, NM

As he waited for his traveling companions, Allen tuned in the car radio's dial to the numbers the cashier at the gas station had recommended just outside of Gallup as they headed north. All he got at eleven in the morning was NPR talk broadcasts. He switched it off. It had been an uneventful four-hour drive so far. The only bright point had been watching the sunrise as he made his way on the two-lane roads outside of the forests toward I-40. Then the blazing sun hit him square in the face for the next couple of hours. It was a relief in more ways than one to turn north and then stop at a gas station with a diner. Though his mother had insisted on making him a hearty breakfast at 5:00 am, her nourishment, both body and soul, only fortified him for so long. He had grown antsy driving while Caroline and Sandy studied documents in the back seat, made phone calls, and tossed legalese at each other. Now, he needed the solace and motivation of music.

Allen reached under the neckline of his black History Rocks t-shirt and pulled out the quartz crystal Toni had given him that morning. It was such an odd thing, coming from her. Very New Agey and not traditional. Toni had only said one thing when she dropped it over his head and under his shirt as she stopped him on the front steps: "We're always near you, my son." Then she patted the bulge under his t-shirt.

Remembering those words, Allen wrapped his fingers around the copper-wrapped long point, letting it warm to his full touch. Warily, he slid his shield down just a bit and opened. Suddenly, he felt a rush of warmth and home. Allen smiled, closing the connection and raising his shield, adding another layer of strength because he had opened it.

The passenger side door opened, followed by the back door on the same side. Sandy slid into the front seat with him and Caroline tucked herself into the back among the small piles of papers she had pulled from both of the women's briefcases. Sandy put two cold drinks into the holders in the center console. "Dr. Pepper, right?" she asked.

"Always. I checked the GPS. It's up to Farmington and then over to Dulce. Maybe three more hours. We should be in there about two."

"Reroute. We need to go to Espanola. The old man is there, not in Dulce. I didn't quite have all of that information this morning. I just got through to my cousin again."

Allen fiddled with the town car's GPS and plugged in the new destination. As it recalculated, a new screen appeared with a new route and then quickly changed to their current location. "Looks like we'll see the two largest cities of New Mexico then, Albuquerque and Santa Fe, before we get to Espanola."

"Sorry. I know you hate driving in city traffic." She looked over at him. "That's why you didn't go to your dad's first thing after Toni left the truck, isn't it? He'd always picked you up for your summer visits and then Toni and Kate collected you."

Allen shrugged. "That and not wanting to get into that continual debate about Logan's testing. It'll finally be over in a few days."

Sandy's hand briefly touched his on the ignition. "And we're taking you away from all that."

Allen moved his hand to the gear shift to put the car into reverse. "I'm glad to help."

"But it's family."

Again, he shrugged as he maneuvered the car out of the parking space. "It's his family."

Shifting into Drive, he swung the big town car around to drive back to Gallup and I-40 and to continue East. Luckily, the sun was overhead now and not in his eyes. He'd face the heavy city traffic on the interstate and whatever else was before him. His right hand touched the bulge beneath his shirt. His family was with him. He wasn't alone.

Chapter Seventeen

"Horses," Logan whispered, his head following the corral fence as the car pulled to a stop in front of the ranch house. He quickly unlocked his seatbelt, swung the car door open, and tumbled out before his parents could even call out a warning to be careful. Logan fitted a sneakered foot onto the lowest wood railing, pulling himself up to the second rail and finally over the top where he secured himself on the fence. He steadied himself with his hands on the top railing while he swung his legs against the rail below.

The four bay horses had watched his approach, their ears flicking in signal, always alert. They were tame souls that were used to being ridden but not so used to small boys, at least not for a long while. The boldest one took a step closer, twisting her head to one side, observing, assessing, ready to signal the others to bunch together. After a moment, she moved forward, her head bobbing slightly with each tread, until she had her face almost against the boy's chest.

Logan mumbled soft words to her, ones Toni had taught him a couple of years ago when he started coming up to go fishing with his brother. It was the only respite he'd had in the ever-present training he had engaged in since he could remember. Reaching both arms to engulf the horse's head into his arms, he leaned in and placed his own head against the great animal's as she pushed gently against his chest. The push, however, was a tad more than the boy could counter since he hadn't tucked his toes around the rail below him. In a breath, he felt himself fall backward.

Toni's swift reflexes caught the boy as he left the rail.

"Hold on there, big fella," she said soothingly, standing the boy onto his feet.

Logan looked flushed and relieved. "I forgot to tuck my toes." He looked up at the mare. "She didn't mean anything."

Toni stooped to talk eye-to-eye with him. He was a little smaller than Allen had been at his age, before that boy had shot up to the six feet he was today. "She was just happy to see you," Toni said. "I think she remembers you from last summer."

Logan looked around. "Where's Allen?"

A frown flew across Toni's brow and then changed back to calm. "He's working with lawyer Lopez."

"Like he did last year?" Logan wrinkled his nose. "He said it was lots of walking around and talking to people. Booorrrring."

Toni smiled. "Yes. Boooorrring. But he said he would be back soon and would take you fishing."

Logan sighed. "The other boys, too?"

"No, just you." She poked his chest, and the boy beamed. "And I found a great place for you to go."

Logan flung his arms around Toni's neck as he had the mare's. Suddenly, he was surrounded by a feeling of warmth and homecoming. Then it was gone as if a cue to step back. When he did, he saw Toni's eyes glistening with moisture.

"Logan!" It was his mother, Marianna. "Come inside and use the bathroom. And make sure you wash your hands. We're going out to eat soon."

Reluctantly, the boy moved away from the corral and trudged across the dirt driveway toward the house.

Chapter Eighteen

Day 2: Monday, midafternoon, Espanola, NM

Allen watched Caroline and Sandy neatening their hair and applying lipstick in the car before they all stepped onto the sheriff's office parking lot. He wished he had changed into a dress shirt at least. He hadn't known they were going to interview their client first thing. Allen had packed professional clothes. It just didn't make sense to drive almost eight hours in a suit and tie on roads that might produce a blowout.

Sandy turned to him and then looked back at Caroline. "Ready?" Without waiting for a reply, she reached for her door handle. "Let's do this."

Allen followed the professionals into the building, feeling like a mascot instead of an equal. Granted, he didn't have their legal expertise, but he was part of the team. Once inside, Sandy got a White officer's attention and asked to see Harley Davidson Manwell.

"Are you a relative?" the young man asked.

Reaching into an outer pocket of her leather briefcase, Sandy produced a business card.

The deputy read it and frowned, looking totally confused. He looked up, "Ma'am, he's in with his lawyer right now."

"Has he been arraigned yet?"

"No ma'am. The old Indian was still drunk yesterday, and he's worse for wear today."

"A drunken Indian? That's an old cliché, isn't it?"

"Well, he—" His voice trailed as he looked further at Sandy and Caroline, aware he had committed a gross faux pas. "I didn't mean—" He swallowed and then tried to justify his remark. "It's a reality on any rez, no matter the location. And it's not just alcohol. It's drugs, all kinds."

Sandy just raised an eyebrow and pursed her lips, making the deputy even more uncomfortable.

"The public defender came this morning, but the old man was just in too much misery. We finally got some food into him."

"Has he been checked by a doctor?"

"He's just hungover."

"He's also ninety-five years old. Do you want a lawsuit on your hands for a death while in custody?"

Once more, the young deputy swallowed. "You can—" he began. "You can talk with the Sheriff if you want."

The lawyer slowly leaned over the counter, letting the full force of her personality propel her face close to the deputy's. Without raising her voice, she said firmly, "I want to talk to the public defender. Tell him to cease what he is doing and come out here now. I will be handling Mr. Manwell's case."

That produced a phone call and the deputy rushing to the door in the back with grillwork over a small glass window. A buzzer sounded and the door opened, swallowing the deputy. A few minutes later, Richard Mason stormed out of that same door.

"What in Holy Hell is going on? I'm Harley Manwell's lawyer."

"Not anymore," Sandy said, handing him her card.

Mason glanced over it. "You don't have jurisdiction here."

Sandy held out her right hand to Caroline who produced several sheets of paper. "I do now." She handed the papers to the public defender. "I've been invited in by the Honorable Hernandez Sandoval. He will be supervising my work here."

Mason jerked his head up. "The Attorney General? What's his interest in this case? We're dealing with a drunk who knifed his lifelong enemy."

Sandy stepped closer to him, her bright red Jimmy Choo's almost touching his highly polished black Salvatore

Ferragamo's. "The particulars of this case should not be discussed in a public forum."

Mason stared her down, only wavering to cast a look of sympathy in Allen's direction. He stepped aside to stuff the papers he held into his briefcase. "Well," was all he said, and headed for the parking lot.

Sandy turned to the deputy. "Now, can I see my client?"

Chapter Nineteen

Day 2: Monday, midafternoon, near Payson

Kate could feel the afternoon sun start to bake her scalp while she stood on the steps of the log ranch house. She had been on the porch peeling apples for pies she intended to bake for Isaiah's wranglers at the horse camp. It wasn't easy to bake out there. She had watched Toni come out of the barn where she had been mending tack when Paul's car came up the drive. As soon as the vehicle had stopped, Logan had raced for the corral and Kate's partner had hurried toward the horses. Toni had impeccable timing or her shields had not been up. They had become accustomed to living fairly open in the solitude of the ranch, only shielding when people visited.

Kate had barriered as soon as she saw the car, knowing Paul's own abilities. She stood now with her arms across her chest, a physical gesture that mirrored the protections she had conjured. Paul and Marianna, who stood in the dusty drive, had not seen Logan's near fall while they greeted Kate and made small talk. Now, as Toni came toward her, she lifted her eyes from them to her partner. She smiled at the confident ease the other woman possessed as she mounted the steps and transferred the black Stetson she always wore when she worked onto Kate's head. It was a playful but practical gesture. Toni casually put her arm around Kate, resting her hand firmly on the side of her wife's waist, as she smiled at their guests.

Paul removed his aviator sunglasses, slid his gaze over Toni, and fixed it on Kate. "So, Allen's working. When will he be back?"

"We don't really know," Kate offered. "Sandy Lopez had work out of town."

He glanced away as if he really didn't believe her and frowned for a few seconds. He snapped his head back toward her. "Then we'll talk business. Logan's testing is in a week. We'll need three horses and a painted pony for Logan."

Toni shook her head. "I don't know where you'll find a pony that's ridable, much less a paint around here. You know we don't deal in ponies."

"You get horses all the time. Go ask somebody."

"Dutch got lucky with Allen's paint. A snowbird had bought it for his daughter and she fell off it so we got it cheap. But we also had more time to search. I don't know what you'll find at the last minute like this. We have riding mares available but nothing small enough for Logan to ride on his own."

"He can handle a mare," Paul insisted.

"No, he's small," Toni insisted. "He needs a mount his size. It isn't like he's ridden all his life like some of the kids on the rez do."

"He's ridden enough."

"On what? A pony?"

Paul's jaw grew tight as his expression grew darker in the long silence that followed.

Suddenly, Toni bluntly said, "We can't help you. You'll have to try another ranch."

Paul fixed the native woman with a piercing stare, not even trying to placate her with his usual soothing psychic projections. It was useless on Toni anyway. He turned his attentions to Kate, making sure he had her full attention. Looking deeply into her eyes, he smiled, took a step up the stairs toward her, and said softly, "It's part of Logan's ceremony, to ride into the encampment as his ancestors did." His tone softened further as he reached a hand to touch her forearm. "As we honored our son, Allen. They both trained for months, for years, for this moment, to participate in this rite of manhood."

Kate felt pulled into his words, into his soft-spoken argument, into memories of her young son so long ago. A

56

cloud gathered around her own thoughts and even her vision. It was an honor. Logan and her precious Allen had prepared for this rite. She must help him.

A strong pressure at her waist, coming from Toni's hand, signaled warning. Of what, she couldn't fathom. The pressure released and then came again as she was pulled closer to Toni's body. A flood of energy washed over her, causing her to shut her eyes briefly. She took a slow deep breath and sent extra energy to her shields. When she opened her eyes again, her vision was crystal clear. Paul was just inches from her face.

"We can't help you," she said firmly. "Try the Ribald Ranch on the other side of Payson. They might know someone. Good luck."

Paul's jaw clenched in anger. "Logan!" he bellowed. "Now!" He swung his body toward Marianna, grabbed her by the elbow, and stormed away.

Logan came running out of the house, an apple in his hand, obviously swiped from the bushel Kate was using for her pies. He sped past Toni and Kate on the stairs toward the car. When he had the door open, he turned, waved at them, and tucked himself inside the back seat with his prize.

Paul wheeled the big car around and sped down the dirt driveway, leaving a cloud of tan dust choking the landscape.

Kate started to shake as the reality of what had just happened came slamming into her consciousness. "After all these years, I still. . . ."

Her partner wrapped her in strong arms. "He's honed his abilities in those years."

"No wonder Allen avoided him yesterday."

Toni rubbed her back. "Don't worry about our son. You'd be surprised what he can do."

Chapter Twenty

"How'd you get the Attorney General to sign off on this?" Allen asked as he and his law companions seated themselves on one side of a grey metal table in a cinderblock-walled interrogation room.

"We were cohorts in law school," Sandy Lopez said, pulling out a yellow legal notepad while Caroline did the same.

"So, there's no state interest?" Allen had nothing before him on the table, since he really wasn't involved with the legal details.

Sandy gave him a motherly stare. "Why would there be?" Retrieving a pen from the side pocket of the briefcase, she continued. "No. I just called in a favor. You can't represent someone in another state if you aren't licensed there unless you're invited in." She rummaged again inside the briefcase. "I just didn't have time to dither about hunting for some local lawyer big enough to get us in here. Caroline remembered typing a congratulatory letter to Hernandez Sandoval last fall when he was elected to the post."

"I wondered why she'd bother, since he's in another state," Caroline said. "Then she told me about her connection. They had vied for first in their class."

"Who won?" Allen asked.

"Mr. Sandoval," Caroline answered. "I think that's why Sandy works so hard."

"I work hard because people like Mr. Manwell need good representation. Actually, we aren't here directly because of the Attorney General. We're here on referral by his law firm,

Torres, Gonzales, and Sandoval. But tossing his name out there helps."

Focusing on Allen, she said. "Just observe and do what you do. I want to find out if a man his age actually could kill somebody."

Allen nodded, frowning. Though he used his abilities in his PI work, he was still uncomfortable. There were ethics involved here that were beyond anything Toni or Great-Gran had taught him. It was one thing to identify the liar in a land title dispute that led to further archival research, and another to decide whether someone was guilty of murder. The old man could wish someone dead without having the means or strength to do it.

The clank of chains as the door opened roused Allen from his brooding. Harley Davidson Manwell shuffled in and sat heavily in the only vacant chair opposite them. He was wiry, with little muscle mass or fat on him. Even at ninety-five, he was handsome, bearing a white mustache that trailed into a little beard around his chin. His eyes lit up as his eyes focused on the women. "*Muy bonita*," he said as a wide grin creased his face. Then he grimaced, reaching both hands to the sides of his head.

"Mr. Manwell," Sandy said quietly. "Are you in pain?"

"*Si, si*," and a flood of Spanish followed.

Sandy turned to Caroline, who said, "He's invoking saints. He says he's hungover."

"Mr. Manwell, we'll have a doctor come and check you after we're done here," Sandy continued. "My name is Sandra Lopez. I will be your new attorney."

The old man looked up, brightening. And then began another string of Spanish mixed with another language, both causing Caroline's brown cheeks to show a definite flush. Sandy chuckled.

Harley stopped talking and then asked something in that strange language.

Sandy shook her head. "No. I only know a few words. I haven't heard some of that since I was a child. My grandmother used that same saying. And from my brief encounter with Mr. Mason, I'd agree."

Harley laughed and then stopped, once more grasping his head.

Caroline scrunched up her face in question. Allen smiled. Even without knowledge of either language it was clear nobody had a good opinion of the public defender.

"Do you know why you're here, Mr. Manwell?" Sandy asked.

Dropping into English, he said, "I was drunk."

Sandy cleared her throat. "No," she began as if she were trying to explain something delicate to a child. "You were found next to Miguel Valencia. He was dead."

The old man took a breath as if to start another string of curses but something stopped him. "Dead?"

"Yes. He was covered in blood. They think he was stabbed."

"Stabbed," he repeated numbly.

"Do you own a knife, sir?"

"*Si*, my pocket knife." Involuntarily, he reached for where his right-hand pocket should have been. "It's in my pants. They took them away."

Sandy pulled a paper out and looked over the list of items that were found on his person when he was arrested. There was a closed pocket knife that didn't appear to have any blood on it. She raised her head. "Tell me what happened. There was a christening party?"

The old man proceeded to tell what happened at the party, about Alphonso's top shelf tequila, and about his trek out into the bush. "I broke the bottle. I was going to offer some to the *hombre* there. If I'd known it was that *puto*, I never would have."

"There was bad blood between you?"

What followed was a long list of Manuel Valencia's transgressions against his daughter, mostly involving his chasing other women. "He didn't deserve my Lucia. And he wanted to go to the baptism? No! I told him not to show his face there."

"You had a public argument with him?"

"*Si*, last week at the store. I was buying flour and sugar and coloring for the cake the Old Woman was going to make. A big sheet cake. Her cakes are the best!"

"Old Woman? Your wife?"

"*Si*, Graciela. And then I see that *puto* and tell him off."

"So, there were witnesses."

"The whole store. They know I hate his guts."

Sandy nodded as she paused. Finally, she said, "Mr. Manwell, I have to ask you this. Did you murder Miguel Valencia?"

"No, but I'd like to shake the hand of the man who did. He's a waste of skin."

The lawyer leaned back in her chair. "We'll plead not guilty at the arraignment tomorrow morning. In the meantime, I'll send a doctor in to check you out and give you something to make you more comfortable. Be ready tomorrow morning."

Sandy nodded at Allen, and he went to the door, opened it, and told the officer outside they were finished. The old man was then helped up from his chair and escorted out the door.

"Well?" The lawyer asked Allen.

"His hatred is real. But he clearly didn't know who he was with."

"That's my read, too." She smiled weakly. "It's good to know my instincts are still good."

"Was that Apache he was speaking?"

Sandy stood to stuff papers into her briefcase. "I haven't heard those idioms since I was young."

"Why didn't I hear it in Payson?"

Again, the lawyer gave him that knowing motherly look and this time so did Caroline. "You introduce yourself as Allen Rodriguez and people take a close look at you. They'll drop into English or Spanish."

"And my Spanish isn't much," he said. "I did understand all of his swear words, though."

Caroline laughed. "Typical boy. That's the first thing any of them learn." Then she, too, stood to clasp her briefcase closed.

"It's just not spoken much by young people," Sandy said, "though there is a movement to rekindle the language. And elders don't use it around outsiders, especially Whites."

Allen looked down at himself. "White?"

Again, Sandy educated him like a patient mother. "Yes. You read White. You are half, and a quarter Spanish, and a quarter something Mesoamerican." Walking toward the door she added. "I know you feel native. You have proper manners and have been taught well. And to many of us, you are."

Properly chagrined, still Allen pursued his curiosity. "Why did he use so much Spanish?"

Caroline explained. "Family ties, like mine, or just being in a dual culture where Spanish is so common."

Sandy added. "He also wasn't sure about Caroline and me. You saw his surprise when I understood what he said. New Mexico is a whole other country. I remember coming here when I was a child and it was always different. More Mexican, really."

Allen nodded. "I'll keep that in mind. I may need to wander about and get a feel of everything."

"Dulce up on the reservation is more native. You'll see. We'll need to go look at the crime scene. Or you should. Let's find a hotel, and I'll call Torres, Gonzales, and Sandoval and find out what you'll need to do legwork here for me. I imagine you'll need to shadow one of their PIs."

Chapter Twenty-One

"Is he in?" Ben Castiano slanted his head toward a closed office door as he leaned on the counter in the front of the county sheriff's office. Not even rising from his desk, Deputy Quintana flicked a hand at him.

Ben took that as an affirmative, hoisted his body off the counter, and crossed to Sheriff Mendoza's door. Offering only the briefest of knocks and not waiting for a reply, he stepped inside to find the portly sheriff elbow deep in stacks of papers. The sheriff glanced up, irritated to be disturbed, and quickly returned to his work.

"Yearly budget review," he grumbled.

"I won't keep you," Ben said. "I just wanted to tell you that Miguel Valencia's body is on its way to OMI in Albuquerque. They called when they left. We should be able to do some preliminary work this afternoon."

"You sitting in on that?" Mendoza asked, still not taking his eyes off rows of figures.

"Thought I would. It's a curious case. Have you heard anything from the crime lab at the Department of Public Safety about test results?"

"Nothing yet."

"Mind if I give them a call? It's not really part of my protocol, but there are some strange elements I'd like to find out more about."

Mendoza grunted. "I wonder if that college boy found the murder weapon yet?"

"I can ask, if you want."

"Sure. Knock yourself out. It'll be another call I don't have to make."

Ben felt a vibration in his shirt pocket. He pulled out his phone to look at the caller ID. "Gotta take this. Talk to you soon, Sheriff." Mendoza waved him off, deeply absorbed in his world of numbers.

"Ben Castiano," the field investigator said into his phone as he walked past the counter and out into the sunshine. It was warming quickly, even up in the cooler regions of northern New Mexico.

"Jim Baxter here. I think I found some information for you. I can either make copies and mail them to you or scan them and email them. Which do you prefer?"

"Email it all to me. My curiosity can't wait for snail mail."

The FBI agent chuckled. "None of us can wait for that anymore."

Ben gave him his email address and then asked. "Was there anything in there about collecting blood?"

"Yeah. It was from the voodoo person and the witch lady. Both of them talked about blood being used in sacrifice. There's a whole description of what to look for at crime scenes for specific groups. A lot of animals — cats, dogs, goats, and of course the voodoo chickens."

"Anything about human remains?"

"Hey, what do you think you've got out there in the wilderness?"

"Damned if I know. This is just a real mind twister. Heard one of the crime scene investigators talking about animal mutilations. There's always all that talk about UFOs up in Dulce."

"Dulce? Not Roswell?"

"Dulce has all the quacks talking about a secret UFO base up there somewhere."

"Where in the world could they hide it, anyway? Isn't all that country turned over in farming, or at least cattle grazing?"

"There's still a lot of heavily forested spots, and houses are few and far apart. But you'd think if a base of any kind was up there, it would be in a mountain like something more in Colorado near Wolf Creek Pass. A place where those UFOs could just fly in and disappear. Not something a farmer could stumble on looking for a stray."

Baxter laughed. "Well, happy hunting, Ben!"

The field investigator laughed, too. "I'm not going to set foot up there again unless we find another body."

"Do you expect to?"

"Naw, this is a one-off. Odd as fuck. But I doubt this will happen again."

After goodbyes were said and his phone was returned to his pocket, Ben frowned. For the first time since his very first investigation, he wanted to find his priest and ask for a special blessing.

Chapter Twenty-Two

Day 3: Tuesday, midday, near Payson, AZ

The aroma assaulted Isaiah's senses as soon as he opened the front door. It was a full-face culinary high. Following the rich apple-cinnamon smell into the kitchen, he found Kate packing foil-covered pies into two slim grocery boxes.

"You are St. Honore come down to earth," Isaiah remarked.

"The patron saint of baking, right?"

"Of course."

"I'll learn them all eventually. Your Rita has been trying to educate me about them."

"Are these all apple?"

"Yes. The two on the bottom of each box are lattice crust and the two on top have the French topping you like so much." Placing the last one, she smiled at the big man. "Will eight be enough?"

"I'll take two for my family, and the men can fight over the other six."

"Your boys sure love the horse camp. You know, I was surprised Rita agreed to set up housekeeping all the way out there when you got married."

"She's a country girl, really. But I guess the boys will want to see the world when they get older. And now that you're back, Rita's really liked visiting you."

Kate smiled. "I like talking with another mother of boys."

"Well, mine are wild and nothing like Allen. I'm glad he's going to be around more for their sakes. He's good with them."

"Have you gotten a new horse gentler yet?"

"Sam's getting arthritic and can't really ride much anymore. He does have knowledge that the gringo wranglers will never know. He needs to pass those skills onto a younger man. We haven't been getting many newcomers for the past couple of years. And nearly all of them are coming from cities with no ranch experience."

"It's good what Dutch began here all those years ago, helping men who'd been to prison or were undocumented."

"Yeah, some have gotten their citizenship papers and then found work with our references. Still, I keep hoping for that one ideal horse whisperer."

"Maybe it'll be one of your sons."

He laughed. "I think Manuel and Alexander would make good sci-fi writers with the imaginations they have." He put a box under each arm and started for the foyer.

Kate followed to open the front door for him. "What kind of games have they been dreaming up now?"

Out on the porch, Isaiah turned. "I don't know where they get their ideas. We don't have TV out there. No electricity. This morning they told me a story about seeing a giant black bird as tall as me around the training corral. Said it was dancing and speaking in its bird language and it mesmerized the horses so they wouldn't make any noise."

Kate shook her head. "Young minds."

"It has to be all those animal books from the library that Rita's been reading to them."

"Maybe she should ask the librarian for books with people in them like *The Boxcar Children* or *Treasure Island*," Kate offered.

"Good idea. I'll tell her. And thanks for the pies."

"Any time."

Isaiah descended the steps and crossed the dirt to the horse tied to the corral fence. Two green panniers across the horse's back were already opened, waiting for their culinary cargo. While he stowed them, he muttered, shaking his head, "Giant birds."

70

Chapter Twenty-Three

Day 3: Tuesday, early afternoon, Espanola, NM

Tucked into a booth at the Green Chile Mexican restaurant near their motel, Allen reached for his soft drink, hoping the good Doctor would soothe his blistering mouth. The middle-aged Latina waitress stood by with a squeeze bottle of honey. When he found some relief, she set it in front of him. "Put some of that on a tortilla. It works better than soda or milk. Though some like sour cream."

He raised watery eyes to the woman, half wondering if she had gone mad.

"You aren't from around here, *mi hijo*, or you'd know we serve the hottest chile in town. We like it hot." She patted his shoulder. "I'll bring you some sour cream, too." Then off she padded to the kitchen.

Sandy, sitting opposite him with Caroline, cringed. "I'm sorry," she said meekly. "I should have warned you. Our Mexican restaurants in Payson don't use chile very much. They make sauces."

Caroline handed Allen one of the tortillas that came with her meal. "You should have gotten a hint from the salsa."

He tore off a piece and squirted honey on it. "It was red. This is green," he said in justification as he stuffed the tortilla piece into his mouth.

"Silly, green or red. It's still chile."

After taking another gulp of his drink, he said, "How would you know?"

"If you had stopped stammering around me all these years and asked me about my family, I would have told you. I have a *tia* and a brood of *primas* in Las Cruces that I visit at Christmas when you're away at school. I hone my Spanish with them. But the food is even different down there than here."

Allen opened his eyes wide, raising Caroline to an even higher pedestal than the one he had already put her on. "Hotter?"

Both women laughed, but Caroline clarified. "No, just different."

"If you survive your lunch, I have some tasks for you," Sandy began.

Allen nodded and looked suspiciously at his meal.

"Boys," Caroline scoffed again, reaching for his plate and his fork. She deftly scraped the green chile off his beef and bean burrito. Carefully, she cut into the rolled tortilla and looked inside and then returned the plate to its place in front of him. "They didn't put any chile inside so you're safe. When you get that sour cream, smother it."

Sandy tried to suppress her smile but really couldn't so she looked away, noticing someone approaching.

"Ms. Lopez?" a feminine voice asked.

"Yes, what can I do for you?"

Allen looked up at a tall, blonde young woman in a black business suit. The collar of her red blouse pointed up, causing his eye to follow the line of the fabric that was unbuttoned unprofessionally low so that the top of her black lace bra showed. The style and colors were the same as Sandy had worn yesterday but had more of a runway flair. The young woman smiled at Allen and then presumptuously sat down next to him, forcing him to slide down the faux leather booth seat. She cleared her throat, and Allen reached for his plate and drew it protectively toward him.

"My bosses at Torres, Gonzales, and Sandoval sent me," she said to Sandy. "I'm their go-to PI. I'm to offer my services to you."

Allen fumbled with his fork, unsure whether it was polite to continue eating and then feeling gun shy about being burned

72

again. The young woman's energy was also broadcasting hard against his shields.

"You'll be working with Allen," Sandy said, nodding toward him. "He's *my* go-to PI."

"Oh?" the woman turned a high-watt smile on him and offered her hand. "I'm Susan Jameson, like the whiskey, street-wise but smooth."

Allen opened his mouth but found himself like a fish on a river bank.

Caroline reached across the table and shook the woman's hand. "Caroline Wolfe. I'm a partner in the firm."

The woman's smile dimmed a few watts as she said, "Well," pulling her hand out of Caroline's and turning back to Sandy. "So, what do you want us to do? Interview witnesses? Verify alibis?"

Sandy glanced at Allen and said, "Actually, I want you to track down our client's relatives and interview them, as well as the grocery store employees who may have witnessed an argument. And I want you to take a look at the crime scene. All that's up in Dulce."

"Oooh. Road trip."

Allen shut his eyes. *How far was it up there? Two-three hours under heavy shielding.* He opened his eyes to see Caroline's face. Her jaw was clenched and her whole body was tense as she studied the PI.

At that moment, the waitress returned with a small dish of sour cream. "Here you go, *mi hijo*. You'll feel better soon."

Allen took the dish and concentrated on his food. He preferred to eat rather than get embroiled in something he knew he wasn't ready to tackle. Shutting out everything that was going on around him, he ate, at first carefully and later enjoying the mix of flavors. He had almost finished the big burrito when Caroline kicked him under the table. It wasn't hard, just surprising. When he raised his head, she gave him another "stupid boy" look that was more of a prompt. Then she nodded slightly toward the PI. He turned his attention to Sandy who was talking.

"—to Dulce tomorrow," Sandy explained. "It might be best to stay in Chama to have some distance from everyone and everything."

Allen smiled at Caroline, warming to the idea of spending time exploring a less populated area with her. He would need her to translate for him. When she glared at him, he scrunched up his face in question.

"Caroline," Sandy drew her from her visual scolding. "Find a hotel in Chama and make a reservation for tomorrow afternoon."

The blonde PI stood and smiled at Allen. "Well, I'll see you tomorrow morning. Pack your jammies. . . . Or not."

When she was gone, Allen, totally bewildered, said, "What just happened?"

"You're going up to Chama tomorrow," Sandy said. "We'll be in court. I don't know why that public defender was hell bent on arraigning Mr. Manwell today. He must be from Albuquerque. I don't how long we'll have to wait tomorrow before we're heard. The court could be packed. I've never heard of a municipal court that only holds arraignments one day a week. Payson isn't much bigger, and it has them every day Monday through Friday."

"But . . ." Grasping for anything to avoid that fateful car trip, he said, "I'll need Caroline to translate for me."

"Trust me," Sandy said, "people will only speak English around the both of you."

"And they won't talk, either."

Sandy leaned back against the booth. "Probably. But you're there to see if what they do say is truthful. I really don't see any surprises. We're just verifying his statements. The PI could do it all herself, but I want you to look at the crime scene."

Allen frowned. "With her?"

Sandy moved closer to him. "When people see you with her, they'll think you're legal here. So, when you do a little poking yourself. . . ." She opened her hands to finish her statement.

It was Allen's turn to rest against the padded booth. "You're sneaky."

She picked up her own drink and took a sip through her straw. "Aren't all lawyers?"

Chapter Twenty-Four

"Those weren't horses," Marianna seethed beside Paul as he drove them away from the Ribald Ranch. "They were big dogs!"

"Shetland breeders," Paul spat out between his teeth and looked out the driver's side window, unwilling to unleash his own anger. Through the trees, he could see patches of meadow creeping up against rising hills dotted with more forest. Once in a while a rock outcropping broke the monotonous green.

"That abominable woman tried to make a fool of you!" Marianna said.

That woman is an enigma, he corrected silently. *She always has been. She was immune to everything I do. But Kate shouldn't have been, and she should have persuaded that woman to agree to the four horses. Logan could ride a big horse! I've certainly paid for enough riding lessons,* he fumed. *The ride to the ceremony grounds was not that far.*

Marianna wailed at her husband. "How are we going to honor our son?"

Horses have to be found. Everything has to be perfect. Logan has to pass this rite and take his place as shaman. There's no room for mistakes this time.

"We don't have long," his wife continued.

Paul knew the window to do this was closing. He was sixty, and after his last doctor's visit, he was certain he wouldn't live to see Logan come into his full power in ten years. And then there were the rumors about Cesar wanting to challenge Logan. *A grown man against a boy!* His anger grew, bypassing his trained control. He needed Allen at the ceremony. Allen had to protect his brother and take over his training. But Allen was as headstrong as his mother. *I need him there!*

"The ceremony begins in a few days," Marianna continued, "at the height of the sun at Solstice. We have to do something."

Paul punched the steering wheel and unleashed his full fury at her. "Don't lecture me, woman! I'm well aware how much time we have!"

In the silence that followed, without speaking, Logan tapped his mother's shoulder with a business card. She ignored him. He continued tapping until she turned on him in rage, "What?" He wiggled the card so she would see it. Grabbing it, she read it. "Where'd you get this?"

"I was petting the horses when you started to leave. The nice people gave me this to give to you. It's another ranch."

Another ranch! Paul ground his teeth.

Marianna reached into her purse and pulled out her cell phone. Luckily, she got a signal and dialed the number.

Drifting from her chatter, Paul allowed a little hope to enter his heart.

After a brief conversation, Marianna beamed at Paul. "They're not far. I'll put the address into the GPS." She quickly punched in the numbers and the automated voice soon notified them of the next turn. "Let's hope they have a pony."

Paul took a deep breath, feeling power fill him again. "We'll arrange for four riding mares. Logan is almost a man. He can have a man's horse."

Chapter Twenty-Five

The room reeked of disinfectant. The pale yellow of the wall did nothing to elevate the coldness of the room. Two multi-bulb Stryker Visum LED lamps were angled from the ceiling at each station, illuminating an empty stainless steel table that was perpendicular to a sink. A bank of lower cabinets separated each station. The lab was empty except for Dr. Angela Morales, dressed in blue scrubs, her long, dark brown hair pulled back with a pink scrunchy. It was an incongruous spot of happy color in the room. She was perched in a chair with casters before a computer screen, which she was studying intently.

Ben Castiano sauntered in carrying a folder of papers in his hand. "How goes it?"

Dr. Morales flashed her deep brown eyes at the field investigator. "I wondered when you'd show up." She looked at the thick folder in his hand. "We went paperless decades ago."

He glanced at what he was holding. "This? Just research a colleague sent me from a conference. He's old school and saves everything. He had all of the handouts and brochures so he scanned them in and emailed them to me."

She looked skeptical. "Why didn't you read them online, then?"

Ben moved the folder up and down, weighing it. "Too much eye strain in front of a computer. This is the kind of reading to do in a recliner with a strong margarita."

She raised an eyebrow. "Heady stuff, then?"

"Creepy stuff. It was a conference for law enforcement on quirky religions and rituals."

"Hmm." Dr. Morales frowned and then motioned for Ben to come closer to the computer. "Look at this. I ran the body through the MRI instead of the CT scanner. The wound was suspicious, so I wanted to know what was there before I took a scalpel to the body." She pointed to an image and waited for Ben to recognize what she saw.

His mouth dropped open. What he was seeing was impossible. Ben twisted his head to look at the doctor. "There's no heart."

Dr. Morales held his gaze and added details. "It was done with surgical precision." She pointed to the screen. "A thin incision line just above the diaphragm and the major arteries to the heart were cleanly cut. I checked it myself when the body came back from the scan. I've never seen anything like this." She leaned into her chair and rolled away a few inches to look at Ben directly. "I swabbed the wound to look for anything that might give me an idea about the murder weapon. It could have been a scalpel."

"Was he sedated?"

She rolled back to the computer and pulled up the toxicology report. "Not anything you'd see in an OR. There was some mescal in his system. But his stomach contents showed something other than your liquor store tequila. It was a whitish pulpy liquid and smelled fermented. I sent that for analysis, too."

"What about the blue paint?"

"Now, that's curious. The results came back quickly. It's a combination of the leaves of the anil plant and a clay, palygorskite. What's odd about that is the anil plant is native to Mexico and the clay can only be found in a deposit that spans a section of Alabama, Georgia, and Florida. Both must have been ordered in."

"Yeah, you can get anything on the Internet now."

Dr. Morales once more moved slightly away from the computer to take in Ben's full demeanor. "Did you find a lot of blood at the scene?"

HANDFUL of DIRT

The field investigator stepped a few paces backwards to lean on a long, stainless steel counter. He folded his arms across his massive chest. "That's odd, too. I should have found more. Wouldn't you think?"

She frowned. "Yes. And there seemed to be old staining from blood on the boulder he was found propped up against."

Dr. Morales sat bolt upright. "You should ask DPS if any other blood samples were sent in." She quickly turned back to the computer monitor. "Ask the local sheriff if there've been missing persons reported up there. DPS has missing persons records, too. I'll search death records here."

Ben shrugged. "Will do. Did you know DPS actually sent investigators up there? Local law enforcement usually collects evidence and sends it to them. But these guys — they were in full PPE, looking like something from a movie set."

"I heard the new director was from Colorado. They have a CSI unit that does the collection themselves. Maybe he wanted his staff to get a feel for what they'd eventually be handling in the lab. It's actually a good idea."

"Well, it's all in Santa Fe, I guess. If they flag a special interest in this, they'll call in cadaver dogs."

"It wouldn't hurt. Seriously. I'll call you if I find anything." Absorbed with the screen, she waved at him and added, "Happy reading."

The file in his hands forgotten, Ben now looked at it as if it might hold more than just academic ramblings about sinister rituals. His face wrinkled in thought. He had a stop or two to make before he went home.

Chapter Twenty-Six

Day 4: Wednesday, afternoon, Dulce, NM

As soon as Susan and Allen entered the supermarket in Dulce, they separated without prearrangement. Susan made a bee-line for the manager's office and Allen explored the store, which not only had groceries but a full hardware section, updating the old-time idea of general store. He quickly found the deli section and looked around for bakery items that often were nearby. Allen found a small white cake with vanilla icing that might serve six people. Next, he looked for a rotisserie chicken. Not finding that, Allen settled for cold cuts. As he ordered ham, roast beef, and two kinds of cheese, he chatted with the middle-aged woman behind the counter.

Allen felt comfortable here among native people, who may not have looked like him but who were more reserved than the invasive chatter he had been bombarded with during the drive up from Espanola. There had been types like Susan when he went to school in upstate New York, but the college was very diverse and he was never in close quarters with them. He always could retreat to the library or his room. Even his roommates had been mixed. Arjun was from India. He talked little, except when he was excited about some aspect of his studies, but he graduated a year before Allen. Jamal, his senior year roomie, was an outrageous extrovert from Brooklyn, who kept wanting to get Allen to party more. He was a serious pre-med student, though, and respected Allen's own reserve. Usually, Allen's heavy shielding and reticence were enough to ward off Susan types. But not this time.

"My cousin that I'm visiting here," Allen said to the woman behind the counter, "said there was a big fight in the store between two old men a few days ago. That's a shame elders do that."

The deli counter worker narrowed her eyes at him, studying his face. "It is. No wonder our young people have no respect."

"My cousin said there'd been some bad blood between them."

"For years. One of them did the other's daughter wrong. A real woman-chaser."

Allen nodded, showing his understanding. "How bad was the fight? They didn't come to blows, did they?"

The woman laughed. "No, thankfully. But one was fit enough to do some serious damage. That old man still thinks he can get women at seventy-five."

Allen smiled. "We all would like to think that."

She cocked her head. "Not you. You're spoken for. I saw that same contentment in my son's eyes before he got married."

Allen actually blushed. "We'll see, ma'am."

She leaned closer to the deli case. "Your heritage is well hidden, but it's there. I hope she's one of us."

He grinned.

Then the woman pointed to shelves of bread. "You'll need that. We make it here. It's fresh."

As he selected a loaf, the woman asked, "Who's your cousin?"

Feigning he hadn't heard, he waved at her and headed for the checkout and eventually to the car. On the way, he called Graciela Manwell to make sure he and Susan could drop in.

~*~

Susan was already inside her Lexus, looking at her visor mirror as she touched up her lipstick. Allen cringed as he had when she had first pulled up at the motel in Espanola. Granted, working for a high-powered law firm made her able to afford a luxury car, but it was incongruous on a reservation. He felt embarrassed as he hauled himself in with his bags and started buckling his seatbelt.

"I thought you were investigating, not shopping."

"We have different methods," Allen replied and then punched the Manwell address into his phone's GPS. "Did you find out anything?"

"No," she said, putting her visor back in place. "They stonewalled me as soon as I walked in." She started the car and hit the AC. "Nobody knew anything. So much for witnesses."

"They're there. Prosecution will find them." He looked out the passenger side window as they drove further into town. "This should be our last stop," Allen suggested, eager to get into his own room to process everything and rest.

"Oh? I thought I was lead investigator. Or do you have more exciting plans?" She gave him a toothpaste commercial smile.

He glanced at her. "We need to get into the hotel at Chama before it gets too late. Caroline said that it wasn't open 24/7. It's historic, and they sort of take that seriously."

Susan harrumphed. "Caroline said."

Chapter Twenty-Seven

Day 4: Wednesday, afternoon, Santa Fe, NM

"Here's the missing persons list you requested." An administrative clerk passed a single sheet to Ben Castiano as she walked him to the lab director's office.

Reviewing the very short list and the dates caused Ben to frown. The dates went back only forty years. "Is this all?"

"That's all that's on the computer. I suppose there might be some on microfiche somewhere," the petite young woman admitted. "I doubt you'll find much. Rio Arriba county is sparsely populated and has had few people go missing." She looked up at the big man. "Despite the fact there's supposed to be a big underground US/alien base up there. Now, cattle mutilations," she began, stepping up to a door, "were reported way back in the 70s. We have those on computer files now. They've been used as part of training exercises." She opened the door to a large lab space. "Dr. Ward's office is in the back."

Ben passed studious young techs pouring over lab stations, either busying themselves with equipment or fixated on computer screens. In the back to the left, he found an open door that led to an office that looked like that of any college professor. Books crammed hanging shelves along one wall, precise and orderly. Two other walls bore antique illustrations of the human body. Ben remembered some of them from his own studies of anatomy. A bank of windows along the remaining wall added brightness to the already fluorescently lit room.

Dr. Ward, now in a lab coat and a plaid shirt and jeans instead of the full PPE at the crime scene, sorted through printouts on the massive desk in front of the book shelves. He looked up when Ben tapped a knuckle on the open door.

"Ah," the young man said. "I got the report from OMI." He gestured to a chair under a sepia-tinted anatomical drawing of the human heart by Da Vinci. As Ben sat, Dr. Ward glanced up at the drawing and back to the field investigator. "Quite curious, isn't it? This case."

Ben shook his head in bewilderment. "I've seen things. But this?"

Dr. Ward separated a paper from those he had been studying. "The blood splatter would be consistent with the victim being forced over the boulder and the heart being removed. But there wasn't enough blood at the scene. Do you think he was moved?"

"I doubt it." Ben considered his next words. "The blood might've been collected."

"Collected? Hmmm." The scientist studied the paper again. "We found a lot of old blood on the boulder. We only took a few samples, but it wasn't the same blood type as the victim's." He looked up at the ceiling, seeming to search for some answer or recollection. "You know," he began and then looked at Ben. "There's a way to see if there might've been other blood on the ground. Old blood. I recall reading a journal article recently about being able to find blood that had been deposited on the ground for up to six years. We could find out if the crime scene was used a lot before. There is an indication that that might be the case. I'd like to get up there again soon. And bring in some cadaver dogs."

"Cadaver dogs? What do you think is going on up there?"

"Might be a serial murderer. They often bury in the same spot."

"This victim was left in plain sight."

"Maybe the murder was interrupted. Maybe the old man the Sheriff picked up stumbled onto something."

"What about the blood on the old man?"

"We took a swab of the man's hands before they took him away, and we analyzed the blood on his clothing and the broken tequila bottle at the scene. There was just the old man's blood on the bottle shards. But he had both his blood and the victim's on his hand and clothing."

"So, he didn't shank him with the bottle?"

Dr. Ward laughed. "Hardly. When I swabbed him, his hands were shaking so much he couldn't even write his name, much less remove a heart with precision."

Ben and Dr. Ward and his team had come on the scene after the old man had been arrested. Ward probably took those samples at the sheriff's office before he came up to Dulce. Ben confronted the scientist facetiously, "So, we're back to aliens and animal mutilations?"

The young man shrugged. "It makes me curious, though." Then, as if remembering something, he sorted through the papers again and pulled another out. "I analyzed the swab from the wound myself. There were microscopic fragments of obsidian there." He looked up. "I remember reading that some cosmetic surgeons use modern obsidian blades because they don't have the drag of a steel scalpel and provided a cleaner line, meaning the patient heals with less scarring. Maybe we're looking at a surgeon."

Ben nodded. "Perhaps. This gets curiouser and curiouser."

"Indeed."

"I wonder if the sheriff's office is prepared for something this puzzling. It looked like they thought they had a slam dunk."

"It isn't. I'll email all this to OMI as well as the sheriff."

"Could you email me a copy, too?" Ben asked. "This one is giving me a nasty itch. It feels. . . ."

"I know," Dr. Ward said. "Isn't that great?"

Ben sucked in a breath in astonishment, realizing also it was time to get home and read all of the research he had waiting in his car. "Thanks. I appreciate your time."

As he headed toward the open door, Dr. Ward stopped him and the field investigator turned. "Do you know who's representing the old man?"

Ben shook his head, curious. Forensics never got involved with the defense.

"I'll call the sheriff's office then."

"Why?"

Turning back to the mess of papers, he threw out, "The victim was HIV positive."

Instinctively, Ben looked at his hands, thankful for the protection of latex at the scene.

Chapter Twenty-Eight

A bright-faced girl of about twelve opened the door of Graciela Manwell's house, an adobe structure at the end of a very long road on the north end of Dulce. She scrunched up her nose at Allen and Susan, who waited under the *portal*. Behind the girl stood an older teenager, who flashed her eyes at Allen and smiled.

"Are you reporters?" the young girl asked.

"No, we're not," Allen said, startled by the rude question coming from this household.

The girl scanned Susan's form up and down. "She looks like one."

"My name is Allen Rodriquez and this is Susan Jameson. We're working with Harley Manwell's defense attorney. May we come in?"

She frowned at him but then eyed the two grocery bags he held in his hands.

"I brought lunch and a cake," Allen added.

As she took the bags, the girl muttered, "At least you got manners." She turned and disappeared into depths of the house.

"At least somebody does," Susan grumbled.

The older girl stepped closer to the visitors. She smiled coyly at Allen and then opened the door wider so they could enter the foyer. "I'll tell Gran," she said closing the door and slipping further into the house. From their ages, it was clear that Graciela Manwell was a many-grand-grandmother to these two.

In the adolescent's wake, Allen and his PI partner stepped into the foyer, and Susan started to move further inside. "We're here to see Graciela—"

Allen's right arm barred Susan from barging in. The action caused his hand to brush against something hard at her waist. He turned, his anger growing, and spread open her jacket to reveal a compact black leather holster at her waist. "You can't have that here. It's illegal on any rez." He spun her around and pushed her toward the open door. "Go put it in the truck. There are kids here."

She started to protest but resigned herself to the legality of the situation. Petulantly, she stalked off to her Lexus.

"Good. She left," the younger girl said behind Allen.

He should have been aware of her approach, but his anger had blotted that out. "She'll be back."

"Not if I can help it." The girl locked the door. "Gran's waiting for you." As she led him into the living room, she added. "Pay no attention to my sister. She gets a crush on anything that breathes."

That produced a much-needed smile from Allen, who was grateful for something to clear away his anger.

The matriarch was stationed in an overstuffed chair in a living room filled with houseplants and statues of the Virgin Mary. The majority were in front of a wide picture window. Tall glass holy candles burned, seeking help from St. Jude, St. Anthony, and Our Lady of Guadalupe. There was even a candle burning in front of a small statue of St. Ives, the patron saint of lawyers. Allen had seen one in Sandy Lopez's office. She'd told him years ago that one of her cousins had sent it to her when she started her law practice. She kept it on top of her legal bookcase.

Allen drew his attention away and focused on Graciela Manwell, who looked older than the ninety years he had been told she was. Dressed in a pink and blue print housedress, she hunched over in her chair. The midsummer heat had caused someone to turn the air conditioning down to polar temperatures, forcing the old woman to pull her purple shawl tighter over her shoulders. She fingered her rosary, either intentionally or just seeking its comfort. She interrupted that action to reach for a cup of hot tea on an end table beside her chair.

"*Ya'ateh*, Grandmother," Allen said respectfully, using one of the two words he knew were spoken by the Apache people in Payson. He knew it was also a Navajo greeting.

Graciela looked up at him. "They say *Da nzho* or *Ha annsi* here. My people would throw you an *hola*." She gestured to the couch that faced the large picture window where the plants and saints resided. As Allen sat, she added, "You're from Harley's lawyer?"

"Yes. Sandra Lopez. We came in from Arizona. She has kin here and was asked to help. I'm her private investigator. I just wanted to visit with you about Mr. Manwell and his trouble."

At that moment, the young girl brought in a plate with a sandwich on it and a glass of fresh-squeezed lemonade. She offered it to Allen.

He gestured to Graciela, meaning she should be served first because she was an elder.

"No, silly. You're the guest."

Chagrined, Allen took the plate and set it on the couch beside him and gratefully started to take a long drink from the glass.

"That other lawyer was a piss ant," Graciela stated.

The lemonade went down wrong, causing him to cough.

"Adam's friend said so. Thought too much of himself. Your lawyer. She of the people here?"

Allen nodded, clearing his throat so he could speak. "She can tell you of her kin, but I can't."

The old woman narrowed her eyes at Allen. "You aren't."

"No." Allen admitted.

"But not *gringo*. Something else. Not Harley's people, though. Foreign. Might be some of mine, too. But you had a teacher."

"A great-grandmother by marriage, not blood."

She nodded her head. "Knocked some manners into you."

Allen smiled. "I guess so. She was a hard teacher."

"You needed that."

"I did."

"So, your lawyer. How much is she going to cost?"

"Nothing," Allen stressed. "She's doing this *pro bono* because she was invited here by her kin."

"That's kind of her."

"It's the right thing to do. Mr. Manwell needs help."

"Got himself into a mess. I told him not to touch Alphonso's tequila. But he has a long-time thirst. He's behaved himself for months now. Maybe saving up his good deeds so he wouldn't have so much to confess when he did go on a bender. But this?"

"I heard that he and Miguel Valencia had a long history of trouble."

"Bad business, that. I worried for Lucia, our daughter. But he was a stallion, that one. Never could keep his pants zipped. I begged her to divorce him. But the priest wouldn't have it. She tried to be long-suffering, but no. She did run him off."

The young girl brought a plate for Graciela. The sandwich had been cut into small squares.

The old woman dropped her rosary in her lap and picked up one of the squares. "Eat," she said.

Allen picked up half of his sandwich and sank his teeth into the pile of meat and cheeses. He discovered heat as he chewed. Pausing, he lifted up a corner of the bread to find a thin coating of green chile on top of the cheese. Mayo was on the bread, too. He took another bite. It was hot but not ulcerative as it had been at the restaurant. He could taste the rich flavors of the peppers.

"So, your daughter ran her husband off."

The old woman nodded slowly. "He tried to come 'round when he was in between women. And he showed up at their oldest daughter's baby christening. The neighbor brought a gift for the baby, and Miguel followed her home and took up with her. Harley was so angry."

"So, this has been building for years," Allen commented to himself. "He has motive."

The old woman grunted. "Motive! We all had motive. If I'd had the strength, I would've shot him years ago and done the penance for it. He broke Lucia in ways only God understood. She withered inside until there was nothing. Once her children had married, it was as if she just gave a deep sigh and left this world." She made the sign of the cross. "I pray for her every day."

"Do you think Mr. Manwell killed Miguel Valencia?"

She shook her head. "Harley gets mad. Yes. But he could never kill anyone."

"Tell me about the christening party for your great-great-granddaughter," Allen said as he pulled a small notebook and pen from his shirt pocket. "We'll need to talk with the guests. That's where Mr. Manwell was last seen."

"Alphonso lives in a big house south of town. You'll want to talk to him. I'm still angry at him about the tequila. Rosa!"

The young girl quickly appeared.

"Write down Alphonso's address."

The little girl fled into the kitchen again.

"Was it a big party?" Allen prompted, looking for more names.

"Twenty people. He wanted to invite the whole casino, to hear him tell it. He's a bigshot there and wanted to impress them or maybe us, I don't know. He's a good man for Sonja.

But thinks too much of himself and his position. He'll tell you who all they invited. Neighbors, too."

Allen nodded, putting the notebook and pen away. "*Ashoog*, Grandmother."

The girl appeared with a slip of notebook paper in one hand and a sandwich in a plastic bag. "*Ahee-ih-yeh*," she corrected. "Thanks to elders. Show some respect."

Graciela laughed heartily. "Still being taught by hard teachers."

Allen smiled at the girl and finally at the old woman. "Yes, I am." He stood. "Sandy Lopez will be in touch to keep you informed of your husband's case. I do appreciate you speaking with me."

The girl led Allen to the front door and handed him the bag. "For the reporter. I don't want her to say we didn't offer her hospitality." She looked up at him. "Now you can say *ashoog*."

Allen laughed. "*Ashoog*, wise one."

The girl rolled her dark brown eyes.

Chapter Twenty-Nine

With his office phone pressed against his ear, Sheriff Mendoza chewed on the top of a ballpoint pen, regretting he'd ever given up smoking those fat cigars he used to enjoy and silently cursing the political-correct *pendejos* who'd pushed to ban smoking indoors. The cocky Dr. Ward from the crime lab kept droning on about paint and ground clay and volcanic glass and how long blood could last on the ground and on rock. *Oh geez-louise, make him shut up.*

When he mentioned HIV and cadaver dogs, the pen fell from Mendoza's jaw. That meant extra expenses on his fiscal year report: HIV testing and a police presence again up in Dulce with all the mileage and extra gas. The dogs came out of DPS' budget. The sheriff ground his teeth. "Well, send the report to the DA's office and a copy here for our files. When are you going up with the dogs?"

"Friday morning," Dr. Wade replied. "I'm emailing the reports now."

"I'll have an officer up there with you."

He slammed the phone down and jerked out a bottom drawer in his desk. "Damn, double damn, hell! Where is that friggin' file?" Wildly, he searched through the papers there, looking for the union rep and the HIV testing site in town. The union rep probably wouldn't be needed, but he thought he'd better pull that out just in case one of his deputies thought about unsafe workplace issues or some other PC ideas. Slamming the file drawer shut, with no papers in hand, he spat out, "Fuck!"

Mendoza hoisted his bulk out of his chair and propelled himself into the main office like a tank. "Somebody get me the hospital and the union rep and patch them into my office." Turning to go back to his office, he spotted Ben Castiano coming in. "I suppose you heard?"

"Yep, can I have a word?"

"Sure," he said, moving back into the privacy of his office. "My day can't get any worse." Once he was settled into the comfortable familiarity of his worn chair and Ben had taken a seat, he asked, "Are you getting tested?"

"No need," Ben answered. "I used proper protocols. But your arresting and attending officers will need to, just in case, as will the tribal police officers. The old man didn't bite anybody."

"Did you hear the banty rooster, Ward, wants cadaver dogs up there? What's he think he's unearthed — a serial killer? The old man knifed the guy. Old grudge."

"It might not be that cut-and-dried, Sheriff. But it'll be up to the DA to look at all the evidence."

"What did you want to talk about?"

"Do you have contact information for the old man's lawyer? Is he one of the public defenders from Albuquerque, like you always get?"

"No, she's a hot, feisty thing from Arizona. She got the red carpet from the Attorney General's office."

"The Attorney General?"

"Well, his law firm. Same difference. She's staying over at the Sunset. That was a surprise. I thought she'd be at the Santa Claran."

"Maybe she doesn't like casinos."

The sheriff grunted.

"Do you have her contact information? I'll walk over the OMI report."

Mendoza grinned, starting to lift up papers on his desk in search of something. "Looking for some side action?"

"I'm a happily married man, Sheriff."

Again, the sheriff grunted, finally locating a business card underneath his fiscal reports. He handed it to Ben.

The field investigator placed the card on his knee and took a picture of it with his phone. Then he handed it back. "You might need it again. This case is getting pretty squirrelly."

Mendoza shoved the chewed pen between his teeth and ground against it as he settled once more into his fiscal spreadsheets.

Chapter Thirty

The slam of the car door jarred Allen from his deep meditation. He had shielded heavily when he returned to Susan's car and found her fuming.

"Well, what you did wasn't legal, either," she began. He sensed he was in for a full-on shrew rant so he had leaned back in his seat and closed his eyes. He cycled through the familiar steps to first enhance the psychic shielding he maintained at all times. It had felt good to relax at the Manwell house. There were enough prayers and good energy there to soothe even his frayed defenses. In the car, he coated his aura with shields of different colors and strengths until he was cocooned so that he could then reach the quiet Great-Gran had shown him. After a while, he could no longer hear Susan's voice. Either she had given up or he was deeply submerged. The car door slam brought him present quickly — too quickly. He opened his eyes and his vision flickered, unable to focus. He immediately slipped back under those deep meditative waters. He took a calm deep breath and let it out, visualizing he was swimming upward, pausing to take deep breaths as from scuba gear. Once he broke the surface, he opened his eyes. He was present, and his vision was normal.

Looking out his window at the side mirror, he saw Susan hauling out her red, hard-case roller bag. He took another breath, opened his door, and stepped out onto the dirt parking area beside the Chama Hotel. He looked around at the historic town, which was more of a village. Immediately, he saw the Cumbres and Toltec Scenic Railroad station and yard; the main reason the town still thrived in the region. The metallic rumble of Susan's roller bag wheels on the street drew him back to the car. Starting to close the passenger door, he noticed the unopened plastic bag with its sandwich. Beside it was a baggie with a slice of cake Rosa's older sister had come rushing out the door to give him before he left. Allen smiled. It was teenage adoration, something he really had never experienced much in school since he had remained aloof as he learned to shield.

Allen picked up the food, pressed the door lock before he shut it, and then came around to the trunk, which Susan had closed. He found his backpack dumped on the ground. Picking it up, he headed to where he saw Susan struggling up the steps with her bag. Allen grabbed the handle and took it up the stairs and into the hotel. From her body language, she was still fuming.

They quickly got their room keys from the owner at a small glass counter filled with souvenirs. Noticing the staircase that went up part way and then did a right angle upwards, Allen decided to continue to carry Susan's bag. She was already mad, so he didn't want that bleeding over into his room through thin walls if the rooms were back to back. A courtesy could temper that.

Finding Susan's room first at the front end of the short hallway, he set her bag down and glanced at the number on his orange plastic key holder. Real keys and not electronic cards were in keeping with the historic tone of the hotel, which the owner had told them had been used by railroad passengers decades ago. He searched the room numbers and found his at the very end of the corridor. As Allen put his key into the lock and opened the door, he smiled, silently thanking sweet Caroline for putting distance between the rooms. He wondered if she was being sensitive to his abilities or if she was jealous. Both ideas made his smile broader.

When Allen had locked his door and took a look at the room, he laughed. It was a comfortable, plain room with a quilt on the double bed and filled with old, but not antique, furniture. It looked just like a railroad tourist's room. He knew it was probably grating on Susan's more high-end expectations.

Pulling out his phone, he sprawled on the bed and called Caroline to report in. When she answered, she immediately passed the phone to Sandy without letting him thank her for the room arrangements.

"It took us all day at the court to get Mr. Manwell arraigned," Sandy said. "No bail, not that he could afford any. So, he'll have to stay in Espanola. How did your day go?"

"Not much to report, Sandy," Allen answered. "There were witnesses to Mr. Manwell's argument with the victim and all the gossip that followed. Graciela Manwell verified the long-time bitterness between them so there was motive. But why would anyone wait forty years to kill anyone? Something doesn't feel right."

"I'm waiting on the autopsy report, and it should be pretty cut-and-dried." She paused, making Allen focus more intently on the phone. There was something in her voice. "I don't normally get twitchy," she confessed. "You and I have dealt with superstitions and some pretty weird family accusations. I mean, elders suspect witches and *brujos* at every turn, but it's usually just some greedy bastard wanting to cheat his relatives. But this one?"

In the back of Allen's mind, something was trying to come forward, but he didn't want to open up to anything other than to see if someone was telling the truth or not. And he definitely didn't want to open up in this hotel with all of its old ghosts. "We'll see what tomorrow's interviews hold," he said finally. "We're going to talk to the party guests. I don't know if that will spin off to other interviews."

"How's it going with Ms. Jameson?"

Allen was hesitant to answer. He only said, "She doesn't understand how to deal with people on a reservation."

"I'm glad you're up there getting to the heart of this."

Suddenly, a flood of coldness sprang from the top his head and coursed down through his body. He barely heard Sandy continue. "It'll take you all day," she was saying, "if you're lucky enough to catch people home. These christenings usually have tons of relatives attending. Stay over another night. You'll need the rest and the isolation afterwards."

Allen took a deep grounding breath and was present again. "I will. I'm glad you understand."

Clicking off the phone, he got up to cross the room and look out the window. All he could see was a grassy area behind the building next door. Beyond that were trees that made him think of water. Slipping down the stairs, he stopped at the glass counter and spoke to the owner.

"You're looking for your dinner, right?" the older man asked.

"Yes, later."

"The Boxcar Café or Fosters are good. Both serve breakfast, too."

"Thanks. Is there a creek nearby?"

"Looking to do some fishing? The Chama River is right behind the tracks. There're some good spots north of town, easy access. You can get an out-of-state license down—"

"Thanks," Allen interrupted and headed to find water.

Chapter Thirty-One

With a slim folder in one hand, Ben Castiano found the two women in a back booth of Mrs. D's Café, which was just beginning to fill with locals for an early dinner. He surmised the older of the two was Sandy Lopez. Neither was what he expected. Pulling a business card from his shirt pocket and handing it to the older woman, he said, "Ben Castiano, Office of the Medical Examiner."

"Sandra Lopez," she said and pointed to the other woman. "Caroline Wolfe, my law partner." She looked at the card and then eyed him up and down. "What can I do for the Office of the Medical Examiner?"

Ben pulled a chair from an unoccupied table nearby, placed it at the edge of the booth, and sat down. "OMI needed your contact information to keep you in the loop. If I may ask, you came all the way from Arizona? Why?"

Coolly, Sandra admitted, "A cousin called me about Mr. Manwell's situation."

"A cousin." He nodded. "How did you get invited in?"

"I knew your Attorney General in law school."

Again, Ben nodded, mulling whether he should show her the information he had brought with him.

"You didn't track me down to ask me whether I've got legal standing, Dr. Castiano. What's on your mind?"

He frowned. He never liked delivering bad news, even though it was part of his duties when dealing with a death in a home. "There are some delicate matters to this case. The victim was HIV positive. The sheriff's office has been notified, but you should have your client tested as soon as possible. The local hospital can send a tech out to do that."

Ms. Wolfe already had a notepad out and was writing down notes. "What's the name of the hospital?"

Ben told her and then turned back to Sandra Lopez. He studied her face. What he would share would probably exonerate her client even though Sheriff Mendoza thought otherwise. Following his gut, he handed her the folder he held. "OMI will email you the official autopsy report. But I thought you should see this now."

She opened the folder and skimmed through the preliminary findings. "This is impossible," Sandra said.

"There's more," Ben added. "At the back. I pulled together a brief report of some initial test results from the crime lab."

Sandra sorted through those. Her head shot up. "What have we stumbled on?"

Ben shrugged. "I have no idea. But your client is in the thick of it. Dr. Wade is bringing in cadaver dogs to search the crime scene on Friday. Who knows what he'll find up there? It's an odd place."

"You've been listening to too many UFO stories, Dr. Castiano. I heard them all myself years ago when I spent my summers up there with my aunties."

"I know. Dr. Wade already mentioned cattle mutilations, and people in his office kept talking about a secret Army/alien base there. Still, there's something. . . ."

"It's a spiritual place like most native land. People don't understand that."

That brought Ben's mind back to the thick folder of conference materials he had in his car. He needed to dive into that later tonight after his kids were in bed. Ben stood up. "I just wanted you to have all of the information. There probably will be more. The paint on the victim is a puzzle, and they haven't found a murder weapon. It sure wasn't a broken tequila bottle."

Sandra's eyes returned to the papers. She shook her head. Looking up at Ben, she offered her hand. "Thanks for bringing this to our attention."

He nodded. "You might want to take a look at the scene yourself."

Sandra smiled. "Thank you. I have a PI who can take a look."

Chapter Thirty-Two

Day 4: Wednesday, late Afternoon, Chama, NM

Water rushed within the narrow banks of the Chama River, soothing Allen. He marveled at its power, though the river's small size had surprised him. He was used to streams this size in the woods behind his Great-Gran's home. He felt a sudden longing to run along that stream, leaping over fallen logs, tapping tall pines as he passed like in a relay race, losing himself within the greenness and water. But he was never lost; uncannily, he always found his way back to Great-Gran as if she had sent out a beacon to draw him home to safety and love.

Allen pulled his phone from his pocket and dialed.

"Hello." His mother's voice was welcome, making Allen smile.

"Hi, Mom. I just wanted to let you and Toni know that I'm okay."

"We were glad to get your text last night and wondered how things were. Where are you?"

"I'm in Chama. I think you'd like it here. Tiny little town with a steam train as the tourist attraction. There's probably a shop selling that homemade fudge you always wanted us to stop for on trips."

She laughed. "I do have a sweet tooth."

Allen paused. "Is Toni around?"

"She's out in the barn. Hold on a sec, and I'll call her."

Allen squatted down on the bank and stared deeply at the patterns the water made as it gushed by. He had no idea what to say to Toni, to explain why he'd called.

After a few minutes, Toni picked up the phone, sounding a little out of breath as if she'd jogged in from the barn. "*Nya: weh sge:no*, Allen."

It surprised him that Toni dropped into that Seneca greeting. It had always puzzled him but showed the great generosity of his step-mom's people. It translated to: *I am thankful you are well,* as if seeing someone was the indication of health and that thinking of the other person was more important than yourself.

"*Nya:weh sge:no,*" Allen replied. "I am well, indeed."

The conversation paused. When Toni spoke again, her breath had become normal. "There is something," was all she said.

"Maybe," Allen replied. "Maybe it's just this land. I was up in Dulce interviewing the client's wife and checking out some leads. We'll do more tomorrow. I'm working with a PI and she's — well — so Anglo."

Toni's chuckle of understanding made Allen smile. They had had similar conversations as he was growing up. Even though he read very Anglo himself, reflecting his mother's Irish heritage, he saw the world through Toni's and eventually Sandy's and Caroline's native eyes. Great-Gran was part of the reason, but it was mostly how he had to live in order to contain and master his abilities.

"Sandy and Caroline should mute some of that for you."

"Yeah, if they were here. They're in Espanola because our client was arraigned today. I'm in Chama now. That's my base while I do all of these background witness interviews."

"So, you're in close quarters with the Anglo."

"Yeah."

Another long pause followed as Allen felt Toni's energy gently touch him. No matter how heavily shielded he was, she was always able to tap against them. He allowed her to wash her protective love over him.

"There is something," she repeated.

"Yeah. Something that's even making Sandy twitchy, and we don't know many of the details yet of the crime. Should be a simple knifing, but it doesn't fit. The client is ninety-five. He's an elder."

"Uh-huh. Must be energy before Summer Solstice. Isaiah's boys were picking up something, your mom said. They thought they saw a big black bird out at the horse camp. That's ominous enough. It wasn't an owl, but even ravens aren't always good omens."

"That's true."

"Speaking of dark omens, your father drove up to try to rent horses. He wasn't happy you weren't here."

"How many did he want?"

"Three and a painted pony."

"Three? Who's the third for? Uncle Juan?"

"I didn't ask. He'll not find a paint in less than a week."

"Well, if they were careful, Logan could ride one of the older mares."

"True, but I sent him elsewhere for his horses."

Allen found that odd, sensing his father had probably tried to throw his weight around as he usually did in Toni's presence. "Just as well. I feel sorry for Logan, but I don't want to be a part of what my dad has planned."

"Frankly, neither do I." Toni let out a grunt as if she'd eased herself up off a chair. "I have to get back to mending tack. If you need anything, just call. Better yet, open up and send. I'll feel you."

"Thanks, Toni. Tell mom I love her." He paused. "And I love you, too."

There was humor in her voice but dead seriousness. "If you send, I'll come running. Love you, son."

Chapter Thirty-Three

Day 5: Thursday, 3 am, near Payson

Thunder rumbled in the distance as flashes of lightning stretched skeletal fingers across the night sky, identifying and selecting the destined. The ground rumbled under Toni's bare feet as if a giant beast were being aroused and at any moment would buck and toss anyone on its back. A heaviness hung in the still air, ominous, both imminent and eminent, calling forth power.

Toni glanced down at her feet and at the embroidered breechclout that hung between her legs from a rope belt. Her flat chest was bare, exposing her scars. She was a warrior but held no weapons. Having another gender than just male and female allowed her latitudes others were not. She touched the cloth, which was more delicate than those used for work, hunting, or battle.

She felt the earth again through her feet, growling like a great feral cat. It was reacting to something, something that was coming. Lightning flashed again as if to echo those thoughts. Behind her, she heard large wings flapping in the air that seemed to hold its aeolian breath, waiting, pausing, preparing to unleash what was being built. The sound of beating wings drew ever nearer, closing the distance, until they were overhead, forcing Toni's head to look up at the starless night sky. Black wings beat overhead, loud and terrible, almost stuck in midair, until they bolted forward toward the lightning on the horizon. Thunder exploded. The earth buckled, throwing Toni to the ground.

Toni jerked awake in a sweat, sitting upright in bed. She gulped air, trying to find calm. Beside her, Kate stirred awake, sitting up, too, but she did not touch her. They had both learned to wait to touch in stressful times, lest what was stressful or perceived by one of them would leak to the other person and they'd feel whatever it was at full intensity.

"What's wrong?" Kate asked.

Calmer, Toni reached over and patted her wife's arm. "I'm okay. Just a dream."

"Do you want to talk about it?"

She turned to kiss Kate and then got up. "I'll go walk among the horses."

"If you're sure."

Pulling on her jeans, Toni said, "Go back to sleep. I'll be back soon."

Chapter Thirty-Four

Day 5: Thursday, morning, near Abiquiu, NM

Ben sipped his second cup of dark coffee, savoring its rich bitterness. His wife couldn't abide the stuff, calling it "truck-driver coffee." She had bought a separate coffeemaker for herself, knowing he would make non-stop pots of it when he was puzzled about a call out.

This morning, Ben fully expected to make another pot as he frowned at the papers strewn across his grandfather's antique desk. It had once borne the heavy burden of medical records that helped the senior Castiano make serious decisions about the life and death of a patient. Even as a boy, Ben witnessed that struggle and observed the anguish his grandfather felt when he lost a patient, verbally and internally asking why.

Ben had never wanted to have to ponder the fate of someone's life or quality of life because of decisions he made. Those early impressions of his grandfather's inevitable *why* colored his own life and caused him to come to the crossroads of patient care and forensics. He was rare in his position as a deputy field examiner because he actually held a medical degree, but he felt his talents were best used in that position to give families not just closure but answers. It was important for him to be at the point of contact with their immediate grief.

He frowned again at the papers on his desk. Not only had Jim Baxter emailed scans of all the handouts from the conference they had both attended, he sent his handwritten notes. Though Baxter was a veritable dark-humored skeptic, his insights were keen. What Ben had read last night and this morning were not just disturbing, they sparked too many grim thoughts about his current case.

Putting his cup down on the desk, Ben checked his watch. It was barely after eight. Dr. Morales should be in her office. He dialed from his cell and waited until she picked up. "Dr. Morales, good morning. Have you received the test results from the crime lab? I stopped by on my way home yesterday."

"Yes, I was actually just looking at the email attachments. Very strange. Dr. Wade analyzed the stomach contents. He mentioned something called *pulque*. It's not a medical or chemical term as far as I know. I'll need to look that up."

Ben jotted the strange word down and read back his spelling.

"Yeah, that's it. Dr. Wade is an odd one. Brilliant, but sometimes off the wall."

"Is he talking aliens and animal mutilations again? The lab was all up in the UFO gossip," Ben admitted.

"Who knows? Is there anything I can do for you?"

"There is, actually. Do you happen to know anyone in the anthropology department at UNM?"

"I know a forensic anthropologist there. She's a great bone man." Dr. Morales chuckled at her description.

"I'm interested in someone who knows about ritual and maybe sacrifice."

"Hmm. Let me ask the forensic anthropologist. She probably knows someone there or else can point you to someone at another university." She paused. "This all does have a ritual feel about it, doesn't it?"

"Could be. Call me when you get that information. And thanks."

"Sure will."

Chapter Thirty-Five

Harley pulled the scratchy blanket over his shoulders. He was cold. The air conditioning in the jail was set to *gringo* temperatures. He liked a little heat. This was what he always had known. A deep rumble in his stomach broadcast his empty belly. He missed the Old Woman's cooking. It wasn't the food his mother and sisters made, but it was rich with the heat of the Old Woman's history — so like her, a warmth that built up over years and lasted, sometimes producing a fiery heat. He chuckled. *Especially when I've been sampling the tequila! But her tongue is as sharp as late season chile!*

Harley shifted in the hard bunk. The food where he was had no flavor, even when he finally could swallow some. The doctor they sent eased the ghosts of his celebratory binge. The hangover was almost worth the taste of that fine liquor. He licked his dry lips as if as he could recapture that distilled quality again. He sighed and opened his eyes in the morning light. They would bring coffee and something soon. He wished they'd bring the Old Woman. He missed her, even if she was a nag. He always knew there was more behind her anger or she wouldn't have stayed with him all these years.

Grunting as his body protested, the old man heaved himself onto the side of the bed. He struggled with the tangles in the blanket as he pulled it around to cover his back and then over his arms. Harley looked at his brown hands, calloused still. A bandage covered his right palm. It hurt like a son-of-a-gun and still bled a bit through the white cotton. Tequila thinned the blood he remembered an elderly uncle telling him. *Nothing to worry about.*

The old man raised his head toward the door of the cell. The brightness beyond hurt his eyes, so he turned away, letting them vaguely focus on a corner of the room where the privy was. The pull of nature drew him up from the bed, leaving the blanket in a pile. He shuffled forward, feeling the blood drain quickly from his head. He started a stream and braced himself by a hand on the wall. As his vision fogged, he saw a figure form in the mist. A black Stetson pulled rakishly over his forehead, Miguel Valencia smirked at him from the gray painted cinder blocks.

Harley gasped then cried out, backing away, his arms flailing before him, leaving a dribbled stream of urine on the floor. Tripping over his own feet, he fell onto the concrete floor, continuing to cry out at the horror.

He barely heard the door open and a corrections officer enter, noisily putting a tray down on the small metal table bolted to the floor. When the officer placed her hands on his shoulder, he tried to scuttle away.

"Are you all right?"

He gasped, his vision finally clearing to see a stout Mexican young woman who had stooped beside him. She looked like the Old Woman had at that age, round and sturdy. He smiled. *"Si, bueno.*

"Let's get you up," the officer said, helping the old man to his feet. "I brought your breakfast. Now that your stomach is better, I got them to make you up a *carnitas* bowl and had them put a fried egg on it."

Harley grinned. *She's the Old Woman come again as a girl.* He settled himself on the bed and the officer brought him his tray.

"Can you manage that?" she asked.

He nodded, blowing on the mug of hot coffee.

"I had them put Christmas on the side because I didn't know whether you liked red or green chile."

"*Gracias,*" he answered, tearing off a piece of tortilla and scooping the mix of meat and beans onto it.

"Your family called and will visit later."

He raised his head, hopefully. "*Mi esposa?*"

"I don't know, but a relative. And your lawyer will be in again."

Harley muttered his thanks again as the officer left and closed the door. *Good food and the Old Woman. What more could a man ask?*

Chapter Thirty-Six

Day 5: Thursday, afternoon, Abiquiu

Ben was waylaid on his path to the coffeemaker for yet another cup of his favorite brew. This time he'd grab a slice of pie.

"Daddy, help," his three-year old daughter quietly pleaded as she struggled to put pink unicorn inflatable water wings onto her arms.

He set his mug on the counter and stepped to kneel on one knee in front of the little girl dressed in a ruffled pink bathing suit. He pushed a swim device up to the biceps of one of her small arms. "There's one." He moved to the other limb.

His daughter put the fingers of her free hand on the plastic bandage at the crease of his elbow. "Owie?"

Ben glanced at it. "It doesn't hurt. I had a test at the doctor."

"Why?"

He smiled. "Just to be careful. To keep us all safe." He gathered her into his arms for a hug. "Now, go swim with the fishes with your brother."

She padded out the screen door of the patio and onto the backyard where a modest-sized above-ground pool waited. Her older brother was chasing a beach ball around the pool like a happy spaniel. He splashed water at his sister as she climbed the ladder, causing her to shriek at him. Their mother, who was repotting a plant at a patio table in the shade of the *portal* that ran the length of the back of the house, raised her head from her task to call out a warning to stop and returned to pressing dark soil around the roots with her bare hands.

Ben had followed his daughter to the screen door and smiled at his family. It had probably been overkill to have the HIV test done, but he wanted to be certain he didn't bring anything home to those precious ones out there. His wife had always told him he was a suspenders and belt kind of guy, making sure every safety protocol was followed. She was a registered nurse and understood his work. Usually, he didn't share much about the death calls he had to service. Sometimes, though, he would speak about a tender moment with a family or an odd end-of-life circumstance. Death was messy even in gentle passings. But this latest one was far from ordinary, poised at being slightly weird, even among the strangest cases he'd seen.

His cellphone's loud ringer drew him back to his office. He found the smartphone on the edge of his desk on an uncluttered part of it. Not paying attention to the number, he answered, "Castiano."

"Ben Castiano?"

"Yes."

"This Dr. Andrea Blakely. I understand you wanted to talk to me."

It was the anthropologist he had called earlier. "Yes, I did. I have a case that has some odd elements to it. Could we meet at UNM sometime soon?"

"I'm tied up for the rest of the week. Would Monday be soon enough?"

"Sure."

"How about 11:00 am?"

"Perfect. I'll be driving in from Abiquiu."

"This case? You're with OMI, aren't you? What are you dealing with?"

"Dr. Blakely, I really don't know. I don't think it's a normal murder, if you can ever say murder is normal." He took a deep breath. "I've been doing a lot of reading from notes from an FBI conference I went to on non-mainstream belief systems and their practices. I think this case might have something to do with some kind of primal ceremony or rite. I have no background. I'm a Catholic. That's all I know."

"Hmm. Modern or ancient rite?"

"You'll have to tell me."

Dr. Blakely released a soft laugh. "You now have me intrigued. I'll see you Monday."

Chapter Thirty-Seven

The heat of the summer sun seeped into Toni's bare shoulders, exposed by the white tank she wore with her jeans. A worn black Stetson shielded her head. For this hot work, she had braided her thick black hair. It felt good heaving the bale of hay into the paddock behind the corral. The physical labor occupied her troubled mind. She had let the mares out to frolic a bit in the new grass that was coming back in after the rains, but it wasn't lush, standing in tufts and clumps. Toni had placed a small armful of alfalfa on top of the bale; both grasses would be an added supplement. She had carefully doled out the alfalfa as if dispensing candy to children. Like youngsters, the mares could really upset their stomachs if they indulged too much.

Pulling out her pocket knife and opening it, Toni cut the binding around the bale, pulling it well away from the rectangle, and stuffed it into her pocket. She proceeded to attack the bale with her knife, separating sections and tossing them to either side. Before she did, though, she checked the bale for foxtails or cheat grass, pulling out a couple of bits. Those weeds were forbidden in horse hay, but sometimes suppliers mixed those bales with hay for ornamental purposes like hayrides and displays. They could cut a horse's mouth badly and do even more damage to the soft lining of the stomach.

The horses had come closer as they watched Toni work. She smiled when she felt a favorite horse nudge her back. Closing up her knife, Toni slipped it in her jeans and turned, holding the small bits of foxtail in her hand. "Hey, you can't have this," she said, putting it behind her back. She patted the horse with her free hand.

Being around these large animals out in the sunshine dispelled some of the worry she had from Allen's phone call the night before. Something — she couldn't put her finger on it — something was off. Perhaps it was only the ghosts that lingered still, ten years after Allen's own testing that haunted her. Perhaps that was what he felt, as well.

Smiling at the mare, Toni continued to stroke the horse's head, but the animal caught the scent of hay and alfalfa and lowered her head to grasp bits with her lips. The woman turned to pass through the corral and put the vile foxtails into a small galvanized garbage can she had placed there to receive it. The foxtails would make good tinder for the next barbecue. Turning, Toni saw Kate come out onto the porch with two frosty glasses of lemonade.

Kate had been resilient these past ten years. Though she had been the one who needed emotional support and understanding, Kate had always been the one to give. Toni had come home to her grandmother, bringing Allen, broken but healing, tied together by Kate, who immersed herself in trying to understand old Seneca ways that had persisted into this modern world. She, more than anyone else from outside, knew that even her academic and personal desire to understand would always be limited because she wasn't of the People. Kate put it well: "I'll always hit a wall because I don't have your blood or your ancestry."

Grandmother had eyed Toni's new woman suspiciously at first, somehow sensing that Toni suffered in a previous relationship with a non-native, even though she had never confided in her about it. Before long, though, Grandmother saw Kate was more Seneca at times than even her own granddaughter was.

As Toni approached her wife, she smiled at how the decade had been kind to her. At 50, Kate's dark auburn had only muddied to a mahogany and her freckles were even more pronounced. The connection between them spiritually and physically was still intense and grew more every day. When Toni reached the steps, she couldn't resist pulling Kate close and kissing her.

It surprised Kate, who was trying not to upset the glasses of lemonade she held in each hand. "You smell like horse," she teased when Toni moved away.

The other woman leaned against the porch railing. "That's why you married me."

That made Kate smile and offer Toni a glass before sitting on the bentwood settee on the porch. She waited a few moments while the other woman drank. "Tell me."

They had agreed long ago to keep a thin thread of connection between their shields. Toni was always startled when Kate read what was seeping through, though Toni never opened up totally except when they were intimate. She looked at her wife, frowned, and then took a breath. "Something is happening in New Mexico."

"With Allen." It was a statement, making Kate nod. "You both were mysterious last night."

"It's his to tell whatever it is."

"But?"

Toni smiled in concession. "Yes, but." She studied Kate's expression. "I'm thinking of making a trip."

"To New Mexico?"

Toni nodded.

"Just you?"

"I can't shut you out from what your own son is struggling with. But—"

"But again."

"Allen is stone closed. I can't read him."

"Neither can I." Kate frowned, clearly troubled. "But he's been closed to me for a very long time. I'm his mother, after all. There are things mothers don't need to know about."

Toni nodded. "Though I'm his step-mom, I've really been his dad."

Kate smiled. "He's needed you."

"But this—"

"Is different. Yes, even I can sense it."

With determination, Toni announced. "I'm going. But—"

"There's that word again."

Moving toward her, Toni put her glass on a big upright log that acted as an end table. She knelt on one knee in front of Kate and took her hands into her own. "I know you're strong. I know you want to be with Allen. But I fear what's there. And I fear leaving you here."

"Why? Because of Paul?"

"Some. My dreams have been troubled. Big black birds and something being unleashed."

Kate squeezed her wife's hands. "Then you must go."

Toni searched Kate's eyes. "I think you should stay with Isaiah and his family at the horse camp. Isaiah is big enough to protect everybody."

Kate nodded. "Okay. When will you go?"

"As soon as we can secure the ranch and move the horses to the horse camp. Probably tomorrow."

"I'll radio Rita."

"No, I'll talk to Isaiah. There are a couple of things I want to make sure he does."

Kate smiled. "You men plotting about how you're going to protect us womenfolk."

"Something like that." Then Toni kissed her intensely.

Chapter Thirty-Eight

Logan spread his ceremonial clothing across his motel bed. He had been left alone to finish his work while his parents took care of some final arrangements. They had finally found horses — four big ones. He wasn't sure how he felt about riding any distance on one of them. They were so big! He wasn't sure the horse would listen to him. This was different from the weekend riding lessons he had taken this spring. When he had finally graduated out of the training corral, the rides were on a trail in a flat meadow next to the riding stable. From what he could see around him in Payson, this was hilly country. He wasn't sure he could handle the horse if it got spooked by an animal or a snake.

Chasing that worry away, he carefully examined his clothing. A sense of pride filled him at his handiwork and at his little defiance. All of the designs were his own. Not only were there lizards on his vest but there were miniature ears of corn he had beaded to attach to the traditional Mesoamerican sandals his father had contracted to be made for him. The sandals had a leather sole and heel that wrapped around the ankle, from which leather laces secured the shoe to the foot. Logan had attached the beaded corn to the ends of the laces so they could be shown off when tied. He could have put some symbol on the heel pieces but felt the corn was appropriate to honor the earth mother, who provided food and upon whose earth he walked. Logan wasn't sure his father would approve, nor whether he would approve of the embellishments the boy had made to the doe skin breechclout. He had continued the corn theme, running a half dozen vertical stalks of the plant across the front of the hide. Below that, he laid a double row of brown beads to represent the earth. From that row he had suspended blue, scrub jay feathers with ends he had beaded also in green.

Logan had been collecting the feathers for the past two years, finding his first accidentally one spring in his front yard while he had been observing Brother Lizard. He had taken one in to his teacher, and she had identified the bird species. She also said that scrub jays weren't appreciated because they were noisy birds, but they were very curious and, like crows and ravens, were intelligent thinkers and could solve problems. Logan smiled, remembering. He was glad he honored those rejected birds as part of his totems. He felt a kinship with them because they were misunderstood.

The motel door opened with his mother excitedly chattering on about food for the feast as his father followed with an indifferent look on his face. That changed when he saw the ritual clothing spread out on the bed.

"You've finished?"

"Yes, Father." Logan stepped back so the whole ensemble could be seen.

Paul picked up the vest. He examined the lizards on each side of the vest panels and then looked at the back, which was blank. "This isn't finished."

"I wanted it blank."

"You have to have protections on your back. Put a jaguar there or a cougar or a snake. You need that energy."

"Ayeee!" his mother reacted. "You have four days before the rite!" She found the pattern book Logan had been using and shoved it into his hands. "Find something and finish."

Logan sighed and went to the easy chair by his bed. He noticed that his father had abandoned his inspection of the rest of the pieces of his costume. That had at least spared him more overreactions. He tuned out his parents' talk about Allen not being at his ceremony. Logan wanted his big brother to be there. He'd be the only person who didn't demand anything from him. He was sad that he'd have to do this alone, just like these decorations. Allen could have given him some good ideas.

Logan paged through the pattern book, which was more the size of a magazine. It was filled with desert motifs. No jaguars were in it at all. He toyed with the idea of putting a big saguaro cactus on the back. It would probably anger his father. Yet, cactus plants had big thorns and could be good protection. But that design like any kind of big animal would take more than three or four days to complete, and he knew there were preparations to do the day before like fasting and doing a sweat.

When Logan got to the last page of the book, he was relieved to find no big animals but also disappointed that he found nothing to cover that blank space. He closed his eyes then and concentrated on cats then wolves and finally any big animal. He remembered photographs he'd seen, the way those big animals moved in movies, and how he had reacted to dogs and cats his neighbors had. The boy remembered seeing paw prints in a neighbor's yard after she had watered her flowering plants. The soft ground revealed a big pad and four toe pads just like both the dog and cat had. The neighbor's little dog, though, had left little toenail marks. Pet dogs and cats were similar to their wild cousins like cougars and wolves.

Opening his eyes, Logan knew what he'd put on the back of the vest. The designs would be easy to bead, and they might even be fun. It was just a matter of drawing the outlines and deciding how the prints would appear on the doe skin. Dogs and wolves were pack animals. Cats were solitary but just as loyal. Finding a piece of paper, Logan began to sketch, sending out a request that these powerful totems would honor him with their protection and give him the strength to become who he was supposed to be.

Chapter Thirty-Nine

Day 5: Thursday, late afternoon, Chama, NM

Allen was dead tired. It had been a long day interviewing witnesses. Susan had thawed a little during their first stop at the casino where they had tracked down Alphonso Torres. She was in her element, flashing lights and direct questions. They had gotten his address and went to interview his wife, who happened to be having her mother and grandmother visiting the new baby. Susan softened a little around the women, who were happily chatting about children, and was able to verify the continued bad blood between Harley and the victim. The women also painted a very warm picture of their patriarch, who was described as gentle and loving, even if he cared too much for drink.

From there, Allen and Susan interviewed all of the neighbors on the front steps of each house, no one offering for them to enter. Allen chalked that up to not wanting to get involved with their neighbors' troubles. Since they had obtained a list of party guests with some initial addresses, the PIs tracked them down. Most of those interviews were done in small groups, as if the reservation telegraph had spread the word that they were working for Harley Manwell's lawyer and that Sandy Lopez was one of them. It made the monotonous work go quicker since they could cross five or six names off the extensive party list at each stop.

The last interviews of the day were at a small café where at least a dozen of the husbands of the women they had interviewed had gathered over coffee. Allen had insisted that Susan sit at a booth nearby to listen and observe while he talked to the men. She fumed at the sexist nature of his request, totally ignoring that she had taken the lead when they'd interviewed these men's wives. It was the only way to handle a discussion with traditional men here in the café. Allen had pulled up a chair and bought another hour of coffee for the men. The café was accustomed to coffee gatherings like this and had posted their rates by the cup or by the hour. His purchase had put a small dint into his credit card, but could be written off as an expense. That group interview only verified their client's love of drink with long stretches of being sober in between. The men also gave very graphic details about the victim's womanizing, but also said that Harley Manwell never got violent.

Nearing six o'clock, Allen just wanted to shut himself in his room and mend his shields. He had opened them slightly at each interview to verify the truthfulness of the witnesses. Still, the bombardment of others' energies left him drained as he followed Susan down the hallway of the old hotel to their rooms. He wasn't alert when Susan abruptly stopped and spun around, making him bump into her chest. The flash of desire more than the predatory look on her face forced him backwards a couple of steps.

"Sorry," he stammered out.

Susan took a step forward. "Why don't we have dinner and drinks and process what happened today?"

In truth, he was starved. He hadn't really eaten all day, only grabbing coffee in the morning before they left and at the café. No one had offered them hospitality, which wasn't surprising since, being with Susan, he was assumed to be non-native.

Allen was struggling to think of words to counter Susan's request. She had already closed the distance between them and was reaching a hand toward his chest when his cellphone rang. He pulled it out and saw that the caller was Sandy Lopez. "I gotta report in. It's Sandy."

Accepting the call, he turned and fled down the way they had come and took refuge out on the upstairs covered balcony.

"Sandy, we finished all of the interviews. Everyone verified the feud between our client and the victim. They picture Mr. Manwell as a loving, caring man, who did like to drink. But he didn't do that very often. It seems his wife kept tabs on him so that he didn't have much opportunity." Not waiting for a reply, he rushed on. "I'll be glad to get back to Espanola tomorrow."

"Have you eaten?" The voice wasn't Sandy's. It was Caroline's.

He took a relaxed breath and laughed.

"You haven't, have you? Now, you listen to me, Allen Rodriguez, you get a good steak in you tonight. Right now."

"I will. I promise."

"Good. Sandy wants to talk to you."

Shaking his head, Allen smiled. Sweet Caroline could be standoffish, but she sometimes let her caring slip out.

"Allen," Sandy said, coming on the line. "I need you and Ms. Jameson to go to the crime scene tomorrow. The crime lab is sending in a team to do a grid search for the murder weapon and to do some extra tests around the actual scene. Something about old blood. They're also bringing in a cadaver dog to see if something might be buried up there."

A sudden chill ran over Allen's shoulders and down his spine. "I—" His throat choked out his voice.

Sandy apparently picked up something. "What is it?"

"I don't know." He took a deep breath and let it out. "I think I got your twitchy feeling."

"Caroline is right. You need to eat. Not just meat but bread, too. Something solid to keep you grounded in this world. You were open all day, weren't you?"

"Off and on."

"Good lord, boy! You have to recover tonight before you set foot out there tomorrow." She paused and pursued a different tack. "Is your PI mate disturbing you?"

He laughed then. "I'd double shield if I could."

"She has big energy. She bleeds all over everybody. Even I can feel it."

"It's been difficult because of the culture here."

"She's more big city than Albuquerque. I'd venture to say maybe Chicago, since she doesn't have an East Coast accent."

"Probably."

"Still, pushy." Sandy paused. "I'm sorry. I need you. But I want you whole and safe."

Allen laughed, "Thanks, mama hen. And the other mama hen."

It was Sandy's turn to laugh. "She is that. More than you know. Let me think a minute."

Allen let the silence pass between them as he turned his attention to the train yard in front of him when a steam engine whistle blew a few times. The black coal smoke from the train rose among the trees to his left. Another round of the whistle finally brought the restored vintage engine and its parlor cars into view. The fresh paint and polished brass fittings gleamed in the early evening light. The train had just completed its tour up the mountains and was disgorging its passengers. Elderly couples, families with small children, even one or two young lovers — all dressed in jeans and t-shirts or other contemporary fare, incongruous to the bit of history they had just stepped from. Allen smiled.

Sandy's voice drew him back to his current, complex situation. "I have an idea for tomorrow. Now, go find food and take it to your room. Strengthen yourself tonight. When you're done up there, come back to Espanola."

"I will. . . . And thanks."

Chapter Forty

"Ben Castiano," the deputy field investigator spoke into his cellphone, surprised at the evening call.

"Doctor, this is Sandy Lopez. I wondered if you could help me."

"What can I do for you, Ms. Lopez?"

"I understand that the crime lab is doing some tests up at the crime scene tomorrow."

"Yes, you'll get a full report from Dr. Ward. I've put you on his mailing list for reports."

"Yes, thank you. I would like my PI to observe tomorrow. It will help me by having a deeper understanding of the case. He's working with a PI from Torres, Gonzales, and Sandoval, who is licensed by this state. So, everything is proper."

"I'm sure it is, Ms. Lopez."

"They're staying at the Chama Hotel. My PI, Allen Rodriguez, is very discerning but sometimes can be sensitive."

"You mean to the sight of blood?"

There was a pause. "Something like that."

"That must be a handicap in his line of work."

"Well, Dr. Castiano, we don't often work with homicide cases in Payson. I'd appreciate it if you'd take my colleague up to the crime scene and look after him. Legally, he would be under your supervision, since his license is only legal in Arizona. His fellow PI doesn't need to be present, since he'll only be observing and taking notes. He's well-disciplined and won't get in the way."

Ben chuckled. "Sounds like a well-trained bloodhound to me."

Even Sandy laughed. "I guess it does. Thank you. Allen will be expecting you. Here's his cell number just in case."

Ben clicked off the call, smiling at his analogy and marveling at how strange this homicide was becoming. A PI who might faint at the sight of blood and yet who wanted to observe a gruesome crime scene and watch cadaver dogs at work. He shook his head. This was just muddling his already confused speculations about this case. Perhaps Dr. Ward's state-of-the-art forensic examinations would help straighten out his confusion or add more to it.

Chapter Forty-One

Day 6: Friday, early morning, Gallup, NM

Watching the sun's rays bursting onto the morning outside the window of a diner near Gallup didn't dispel the dark brooding Toni felt as the day began. She had been on the road since 5:00 am, after packing a bag and securing the ranch house and barn. She and Kate had herded the mares to the horse camp the evening before and made a hasty goodbye. Toni had refused a ride back to the ranch in an ATV, opting to hike the way back as she sorted through her thoughts, trying to let the quiet of the night soothe her. It didn't, but the physical activity attuned her body and spirit to what she needed to do, and the physical activity helped her sleep.

Toni returned to the coffee cup beside the remains of her scrambled eggs and hash browns. She really didn't have much appetite, but realized she would need the energy later — if not today, then another day, as whatever this was unfolded. The coffee was bitter no matter how much cream she added.

Pulling out her cellphone, she dialed Allen's number. It was around 8:30. He should be awake.

"*Nya:weh sge:no*, Allen."

"Toni, what's up? What's wrong?" Allen answered.

Toni heard the clatter of dishes and muffled voices in the background. Allen was probably out having breakfast, too. "I just wondered where you'd be today. Are you going back to Espanola?"

"No, I'm still in Chama. I'll be going back down there later today."

"So, you got your investigating done?"

"Pretty much. We did all the witnesses over the past two days. I'm going up to see the crime scene this morning, up near Dulce. I'm waiting for a deputy field investigator from the Medical Examiner's office to take me up there. I'm not sure why he's doing that."

"Maybe he wants another look see himself."

"Could be. He called and told me to just check out, and he'd take me back to Espanola. I'm here in a café, waiting. Maybe he wants to talk to Sandy. I don't know."

"How's it going with the PI up there?"

"She's really been pushy. Doesn't understand native people at all and—" Allen stopped short.

"And?"

"She's aggressive."

Toni chuckled. "Not quite like Ms. Caroline, right, who pretends to just tolerate you?"

"She's maddening. They're both maddening."

"Is she coming with you and the guy from the ME's office?"

"No. He said that because I'm observing and not interacting with anyone, I didn't need to be with the other PI."

"I see."

There was a long pause, while Allen waited. The early call had set off an alarm in her step-son that Toni hadn't intended. "Be careful up there. A crime scene holds ghosts."

"Yeah." Allen's response with a slight laugh indicated nervousness.

"Don't open up when you get there."

"Sandy wants me to. It could help the old man, who's our client."

Suddenly, Toni had a copper taste in her mouth as if she'd bitten her tongue. "You can't trust the earth up there."

"But that's how I ground."

"One way."

"What do you know? What are you sensing?"

Unable to define what she felt, she could only say. "I'm coming. I'm up in Gallup right now, but I'm taking a route north through Chama. I hate city traffic as much as you do. I'll meet you in Espanola later." Toni could hear Allen release a held breath.

"We're at the Sunset."

"I'll find you."

Chapter Forty-Two

Day 6: Friday, early morning, AZ

Cesar straddled the kitchen chair, his hands on his knees, his exposed back now a raw portrait of twin feathered serpents intertwined like a reptilian yin/yang symbol. Mala inspected how the irritation process of the ancient scarification was proceeding. This was the last day. Then it would be exposed to the air for two days as scabs continued to form.

She had already washed the design and patted it dry. Now, she would apply the last irritant. Putting her own hand into a bowl of freshly grated horseradish, she scooped up a large portion.

"You honor your ancestors, my son," Mala said, before pressing her hand over the raw wounds.

Cesar ground his teeth together, grabbing the kitchen chair as his back reflexively arched. He didn't cry out.

Mala closed her eyes and smiled, enjoying the act of power she participated in. She grabbed another handful and another, pressing the irritant deep into the wounds. She knew that the initial pain would numb the rest of her ministrations. The work had been done by the same artist who had embellished the rest of her son's body with sacred art. She had rejected the medicinal ointments and even the irritants with numbing agents, preferring to treat these sacred images with older remedies.

Once more, Mala washed the wounds and patted them dry. She placed a large sheet of plastic wrap over the ancient art and secured it with surgical tape. Then she helped her son put on an over-sized shirt.

"You must eat," Mala instructed. "And then we will sing the chants for the rite. They must be flawless pronunciations."

Standing, Cesar turned to his mother. "I will not fail you."

She smiled. "What would you like to eat today? There's a bear steak I pulled from the freezer. You should take in that animal's fearlessness."

Cesar grinned and looked at the near-empty bowl of horseradish. "And smear it with that," he said. "It will temper my insides."

Mala marveled at her son. It had taken time to harness the wild, reckless spirit of his younger years. That bold rashness had won him followers. Many followers. But she had had to shape and mold that energy into an instrument of power in order for him to become the man who would lead those followers and provide her with the place of honor she had sought all her life.

She had been the older twin. She should have been the shaman. But her people were not matrilineal. Paul had been selected because he was male. His sons, first Allen and now Logan, were in line to lead.

Allen had been a surprise. No one knew he had that much power, and it had scared the boy and his mother so much they took him away from Paul, away from his home and people. They hid him away to become something else. Now, Logan was to be tested, but he seemed to be only a boy, with little power.

Cesar had been tested again and again. First with Allen and then later among other native people. Mala had taken him to the far North among the Plains natives and he had danced three Sun Dances at different ages. Cesar had sweated among those people and others and had fire walked in the Pacific. He had gone on vision quests every summer for ten years. Cesar had even studied karate as a way to harness the rage boiling deep inside him, earning a black belt, and eventually making a living teaching the art to adults.

Mala smiled proudly. He was a wild animal who had learned to live among people, but he would never be tame.

Chapter Forty-Three

Day 6: Friday, early morning, near Dulce

Ben looked over at Allen, who sat stiffly in the truck seat. The young man hadn't said very much since he picked him up at the café, two blocks from Hotel Chama. Ben had wondered why Allen hadn't just eaten at the restaurant across the street. Maybe the food was better there. His companion seemed tense, perhaps because he wasn't looking forward to seeing blood on the boulder at the crime scene. Ben absently patted the bottle of smelling salts he had tucked in the shirt pocket that didn't hold his phone. He was glad he had it handy. The boy might need it.

"It isn't far now," Ben announced.

Allen only nodded, turning his attention to a small pile of palm-sized river stones in one of the cup holders.

Noticing, Ben explained, "My kids pick up rocks all the time. Those came from Abiquiu Lake when we went swimming a couple of weeks ago."

"Is that a natural lake?"

"No, it's man-made. Most lakes are, here in New Mexico."

Giving him another thorough scan, Ben said, "You seem young to be a PI."

"I've been working as one for four years, ever since I got my license."

"How'd you get into that line of work?"

"I'd been working in Sandy Lopez's office in Payson since high school, doing clerical work, filing, running errands. She and her legal partner eventually took me with them when they did some interviews. I learned a lot."

"Get many homicides out there?"

"No. We mainly handle land disputes, some domestic cases, and sometimes a teenager in trouble."

"Payson? That near a rez?"

"Yeah. A couple, really. Our clients are mainly Apache."

"Must be hard for you, getting their trust."

"It's a matter of manners," Allen answered.

"I suppose so."

"But I have some native in me."

"Oh?" Ben was surprised and then chided himself. Most people who were born and raised in New Mexico, even with very Hispanic names, had a trace of some native blood. especially those with Mexican ancestry.

"What about you? Apache, maybe?" Allen asked.

Ben chuckled. "Why would you say that?"

"Your height. A lot of people with Mexican-Apache blood are very tall."

"Well, there are stories," Ben admitted, "but we have no direct enrollment in a nation. My people have been here for hundreds of years. We had a large land grant holding that was eventually sold off."

"So is Castiano Spanish and not Mexican?"

"We had a Mexican land grant, not one from Spain directly. My ancestors came from Mexico City and claimed their Spanish ancestry."

Allen smiled. "There may have been some more recent romantic entanglements then."

Ben laughed. "Probably." He looked at Allen with renewed respect. "You're good. I've never talked to a stranger about my history before."

Quietly, Allen said, "You seemed open to talk."

Ben swung his pickup truck off the road and onto an open field where three other trucks were parked. Two German Shepherds scrambled out of the back seat of a dual cab and waited as their trainer clipped leashes on their collars. Another man joined him, taking one of the leashes from the trainer.

Five other people were pouring over a large piece of paper that had been spread over the hood of another truck. Against the front fender of the third truck clearly marked with Rio Arriba County Sheriff's Office, a young deputy lounged, drinking from a thermal mug.

Ben stopped and turned off the ignition. Before opening his door, he turned to Allen. "The crime scene is really a big boulder with blood on it. Are you going to be okay with that?"

Allen looked out over the activity in front of them. He took a deep breath and then glanced at the stones again. "This may sound odd, sir, but if something happens to me, don't touch me. Would you put one of those stones in my hand?"

Narrowing his eyes at Allen, Ben reached for the largest, smoothest stone. He offered it to Allen. "See how it feels first."

Allen weighed it in his hand and closed his eyes. The young man's face relaxed, and he smiled. "You've got happy kids. Two."

Ben raised an eyebrow, realizing that there was more than fainting at the sight of blood going on here. He pulled the smelling salts from his pocket and put it in the cup holder. "This wouldn't help, would it?"

Letting out a nervous laugh, Allen admitted, "I don't think so."

"I had a *tia* who always knew who died before anyone else in the family found out." Raising both hands in front of himself, Ben said, "I don't need details. Just tell me what you want me to do. I am a medical doctor."

Shyly, Allen nodded. "Yes, sir. Thank you."

"And call me Ben, please."

Chapter Forty-Four

"But—" Sandy tried interrupting for the third time. "Ms. Jameson—" She rolled her eyes, making Caroline stuff a laugh as she studied the breakfast menu at the restaurant. "Ms—" Finally, Sandy was done being polite. Raising her voice a notch higher, she blurted out, "Ms. Jameson, I know perfectly well where Allen Rodrigues is and who he's with. He is not conducting interviews, and no, he does not require your presence. Thank you very much for your services. Please file your bill with your law firm and have them forward those charges to my office in Payson." She clicked off the call and very nearly tossed her phone across the crowded room. If it weren't for the possible lawsuit from potential injury, she would have.

"Well, Ms. Jameson seems to be upset because she didn't get her way, poor baby," Caroline said innocently as she put down the menu, having made her decision.

"Ms. Jameson can go—"

"Uh, uh, uh," Caroline warned. "We must maintain some sense of lawyerly decorum."

"You've been grinding your teeth ever since Allen's been up there with her." Sandy pulled out papers from her briefcase and handed a small stack to her legal partner.

Taking them, Caroline declared, "He's not eating. And what he'll do today is dangerous."

"That's why I sent Ben Castiano up there with him." She sorted through some of the papers that now included some crime scene photos. She grimaced. "It won't be easy for him."

A waitress appeared with a coffee pot. At Caroline's nod,

the woman filled both their waiting cups and then took their orders.

When the server had gone to the kitchen, Sandy confessed. "There is something. . . ." She shook her head.

Caroline looked over the autopsy and crime lab reports. "I know what you mean. This incision. There's no way our client had the skill or the steady hand to do this."

"Despite the long feud, no, he couldn't do it."

"We should get a statement from the doctor who examined him in the jail. Surely, his medical report would tell us that he wasn't capable of doing this."

"It will add some strength to our case."

"And what did he do with the heart?" Caroline asked.

"Good point. It wasn't found at the scene. Unless there were more people involved."

"But if the old man had help, why would they leave him there?"

"That's just it. From what I can see, either the victim would have had to be totally incapacitated or half-drugged and then the killer would have had to have people help do the deed."

"You mean like a killer duo, a couple, or a killer and his protégé?"

"I don't think so. . . . Maybe a group."

"A cult?"

There was a long pause as Sandy cast her mind back to stories from her childhood and classes she had taken as an undergraduate student.

"What was that white substance in his stomach? Wasn't it fermented?" Caroline asked.

"We'll need to research that. Maybe we can get Ben Castiano to help us with that, maybe point us to someone who could help."

Caroline leaned back against the cushions of the booth. "I wonder if they'll find the murder weapon up there."

Sandy pushed her pile of papers to the back edge of the table and reached for her coffee. "I doubt they'll find it." She took a sip of the hot liquid. "I wonder what the dogs will find up there."

Just then their food arrived, and they pondered Huevos Rancheros and Breakfast Enchiladas, letting the heavy food keep them rooted in reality instead of in wild speculation.

Chapter Forty-Five

Day 6: Friday, near noon, Payson

"Where are you calling from?"

Kate heard the panic in Toni's voice. There was no cell service at the horse camp so she understood her wife's concern. Isaiah had a short-wave radio he used once a day. He'd said that ham operators had better real-time information than even weather services. Isaiah had once told her that he had been visiting his adoptive grandparents in Wisconsin one summer after he was first married, and there had been warnings of tornadoes in the area on the local news station. His grandfather had tuned in his ham radio, and local operators were reporting real-time sightings of the storms that were being fed to the local emergency numbers. Though a storm hadn't been projected for the area where he was, the ham operators sighted one just three miles away. They had time to get into the basement and take shelter before it hit. That experience had sold him on the short-wave grapevine.

"I'm in Payson with Isaiah and Rita and the kids. The boys enjoyed me reading to them last night, so I went to the library while they did grocery shopping," she explained, standing outside of the library. "It's been ages since I've been in the children's section. There are so many new authors and new books! And they're readable. I remember Allen struggling with some classics when he was little before Paul restricted everything he read to preparations for his rite. He picked his own books when we were in New York, remember? I found an illustrated *Treasure Island* that I thought I'd start reading to the boys tonight."

Kate stopped her babble even though she was enjoying the distraction of young children. She had only called to see where Toni was. She hadn't heard anything from her since last night, when they had brought the horses and a few of her personal items to the horse camp.

"I'm sorry," Kate continued, starting to walk the two blocks to the grocery store. "Rita was excited, and so was I. She wants me to homeschool the boys in the fall. Where are you now?"

"I'm heading toward Dulce. It's beautiful country here. You'd love it. If there weren't an arbitrary state boundary, you'd think this was Colorado."

Kate now noticed the road noise and the old truck's loud engine.

"I called Allen this morning," Toni admitted. "He was supposed to be in Dulce at the crime scene. I don't know how I'll find him in this open country."

"Maybe the tribal police can help you."

"Even if they aren't involved, they'd probably know," Toni conceded. "You can't keep something like that a secret on a reservation."

"That area will probably be off limits."

"True." Toni let out a loud breath. "How in the world would I ever convince them to show me? My skills don't involve mind control like Paul's."

"I'm glad they don't."

There was a pause, and when Toni spoke, it showed her frustration. "Allen's probably gone by now. It's coming up on noon."

"But he hasn't opened, has he? You're closer. You'd feel it."

"No. There's been nothing. At least I know his shielding is holding."

Another pause continued far longer than just gathering thoughts.

"What is it?" Kate asked with an edge of worry.

"I need to see that place."

154

"Whatever for?"

"I—," she began, then let out another frustrated breath. "This is enough to trouble Allen. I need to find out what it is."

"But it's really none of our business," Kate said, sighting Isaiah's pickup in the grocery parking lot. He was loading kids and groceries inside.

"No, it's not," Toni admitted. "Except for how it affects Allen."

The road noise grew louder in the silence that followed.

"Maybe you can try Allen's cell or—"

"Or open to him? Kate, I've never invaded his privacy. But he used to broadcast even louder than you did when I met you. Grandmother taught him control."

"Well, if you open to what's out there, whatever it is, you'll open to him if he's listening. And he might send to you since you gave him permission."

Toni emitted a light laugh. "I did. I think that may have shocked him."

Kate smiled. "He may not be your blood, but he is of your spirit. Please be safe."

"And you do, too."

"The worst I have to worry about is getting in the middle of a fight between the two boys. They can be so rambunctious."

"We'll connect whenever either of us can get a cell connection."

Chapter Forty-Six

It had been a very long morning for everyone at the crime scene. The overcast skies were the only blessing, muting the growing heat of the day.

Ben and Allen had joined the crime lab team and the deputy in the search for the murder weapon. They had spread out, three feet or more apart, and walked several yards, first north to south and then east to west, around the central boulder. All of them kept their attention on the ground, looking for some kind of knife. After well over an hour, they had found nothing.

The dog team, however, had better luck. They followed those looking for the murder weapon and had identified six areas on the property where yellow identity flags now sprouted. Their work finished, the dogs and their handlers were allowed to leave.

The rest of the crime lab team, however, remained to conduct further tests. Ben and Allen leaned against Ben's truck, watching while a man and a woman scraped away the top soil from a staked off, three-meter square around one of the yellow flags. Nearby, Dr. Ward and two men sprayed a liquid all over the boulder and in a circle on the grassy ground about six feet around it. When they were done, Dr. Ward's helpers unfolded a thick black tarp, holding it at various angles to create a shadow over their previous work. Dr. Ward swung a battery-powered light over the boulder and on the ground. Bright splotches covered the boulder almost entirely, except in a void in the middle. The ground around it held varying degrees of brightness in irregular patches.

Dr. Ward waved at Ben and Allen to come over.

"I'll go," Ben said, starting toward him, and then heard Dr. Ward's shout.

"Bring my camera. It's on the front seat."

Finding a camera case in the forensic scientist's truck, Ben brought it to Dr. Ward, who didn't reach for it.

"You're experienced taking crime scene photos. If you could give me a hand here."

Ben removed the digital camera from its case, noting that a lens was already attached. "Do you want another lens?" he asked.

Dr. Ward glanced at it. "It'll do."

Ben checked the settings and took one shot of the three men. He checked the photo on the camera to see if he needed to make any adjustments. Dr. Ward then started giving instructions to the two other men to move the tarp, and then more to Ben. This was precise work, with Ben checking nearly every shot and conferring with Dr. Ward on several to see if they warranted retakes.

When the other crime scene members had folded the tarp and were storing it away, Dr. Ward and Ben walked back to the truck.

"Was that luminol?" Ben asked.

Dr. Ward nodded. "The boulder was an obvious use. We don't normally use it on the ground, but a recent study showed that, though there isn't visible blood on the ground, it can show up as old as six years before. Newer research is being done to see if even older blood could be found." He turned back to the boulder. "It's clear that we aren't dealing with a single crime of passion. Something has been going on here for a long time."

Ben looked over at Allen, who had overheard. The boy now made his way around the vehicles, giving the boulder a wide berth, heading toward the little stream that they had been told this morning separated this area from native land. He squatted down by the water, watching its slow meandering.

Ben followed him to the stream. "You okay?"

Allen nodded. "Water helps."

"We can go anytime you want."

"I know," he said. "I'm not done here." Slowly, he turned to the shallow pit the man and woman were working on.

Ben followed his gaze. "Are you ready for that?"

Allen moved his head toward the boulder. "It can't be any worse than that."

"Okay," Ben said. "We'll go have a look see."

When they reached the square that had been dug down about two feet, Dr. Ward was bending over the contents, blocking their view of what, if anything, it contained. The forensic scientist swung his head at their approach. He looked like a kid who'd just found buried treasure.

"We'll have to call in a forensic anthropologist, but maybe you can give us the benefit of your experience, Dr. Castiano."

Ben squatted down next to Dr. Ward for a clear view. Below him were the skeletal remains of what was probably a man with scraps of what may have been jeans and a belt. "Well, it's definitely not recent. I'd say by the deterioration of his clothing and the cleanness of the bones the body has been in the ground about thirty or forty years."

"We won't touch it until the forensic anthropologist gets here. We'll have to cover it and post a guard."

"The sheriff's office won't like the overtime," Ben pronounced.

"Well, we need to tell if it's native and whether there was foul play."

"He is," Allen said in an odd tone behind the two men.

Ben twisted his body slightly toward Allen and looked at him.

"But he's not local." Allen's face contorted in a grimace of both pain and fear. He slumped to his knees, tottering there for a while as if fighting to stay upright, and finally losing that battle of will, he fell forward, face first onto the hard ground.

Chapter Forty-Seven

"She'll be driving six white horses when she comes," Isaiah bellowed out, coming up the drive to the ranch house. Manuel and Alexander all whinnied on the response instead of the traditional "Whoa there!"

"She'll be driving six white horses, she'll be driving six white horses, she'll be. . . ." Suddenly, his deep bass drifted away as he slowed the double cab truck. A familiar car sat in front of the ranch house. Paul came rushing down the front steps. "Kate, get down on the floor," Isaiah ordered. "Boys, cover her up with the horse blanket back there."

"Why, Papa? Are we playing a game?" Alexander, the youngest asked.

"Yes, you're hiding the fair maiden from the pirate."

The boys giggled and helped cover Kate as she curled herself into a ball on the truck floor.

By the time Isaiah had pulled up near the barn, Paul had crossed the distance and had his hand on the truck's door. Isaiah opened the door and stepped out.

"Where are they?" Paul demanded.

"I haven't seen Toni since yesterday." Isaiah said truthfully, as he pulled a set of keys from his pocket and walked around the front of the truck to the barn door.

"Did Allen come back?" Paul asked.

"Nope," Isaiah said as he applied key to padlock on the big double doors. "I heard he was off working with the lawyer in New Mexico somewhere." Removing the lock, he opened one of the doors and swung it fully open.

"Did they follow him there? Everything is locked up tight here. Even the horses are gone."

Isaiah walked the other door to a wide-open position. "You'd have to ask them. I just came to pick up some alfalfa." He returned to the truck and opened the door to climb back in. The boys were trying to stifle giggles in the back but a few slipped out. Their noise seemed to irritate Paul. "If you see them, remind them that Logan's rite is Monday."

"I'll tell them," Isaiah said, closing the door as he stuck the keys in the ignition. He watched as Paul stalked to his car, entered, and slammed the door. While he was turning the car around, Isaiah slowly backed the truck deep into the barn. When Paul's car sped past and away from the ranch, Isaiah shut off the engine. "All clear."

"We saved the maiden from the dreaded pirate!" Manuel said as they unbuckled their seatbelts from their car seats and scrambled out.

"Everybody, grab a load," Isaiah instructed.

Kate untangled herself from the horse blanket and climbed out, too. Isaiah passed her on the way to the back. "You didn't have to hide me," she said.

He flashed her one of his pure-white, angelic smiles. "I've got strict instructions that no one knows where you lay your head."

Kate just shook that head as she busied herself with folding the horse blanket while the others loaded the groceries into the cargo carrier of one of two hardtop UTVs. She put the blanket back into the truck and pulled out a cloth bag full of books she had borrowed from the library. Looking in the truck bed, she found the last remaining bag of groceries and headed for the UTV where Rita was organizing what the boys had brought her.

Isaiah lifted a bale of alfalfa from a built-in shelf in the back of the barn and put it in the carrier of the other UTV. He smiled at how his family worked together. As he was about to call his boys to ride with him, he saw Kate grab the side of the other UTV carrier as if to steady herself. Then her whole body began to shake as she gripped the metal and her legs began to lose strength. Isaiah sprinted to her and caught her before she fell hard, moving to stretch her out on the ground.

"Just hold her close," Rita said as she and the boys gathered round, touching Kate's hands and legs.

Isaiah knelt on one knee behind Kate, pulling her body against his chest and wrapping his arms around her. At first, he thought it was a seizure, but it wasn't. Kate's body hadn't continued to shake as she would have during one. She gasped, her eyes wide open, a look of terror stretched across her face, as if she was trapped in a nightmare.

Rita made the sign of the cross and began to pray. Manuel and Alexander copied her movements and began to pray the Lord's prayer, the only one they knew. Isaiah just held on, feeling responsible, not wanting to have to make a heartbreaking phone call to Toni.

Chapter Forty-Eight

Frustrated, Toni switched off the radio in her old truck. Reception had been spotty since she left Gallup. She'd caught a few *Norteno* songs passing through that town, but they had come ghosting in with a strong easterly wind, fading in and out, until they totally disappeared the farther North she drove. She'd caught some country and rock stations around Farmington and even tuned in to the native-run Dulce station. At this hour, though, it was a call-in program and the vocal nattering irritated her. Not that she didn't have empathy for their community concerns, but the bickering reminded her of generational wounds inflicted by governments and between peoples. They weren't new and couldn't be solved with simple answers or a radio airing of those grievances.

Toni had enough to occupy her thoughts at the moment. She was worried about Allen and whatever this case was doing to him. As she passed through the edge of Dulce heading East, she wondered if Allen had found answers there or out wherever the crime had been committed. Traffic had dwindled almost as soon as the old truck cleared the city limits. Had Toni known where to go from there, she would have shifted into fourth and challenged the speed limit. But she didn't know where he was, so she chose to scan the road ahead at a modest thirty-five miles per hour.

She only had a sense she was headed in the right direction, logically thinking that surely official vehicles would be pulled off the main road or that she could see them from her route. The two-lane blacktop she was on had few side roads sprouting from it, mainly dirt access lanes that led to open land or a cattle trough. It was pretty country, as she had told Kate. Too bad it had been marred by violence, brutal killing, blood, dark birds.

A barrage of images assaulted Toni, coming way too fast to even register or recognize. Then heat alternating with intense cold flooded her, forcing her focus on her physical body. Fear and pain pummeled her. Every muscle ached and a sharp searing slashed across her chest. Toni struggled to shut down these assaults, patching any leaks in her shields, fortifying them so that she could gain control. The only control she found was in her feet that slammed on the brakes as the truck slid into the grassy berm, edged by scrub trees. She just managed to put the car in park and switch off the ignition before she blacked out.

Chapter Forty-Nine

Ben slapped Dr. Ward on the arm and stretched out his hand. "Got extra gloves?"

The forensic scientist, looking horrified at Allen, who was planted face first into the grass behind him, reached into his pants' pocket and pulled out a pair of blue surgical gloves. He handed them over. "What happened to him?"

Stretching on the gloves, Ben stooped over Allen and gently rolled him to his side and then stretched out the young man's legs so that he could roll him onto his back, trying to touch him as little as possible. He scanned the body, making sure Allen was breathing and had no other injuries. Then, remembering the smooth stone in his jeans' pocket, he put it carefully into Allen's hand, curling the boy's fingers around the rock.

"Maybe the deputy can call an ambulance on his radio," Dr. Ward said.

"Just wait," Ben cautioned.

The forensic scientist started making speculations. "Is he ill? Does he have a condition? Epilepsy? It can't be the heat. The temps aren't that high today. It could be the altitude or maybe it's a blood glucose issue. We've been out here all morning. It's time for lunch."

Ben turned his stoop into a squat as he waited beside Allen. He shook his head at Dr. Ward. "Maybe it's aliens."

"Well, there could—" The scientist caught the sarcasm and stopped talking.

"Are you always that eager to find answers?" Ben asked him, shooting him a glare.

Ward smiled a little sheepishly. "All my life."

"Well, focus your questions on the remains over there. I'll tend to the living, if you don't mind."

"That'll be a switch for you, won't it?"

"The Doctor in front of my name isn't a Ph.D. like yours."

Dr. Ward raised an eyebrow. "Why are you just a field investigator, then?"

Turning back to Allen, he muttered, "I have my reasons."

The boy's body twitched once in a while like a dog dreaming, but otherwise didn't seem affected more than with just a faint. Ben wished he hadn't left the smelling salts in the truck but figured bringing Allen back from where he was might be dangerous. His *tia* just would wake from a dream in the middle of the night and walk the floor until the phone rang. This was different.

Checking his watch, Ben calculated that it had been about ten minutes since Allen had last spoken. He decided to wait five more minutes. When that time had lapsed, he leaned over the boy and spoke into his ear. "Allen Rodriguez." He waited a few seconds and repeated the boy's name. "Come back now." This time, he shook the boy's shoulder.

Allen's eyelids fluttered for a few seconds and then slightly opened.

"Are you okay?" Ben asked.

Allen looked around and then noticed Ben's gloved hands. He nodded at him and slowly sat up.

Ben stood and then hooked a hand around the boy's closest arm and helped him to his feet. "Let's get some water in you first and then a soda. I have some in a cooler in the truck."

Allen accepted Ben's guidance as he pointed him back toward where the vehicles were parked. He stumbled slightly as if he were groggy after a long sleep.

"We'll get some food in Chama."

Allen shook his head. "I need to tell Sandy."

"I'll call her on the way. You need rest and food."

When they got to the truck, Ben unlocked the door for Allen. Helping him into the seat, he held up his gloved hands. "Can I take these off?"

Allen offered a half smile and nodded. "Good call," he said.

Chapter Fifty

The butter, vanilla, and confectioner's sugar blended gently. Kate lifted the old-fashioned, hand-operated rotary beaters, ran her forefinger across the gadget's ribs, and tasted the mix. She nodded in satisfaction. Spying two sets of eager eyes on the other side of the wooden table that had been set up in the outdoor kitchen, Kate grinned and handed the beaters to Manuel and Alexander. "Hold down the handle so you don't get your tongues caught."

Nearby, with a large wooden paddle, Rita pulled out two blackened cake tins from the adobe *horno* that complemented the permanent, rock-rimmed firepit at the back of the wooden *portal* that comprised the outdoor kitchen. She slid the cake tins gently onto the end of the table. "They might have a little ash on them, but I think that can be dusted off."

"When they're cool, we'll see if the boys want to help ice the cake."

Rita laughed. "Of course, they will. But I can't guarantee how it will look."

"They won't mind, as long as they get big pieces!"

Propping the wooden paddle against the side of the table, handle side down, Rita moved to Kate's side and stuck her own finger into the icing for a taste. "Hmm. It's good." She squinted at her friend. "I'm surprised you're out in this heat doing this after. . . ."

Kate herself was surprised how a little therapeutic baking and the energy of two young children could soothe her frazzled nerves. She smiled. "I needed this." Now that the baking was done, though, she suddenly felt shaky. Seeking the solidity of a vintage highbacked porch chair, Kate sat down heavily.

Rita frowned at her, folding her arms across the bib of her long apron. "Manuel, go in the house and get a can of V8 for *Tia* Kate."

With the gooey evidence all over his face that he had clearly licked his beater well, Manuel scampered into the single-story adobe house.

Kate admired Isaiah and the ranch hands' handiwork on the house. Rita had nudged her husband into moving out of the cookhouse after their first child had been born. They had moved in there after they were married, sharing it only for a few months before the ancient Mexican cook passed away. Rita had taken over the cooking, which she didn't really mind, since she came from a large family and was used to cooking for her four brothers and little sister. An extra handful of beans in the pot for any extra men was an easy adjustment. After Alexander was born and Immigration had plugged the flow of newcomers from Mexico, that task had lightened, even though their family had grown. Only occasionally now would they get a man good with horses who hadn't been able to find work because of his prison record or his lack of understandable English. Though Kate's experiences with the men had been limited over the years, she never felt in danger. The hands were happy to have work, especially those who were sending money back to their families in Mexico. Because of their work history at the horse camp, a few of the ex-cons managed to find jobs in larger communities that offered better benefits, and one or two married and even were able to buy houses. Kate smiled. It was a good work that Dutch had begun there.

As soon as she thought of Dutch, she was drawn back to the barn at the ranch house, and a shadow passed over her mind. Black wings. A bird feather cape. The glint of a knife. A sacrificial stone upon which Allen had been conceived. Old images superimposed on the new. Then blood . . . blackness.

Feeling her own blood draining from her head and her vision darkening, Kate spread her jeaned thighs apart and dropped her head between them. She heard the rush of feet and an aluminum can lid pop open. A cool can was shoved into her right hand.

"Drink," Rita commanded.

When her vision had cleared, Kate raised the can to her lips and took a long gulp.

"You're dehydrated," Rita diagnosed. "You've lost potassium. It happens to me when I don't take care of myself."

Kate finally straightened and leaned back into the chair.

"Drink more," Rita urged.

Complying in order not to have to explain, Kate drank. She wasn't sure if what she had felt and sensed in the barn wasn't just her own dark memories and her past worries about Allen when he went for his manhood rite, as Logan was going to do in a few days. As she sifted through those images, recognizing the familiar ones, she identified wisps of others that were not her own. There was a connection to Allen, but not directly involving him. There was something ancient about them, as with images she used to pick up from artifacts and from the shaman stone Paul always wore. But today, these had come on the wind, not from an object. They had come like the sending Allen had done during his rite that Toni had brought her out of. If Toni hadn't swept them off to New York and her grandmother, Allen could have been lost down a dark road forever.

"You need to put your feet up," Rita continued to mother her. "Alexander, go bring me that big piece of log over by the fire that your father hasn't split yet." Turing to Kate again, she added, "I'll finish up the dinner preparation. You're our guest; you shouldn't be cooking, anyway."

Kate smiled. "Rita, you know no woman ever stays out of a Mexican kitchen, guest or not."

Rita laughed. "You have become one of us."

"I should hope so. I'm not *Tia* Kate for no reason."

"And you will become Teacher Kate in the Fall."

Before emptying the can of V8, Kate added, "I think I'm going to enjoy that."

Chapter Fifty-One

Day 6: Friday, early afternoon, near Dulce, NM

The truck engine roared to life. As Toni put it into gear and pulled back onto the asphalt, she wished she had as much energy as the old truck claimed to have. She was drained from being bombarded, forcing her to fortify her shielding and keep holding it constant. Toni had slipped into a dark void, almost as an instinct. She chided herself for not opening fully to experiencing the impressions she had been sent. Humbly, she realized her grandmother had been right when Toni had returned to her homeland with Allen and Kate and then finally confessed to why she had fled to somewhere so far away. Her grandmother had simply said, "The spirit retreats when it must." Toni had retreated physically to heal. Perhaps now her spirit had escaped to oblivion to protect herself from another kind of harm. Today, she felt she had acted cowardly and had somehow failed Allen.

Sensing a remnant of Allen's signature left in the energy in the cab, Toni continued down the two-lane blacktop, edged on the right with low scrub, having no clue how to find him and the place he'd come up there to sense and feel. After driving some distance, Toni saw the highway end at a T-intersection. She'd missed the place somehow. Swinging the truck into a wide U-turn, she headed back up the way she had come, searching the countryside. About half way back, a truck with emergency lights on the roof and a huge ram bar over the front grill came into view. It slowed and then swung left off the road onto an open field that had been hidden from view by the overgrowth along the side of the road. Along the vehicle's side, lettering identified it as tribal police. There were depressions in the low grass where other vehicles had recently passed, providing a clear track that led somewhere.

Looking beyond the police unit from her new vantage point, Toni spotted people working around some staked-out rectangles that looked like an archaeological site. Coming west the way she had come, all that activity had been hidden by bushes and trees along the side of the road.

Toni turned off the asphalt and followed the path the tribal unit had taken until she brought her truck to a stop next to three other vehicles — the tribal police one, a unit from Rio Arriba County Sheriff's Department, and a truck with a New Mexico Department of Public Safety logo on its side. She waited a moment as she watched the tribal police officer leave his vehicle with a bag in his hand and greet the deputy, who was leaning against the hood of his unit.

Tossing a brown paper bag to the deputy who caught it, the tribal officer teased, "How's your stomach?"

The deputy removed what looked like rolled frybread from the bag. "Shut up. They're just finding bones. No blood this time or bodies. They had the dogs out this morning." The deputy unwrapped an end of the roll and bit into it, releasing meat and beans that almost dripped onto his uniform shirt. A skillful step back avoided that embarrassment. Adjusting the paper wrapper and his stance, he bent over and dived in for another bite.

Toni opened her door, stepped out, and walked toward the two officers. "*Ya'ateh*," she spoke in greeting.

The men turned to her. The deputy choked down his last bite to do his duty to protect the crime scene. The tribal officer stepped ahead, "Eat your lunch." He walked to meet Toni. "You can't be here. This is a crime scene."

Toni noticed the lieutenant bars on the collar of the tribal officer's uniform and a name tag over his pocket that said

Lucero. She was well aware Lt. Lucero was inspecting her just as closely, probably puzzling at trying to identify her gender. When his eyes slid to the flatness at the chest of her western shirt, Toni cast her eyes out over the activity in the open field. Three squares were staked out and exposed. Three more places scattered about had yellow flags in them. There was an electricity in the air that made the hair on Toni's arms stand up. She doubted anyone else felt it, but it made her reluctant to talk. Out of the corner of her vision, she saw Lt. Lucero crane his head slightly to look around her at the Arizona license plate on her truck.

"Long way from home," he commented quietly.

Turning back to the officer, she said. "I am."

They eyed each other in silence for a couple of long minutes. Lt. Lucero crossed his arms over his chest in a quiet stance of power but not ego. "You'll have to leave."

Taking off her black Stetson, Toni looked up at the overcast sky, hoping what she was feeling was an approaching storm and not what she knew deep in her bones was something darker. She wiped her forehead with the back of her hand and replaced her hat. "I'm looking for my step-son, Allen Rodriguez," she finally explained. "He's a PI working with a lawyer on this case. I was told he was here."

The officer swiveled his head and called behind him. "Quintana!"

The sheriff's deputy wiped his mouth with the fingers of his free hand and came closer, holding the wrapped Indian taco in front of him. Red chile sauce dripped down the side of his hand.

The sight of it forced Toni to swallow hard. She pumped more energy into the shields in front of her as he neared. Feeling the soles of her worn boots on the ground, she willed up energy from the earth, but it was like sucking a frozen malt through a straw.

"Was anyone else here beside the dog handlers this morning?" Lucero asked.

"Yeah, that OMI field investigator came up and observed. He had a kid with him. Hey, everybody made fun of me when I saw the body Sunday. I couldn't help it. I'd never seen that much blood before. But it was nothing like what happened to that kid."

"What—?" Toni said taking a step forward.

Lt. Lucero put up a hand to stop her. "What happened?"

"When that kid saw the bones in one of the trenches they'd opened up, he just faceplanted right onto the grass. They were just bones. It wasn't like seeing a real body covered in all that blood and all over that stone." The deputy looked a little green. He fled to put the taco back into the paper bag he'd left on the hood of his unit. Finding a napkin, he wiped his hands vigorously as if imitating Lady MacBeth.

In truth, Toni was beginning to feel shaky herself. She managed to ask, "Are they still here?"

Deputy Quintana looked up from his scrubbing. "No, they left a few minutes ago."

"Were they going back to Chama or Espanola?"

The deputy looked confused. "Uh. Espanola, I think."

Confronting Lt. Lucero, Toni asked, "How do I get there?"

The officer moved toward Toni's truck, causing her to move with him. "That road you're on is 64. Just follow it. Go down to the T and turn right. When you get to Chama, there's another T. Turn right again. There'll be a sign later on where 64 turns off to the left. Keep going straight toward Espanola. You'll be on 84 then. It'll take a couple of hours."

When Toni opened the truck door and took out her keys from her pocket, he asked, "Do you know where to go when you get there?"

"I'll call the lawyer."

"No cell service right here. You'll have to get closer to Chama."

"Thanks, Officer," Toni said and climbed into the truck. When she had closed her door and stuck the key in the ignition, she noticed Lucero studying her closely.

"There's a gas station and a grocery store right near the T when you get to Chama. Get yourself a cold drink. People forget to hydrate out here."

Toni nodded.

"And maybe some food, if you've been driving all that way from Arizona."

Starting the truck, she said, *"Nya:weh sge:no."*

"That's not Navajo or Apache," Lt. Lucero remarked.

"It's *Onandowaga*, the 'great hill people.' Better known as the Seneca."

"You *are* a long way from home." Lt. Lucero stepped away from the truck. "Travel in beauty."

Raising her hand in final greeting, Toni put her truck in gear and spun it around the grassy field, heading for 64 and sustenance and ultimately to Allen.

Chapter Fifty-Two

Day 6: Friday, early afternoon, near Chama, NM

As the cellphone in the holder on his dashboard dialed Sandy Lopez, Ben scrutinized Allen in the passenger seat beside him. It was a swift but experienced glance that noted Allen's breathing rate and his posture. His companion had dutifully accepted water and then downed half a can of soda after he had dragged himself inside the truck. Allen's hand had shaken when he had put the can into a cup holder in the console between the front seats. When Ben had finally pulled the truck out onto 64, Allen leaned back and closed his eyes. It wasn't another slip into unconsciousness, just exhaustion. Soft snoring sounds could be heard over the roar of the tires on the roadway. Ben wondered what Allen had seen or felt that had so shaken him that he'd blacked out.

"Sandy Lopez." The voice interrupted his thoughts.

"Ms. Lopez, Ben Castiano. We just left the crime scene. The crime lab is still working there."

"Was your morning productive?"

"It was . . . educational."

"Oh?" she prompted.

"I've never seen the techniques used."

"Did the dogs find anything?"

Ben felt reluctant to detail their day, especially with Allen nearby, who might not be as asleep as he thought, but listening to every word said. Still, he needed to process some of what happened, even if the lawyer wasn't able to make sense of the experiences up there. *Shoot, even I don't know what happened up there and I saw it.* "I—" He just had no words, though he searched for appropriate ones, accurate ones.

"Dr. Castiano, I didn't get the impression that you ever were shy with words. You're very articulate." Then she paused as if her mind traveled along a different path. "Is Allen all right?"

Medical issues were familiar and helped him focus. "He's stable for now. He picked up something there that—"

"Picked up?" Evident surprise was in her voice. "Did he tell you he picked up something? An object?"

"No, nothing physical. It was another kind of picking up," Ben admitted. "He told us the remains were native but not from here."

"Remains? There are more bodies up there? The dogs found more bodies? I think you had better start from the beginning."

Ben told her about the forensic tests for detecting years-old blood on the ground. Then he told her about the grid search for the murder weapon that hadn't produced anything. Finally, he told her about the six targets the cadaver dogs had found and how Dr. Ward and his team were uncovering remains at that moment.

"In the first square they cleared, there were the remains of a male who'd been there for about thirty or forty years, I'd guess." He paused. "Your client is ninety-five. It's still within his range of opportunity."

"I don't believe that."

"I'm just stating facts. We don't know how that man died. Only a forensic anthropologist could tell us if there was some sort of trauma or disease that left indications on the bones or whether a knife had nicked a rib. I need to call OMI and see who's available to help Dr. Ward up there. But it's evident from the number of targets and the amount of old blood found on the ground that this wasn't an isolated incident based on an old man's grudge against his son-in-law."

Sandy Lopez didn't answer for a long moment as she absorbed what he had shared with her. "Where did Allen pick up what he did? Where our current victim was found?"

"No, he avoided the big boulder. He came over to look at the open forensic excavation and that's when he identified the remains as non-local native."

"What happened to Allen after that?"

"He collapsed. He was unconscious for several minutes. He asked me not to touch him, so I put on a pair of surgical gloves and got him into a more comfortable position." He paused. "I put a stone in his hand that my kids found at a lake far from here. He had asked me to, if something happened to him." Then, he added with a touch of incredulity in his voice, "He read the stone my kids had handled. I figured he didn't want to read me, and that's why he didn't want me to touch him. Wearing surgical gloves was the only way to turn his body. He landed on his face . . . I'll need to examine his nose. He might have a nasty bruise there later. I got water and some soda in him, but this is more than dehydration."

"You need to get food into him as soon as possible," the lawyer urged. "The heavier the better. Food seems to keep him from retreating into what he saw or just slipping away somewhere."

"And you don't mean hitchhiking on the highway, do you?"

Sandy Lopez released a small laugh. "You know more than most," she admitted. "We researched your background and found your medical credentials. I just wanted Allen to get care on site in case he got into medical trouble. I didn't think he'd share with you or that you'd understand."

Glancing back at Allen again, he turned his eyes to the road. "I deal with death. You'd be surprised what I've seen and heard."

"I need to get his parents here. They know better than I do what to do with Allen. I've just seen him get tired after an interview, where he'd tell me the witness was lying his head off."

"Are his parents like him?"

The lawyer laughed. "You need to meet Toni. Bring our boy home. You're — what? — two hours away?"

"Maybe a little longer with getting food."

"Don't take him into any place. Just grab a burger or something."

"Will do. See you in a few— Wait, where do I take him?"

"Sunset Motel. It's not far from the restaurant where you brought us that information. Room 17, in the back."

Chapter Fifty-Three

Caroline swung open the outside motel door before Toni could knock. The way she squinted, Toni wasn't sure if it was the bright sunlight behind her or if she was giving her the kind of fish eye her Grandmother did when she'd gotten into some mischief playing too roughly with her male cousins. Instead of trying to read emotions, Toni opted to look over the lawyer's head for a visual sweep of the small room. The night stand bore only the customary phone and lamp, the bed was crisply made, and the area around the TV perched on a dresser was void of any sign of occupancy. Even the sink counter in the back of the room had nothing marring the handiwork of the housekeeping staff. A quick swing of her eyes to the left revealed Sandy Lopez and a big Latino, who reminded her a bit of Isaiah, crowded around Allen, who hunched over a small round table where his backpack sat.

Relief quickly changed to concern when Toni examined Allen's body language, especially his clenched fists on the table edge, and his face. She was sure he'd seen what she had so desperately tried to keep out.

As Caroline stepped back to let Toni in, she muttered, "You look like hell. Another psychic casualty to take care of."

Toni swiveled her head to give the lawyer a look of surprise, and then frowned. She chided herself for not taking better care of her own circumstances before trying to come to Allen's rescue. When Allen raised his troubled eyes to hers, she knew he clearly needed someone who understood what was happening on a deeper, personal level. Striding slowly, calmly, to him, she finally squatted next to his chair. "How ya doin', Alley Cat?" she said softly, knowing how he had hated the nickname his mother gave him when he was very young.

Allen grunted out a laugh and actually smiled. "This alley cat's been prowling that back fence too long."

Toni smiled, too, and nodded.

"I'm glad you're here," her step-son almost whispered.

"We both need Grandmother's healing."

"Did you see?"

"No," Toni admitted, trying hard not to reveal her fear. "I got hit by something."

"Was that me?" Allen asked.

"No. This was something else. I would have known your energy."

"I tried to shut it out."

"So did I." Toni reached a brown hand to touch Allen's knee in reassurance, but he moved it away reflexively, leaving her hand in midair. She had always been able to touch him, even as a boy, without either of them picking up from the other. Reluctantly, Toni rested her hand on her own knee. She was aware he didn't trust himself not to broadcast like Kate used to do. Though his mother had learned control, she still slipped, even today.

Using her hands on her knee, Toni pushed herself upright and faced Sandy and the stranger. "Did you find out what you needed to know?"

Sandy shook her head, her face lined with worry as she focused on Allen. Finally, she seemed to break out of her thoughts. "I'm sorry. Toni, this is Dr. Ben Castiano."

Dr. Castiano reached a hand toward the woman. "Ben. Office of Medical Investigations."

The hand and the title suddenly triggered a memory of countless faculty cocktail parties where Toni had had to introduce herself as Dr. Antoinette Houston, Indian Studies.

That had been two decades ago, long before she had met Allen and Kate, who herself also bore that title for Anthropology. As she took Dr. Castiano's hand, she simply said, "Toni Houston. Allen's my son."

"Ben was up at the crime scene with Allen," Sandy explained.

"I tried to get him to eat, but he slept mostly on the way here," Ben rushed to defend himself. "Medically, he's OK, except for extreme stress. But. . . ."

"Yes, but," Toni echoed.

"We need to get him to eat," Caroline interrupted. "Why don't I go get something for us all?"

"I'll go with you," Sandy said.

"Just a coffee for me, thanks," Ben said.

"Could you stop somewhere and get some Jameson?" Toni asked.

"Jameson!" Caroline fumed. "I'll tell you what I'd like to do to a certain Jameson."

"This is medicinal Jameson," Sandy chided, ushering her law partner out the door.

When the lawyers left, Toni noticed Allen slowly unclench his fists, unfurling his fingers so his hands flattened on the table. "Are you ready to do this?" she asked Allen gently.

Looking up, he shook his head.

"You can use me as a conduit. I'll bleed off the emotion and ground it. Telling what you saw will—"

"You can't. You're not at power."

Embarrassed that he could see through her sham of strength so clearly, she bowed her head. It would be foolhardy to try to do this now. But she worried that he would internalize what he had experienced, not knowing fully what it was. She had lived with such an internalization for seven years and it had taken Kate to stir it out of its darkness and Grandmother to bring Toni to wholeness.

"If you're thinking of doing something to retrieve or relive these . . . experiences, the boy is right," Ben said. "Both of you look weary to the bone. Food and rest will help. And lots of water."

Toni nodded. "Tomorrow then."

"Uh," Ben began and hesitated, causing Toni to look up at him. "It might be helpful if I were here tomorrow. Just to monitor you both in case something goes awry. . . . I can at least take notes."

Reading something from him, Toni smiled. "You're curious as hell, aren't you?"

It was Ben's turn to look down in embarrassment.

Toni chuckled. "At least you aren't thinking about calling an ambulance and measuring us for white jackets with extra-long sleeves." Out of the blue, Toni reported, "You had a relative with abilities, didn't you? Mother?"

"Aunt," Allen answered.

"But not you?"

Ben released a nervous laugh. "No, thank God. I've got both feet in the practical." He paused, then said, "My *tia* never spoke about the gift. I never really saw it work. She just shared her pronouncements."

At that moment, Allen hoisted himself off his chair, causing Ben and Toni to straighten to alert. "Too much water today," he explained and headed to the bathroom in the back.

When the door was shut, Toni turned to Ben. "Can you tell me what happened up there? I stopped by the place, looking for Allen. It's . . . unsettling."

"You got that right," Ben admitted, but still looked askance at Toni. "I probably shouldn't share anything."

Toni nodded understanding. Then she suggested, "Come tomorrow. Anchor for us. Take notes. Make sure we're both safe. Then see if you can fill in the gaps."

It was Ben's turn to nod. "Sounds good." Then he asked another question. "Did Allen's abilities manifest early?"

"I've been told, yes. But not fully until he was ten, after his manhood rite when I came into the picture."

"You're not his. . . ." Ben looked as if he were struggling for a word that didn't involve gender.

"Biological parent?" Toni offered. "No, his abilities came mostly from his mother and some from his dad. I've filled that capacity in his life since his mom and I married."

"Did your abilities hit at your manhood rite?"

Toni laughed, shaking her head. "Do you know what two-spirted is? Or third or fourth genders?"

Ben's eyes widened. "But you—"

"I have male energy, too. And it's confusing."

"I'm sorry. I didn't want to mis-gender you before."

"Don't be embarrassed. Native people have understood Otherness far longer than most other cultures, and welcomed it."

The bathroom door opened, drawing Ben's attention. Turning back to Toni, he asked, "Do you want something for sleep tonight? I can get you something over-the-counter with my suggested medical dosage. It might help."

Toni grinned. "No, I think a couple of shots of Jameson will do."

"Are we bonding again?" Allen asked as he stumbled to the foot of the bed and started taking off his shoes.

"In many ways, my son."

Chapter Fifty-Four

Day 6: Friday, late afternoon, Espanola, NM

The aroma of food filled Sandy's town car. She suddenly realized that she was starving, since she and her law partner had worked through lunch as they pored over notes and reports in their hotel room. It was a way for both of them to avoid worrying about Allen. She'd sent him alone before to take witness statements, but those PI tasks had been activities in the normal world, not what they were dealing with in this case. Sandy was glad to have his expertise, but she began to think that they all were in over their heads. She'd reviewed the preliminary report from the medical examiner and some initial findings from the crime lab. This wasn't a crime of passion; it was beginning to look more and more like something she had no name for. Ben's brief statement today added another layer of hinky to something she didn't want to even think about. Old blood and more bodies. She didn't think for a minute that her client could have done what was done to the current victim, even though he had a long-standing feud with him. He could have had help, though, and it was looking like maybe more than one person was involved. The thing that she couldn't get her mind around was the fact that there was no heart. *A trophy? Or a message, as in "heartless bastard"?*

Then to send Allen up into that without anyone there who knew what his skills were. Hell, she didn't even know the extent of his abilities. When she saw the state Allen was in on his return to the motel, her guilt mounted. Toni's unexpected appearance was a relief, but she looked as if she'd been through some of what Allen had. Sandy was grateful that Ben had been with Allen and was now with him and Toni.

When Caroline returned to the car with the pint of Jameson Toni had requested, she fussed, "I hope Allen doesn't think he's going to get drunk on this. How can that help? Or Toni, for that matter."

When she put the bottle on the seat between them to fasten her seatbelt, Sandy eyeballed it. "I doubt both of them will get drunk with just a pint." She gave Caroline the fish eye. "You do realize that you're breaking a few laws with that up front here."

"We're only going two blocks," Caroline countered.

"It's obvious you don't drink," Sandy said, "or you've never been pulled over for a DUI. We're guests in this state." She took the bottle and put it in the trunk of her car.

When she returned to her seat and started the engine, Caroline muttered, "I never realized you were such a legalist. We've split hairs over the law so many times in court."

"That's when we saw different sides of the law, Caroline. We've never purposely broken the law. We can't."

Caroline didn't answer but sat smoldering.

"You're angry at me about Allen, aren't you?"

Caroline turned to look at her law partner. "No, I'm angry at him. He should know better than to put himself in danger. You saw him! What if he isn't normal after. . . ." Her voice caught, forcing her to turn to stare out the windshield. She swallowed hard as if to keep from shedding tears.

Sandy reached over and covered Caroline's wrist with her hand. "We will be strong women for him. Toni is here. She understands this in ways we'll never be able to. And Ben said Allen was just exhausted."

Caroline sniffed and reached for a napkin in one of the bags of food. She blotted the corners of her eyes and patted her nose.

"Now, stop acting like his nagging big sister and start acting like his woman. Find that fierce power you display in the courtroom and season it with some tenderness. He needs your strength now."

"All I want to do is take him in my arms and make it all better. . . . He couldn't even let Toni touch him."

Sandy soothed. "There'll be time for that. And when you do, fill your heart with love and not worry. There's healing in that."

Chapter Fifty-Five

Finishing up the postmortem on yet another homicide in Albuquerque, Dr. Morales hit Send on the report. She'd seen so many gunshot victims in her ten years as the state medical examiner that they had become routine, just a parade of bodies with the only differences being where the victim was shot and how many times. The weapons were nearly always similar. She worried about becoming dulled to the carnage and insensitive to the families of those involved — victim and shooter. Often it was some family dispute. Somebody's brother didn't pay back a loan. Somebody's girlfriend was caught flirting with someone else. A son felt slighted by his father about something. Usually petty reasons, built-up injustices over time, and too-handy weapons. Far too many young people. Standing up to stretch her back and retrieve her suit jacket from a hook behind her desk, she realized that she had indeed developed a thick hide over all these years — and maybe boredom at the routine of it. Rarely did she find a case like the one Ben Castiano had brought her.

The jangle of her office phone caused her to look at the wall clock that showed it was three minutes before five. Time to go home and immerse herself into the liveliness of her two elementary-school-age boys and the funny work stories her building contractor husband often shared. The insistence of the phone drew her back to her desk.

"Dr. Morales."

"Glad I caught you. Can you give me some names of local forensic anthropologists?" The rushed request came without prelude or pleasantries.

"Dr. Ward?"

"Oh, sorry. Yes. From the crime lab. Can you connect me with a local forensic anthropologist? Otherwise, I'll have to import one of my colleagues, and that might ruffle some feathers."

Dr. Morales rubbed her temple, trying to search for the name. "There is one attached to UNM's anthropology department. She does some work when we have cold cases and remains are found. Doesn't happen too often here. Although there was that cache of bodies found in West Mesa in 2009 that's still an open cold case. Her name is Dr. Louise Brookman. She's originally from New York or some place on the East Coast. She's pretty intense. I think you and she would work well together. Call the Anthropology Department and see if you can locate her." Then it occurred to the medical examiner why Dr. Ward asked. "You brought in cadaver dogs?"

"Yeah, got six hits in a spread of about a thousand yards on the south side of that big boulder where the body was found. Who knows how many might be farther away? We may have to get ground-penetrating radar out there to see just how big the burial field is."

"That could get tricky. Is the site on reservation land?"

"No, it's outside the boundary but, yeah, that could get dicey if these are native burials. But I doubt it. Well, I doubt they're natural deaths. We removed the top soil on three of them and one was at least thirty or forty years old. Or that's what Dr. Castiano said. The clothing looked about right. The others seemed older, at least the remains and the clothing were more degraded."

"Did you see any evidence of trauma?"

"What we could observe visually was no head wounds on the front of the body or visible on the exposed bones. Funny, though, they all had the remnants of pants but no shirts that I could see."

"Do you think a serial killer has been operating up there?"

"It would have to be a very long-lived one, or maybe a killer who trained an apprentice. But you know those are rare as hen's teeth — paired killers."

"What else could it be?"

There was a noticeable pause before Dr. Ward offered, "There was older blood on the boulder where our current body was found and lots more all around on the ground . . . A ritual, maybe."

"Well, there are some strange elements found on that body in any case. It could be a ritual of some kind, but I can't figure out what kind, yet."

"Maybe Dr. Brookman will be able to enlighten all of us."

"I hope so. But I have a feeling that this has turned into a bigger case than any of us thought and may take a long time to find answers to."

Dr. Morales heard her colleague release a small laugh. "There'll be quite a few journal articles in this, I'm thinking. We'll all be famous."

"As long as we find the murderer. That's all I'm concerned with." Dr. Morales put her phone back on its cradle and stared at it, wondering if this would really turn out to be a long-term cold case. Frowning, she rushed out the door to the happy oblivion of boisterous boys and long-winded tales.

Chapter Fifty-Six

The sound of horses trumpeting and screaming woke Kate before dawn. Her other senses picked up a definite threat, causing her to jerk on her jeans and shove tennies onto her feet. She rushed into the living room as Isaiah pulled one gallus of his overalls onto a bare shoulder. His boots were already on his feet. Rita followed close behind, barefoot in her cotton nightgown.

Isaiah was already at the gun cabinet, reaching on the top of it for the key. He got it open and pulled out a shotgun and then unlocked a drawer for ammunition, finally shoving two big shells into the chambers. He handed it to Rita. "Keep the kids in their room. Whatever is out there isn't just a rattler." Then he reached for a rifle and loaded it.

When Kate picked up the big battery lantern Isaiah kept by the door, he challenged, "Where do you think you're going?"

"You can't see out there. You'll need two hands to operate that monster." She nodded at the rifle in his hands.

Only a second or two passed as he considered what she said. "Stay behind me."

Kate waited until they were outside the door before she switched on the light. She'd forgotten it was an LED light that could throw out 1100 lumens at several yards. It practically lit up the entire horse camp. When Isaiah plunged off to the corral at a hard run, Kate was pressed to keep up. On the edge of the light, a dozen horses could be seen as shapes rushing around the wood corral fencing. As their forms came into light, it was clear they were in a panic. Their bodies struggled against one another, trying to break through the fence. Kate cast the light around the corral as she approached, projecting giant horse shadows against the sandstone outcropping behind them.

Added to them was another shape, smaller, sleek, crouching, waiting. It took her a few seconds to realize that the new shape was not a shadow but something solid on the rocks behind the corral. She flashed the powerful light in its direction. That's when she heard the animal's cry as it opened its dark mouth, studded with sharp teeth, angry at being discovered. Its black fur looked oily in the light but couldn't camouflage the hard, feral muscles underneath. For a moment its beauty struck her, then her belly ran cold as she realized exactly what it was. A flood of ancient lore and symbolism filled her mind: The black jaguar, ruler of Xibalba, the underworld of the Aztecs, and the Mayan symbol of the Ocelotl cult of ferocious warriors. Other images filled her of black wings and a sharp obsidian knife poised over her.

"Hold the light steady!" Isaiah barked, trying to take aim.

Kate hadn't realized she was shaking. Putting her free hand underneath the lantern to steady it, she willed her body to calm. Feeling her feet in her thin shoes on the dusty ground, Kate sent her energy deep into the earth to anchor herself. She was concentrating so hard she jumped at Isaiah's rifle report. Two shots.

"Damn!" he responded.

Unnoticed by Kate, three wranglers had rushed out of the bunkhouse and stood muttering in Spanish behind her.

Isaiah barked some orders to the men. Kate only understood *andele*, meaning *hurry*. The men didn't hesitate, running to the corral, trying to soothe the frightened horses. Then, the big man turned to Kate, looking as worried as he had when she'd come out of her faint yesterday. "You okay?"

She took a shaky breath and nodded. "Did you kill it?"

"No, but I think I nicked it."

"That can't be good."

200

"No." He stared back at the corral. "We'll need to set a watch." Putting a strong hand at Kate's back, her turned toward his house and his family.

"A black jaguar here?" she questioned in disbelief.

"I've heard stories," Isaiah said. "They come out of Mexico sometimes. Panthers. Mostly spotted, though."

Before they reached the door of Isaiah's house, Kate muttered, "This isn't good. Just before Logan's rite."

Isaiah released an uncomfortable laugh. "Last time, didn't they broadcast animal roaring noises and images, like on a movie set? Guess they wanted the real thing."

Kate looked up at his face. "Would they do that to a boy? He doesn't have Allen's abilities. He doesn't have any abilities that I've been able to see."

Isaiah grimaced. "I've never begrudged anyone's beliefs before, but I think your ex is nuts." He reached for the door knob and paused. "I'll protect what's mine. But I may take Rita's lead tonight and invoke Divine help." Slowly opening the door, he made the sign of the cross and prayed loud enough for Rita to hear so she wouldn't shoot him accidentally, but Kate suspected for his own comfort. "Protect me and mine and all men during this night and through the intercession of the blessed Virgin Mary—"

Coming out of their boys' bedroom, Rita took up the prayer, "preserve us from all dangers of body and soul. Keep away from us sickness, fire, and calamities of every kind. Protect us against the assaults of the wicked and of Satan. O Lord, visit this household and repel from it all the snares of the enemy; let your holy angels dwell here to preserve us in peace, and may your blessings remain with us forever."

Chapter Fifty-Seven

The only sound in the motel room was the fan of the AC unit. Ben sat with a notebook propped on a leg crossed over his other thigh. He'd thought about sitting behind the table to take his notes, but he felt that his presence was already an intrusion. Sitting like a clinical psychologist — or worse, a reporter — behind a desk would add more tension to the room and further impede the naturalness of what was about to happen. Clearly, Toni and Allen didn't want to do what they had to do today, but it was necessary for them as well as for himself.

Knowing he was clearly out of his depth here, Ben agreed to Toni's terms, which were mainly to monitor their physical health and to document what was revealed. He wasn't to interrupt or ask questions.

They both now sat on the bed, shoes off and cross-legged. Allen leaned back on several pillows pushed against the headboard. Toni had positioned herself about two feet away from him, apart but within reaching distance if she or Allen chose. In that gap between them, Allen had asked Ben to bring in four of the river stones from the cab of his truck. Toni had explained that they would normally do this on the ground, but they were in foreign land. So, the smooth stones would be their connection to earth.

Toni began, first with some simple deep breathing and relaxation.

"Don't be afraid to let go," Toni said. "I know you're heavily shielded, and so am I. You can't hurt me or Ben because this is only a memory of what you felt."

"My mind knows that, but—," Allen admitted.

"But the rest of you isn't so sure. I will anchor for you. And then I want you to anchor for me."

Allen closed his eyes, and they continued to breathe together. Then Toni said, "I'm going to open to you and share my shields." She closed her eyes then and concentrated.

Allen smiled and visibly relaxed.

Ben scribbled a note that this resembled a type of hypnosis but was different.

"What were your first impressions up there yesterday?" Toni asked.

"I could feel the energy well before we even got there. It's a dark place, an ancient place."

"I sensed that, too. Tell me what happened when you got out of Ben's truck and put your feet on the ground. What did you sense? What did you smell?"

Ben noted that this was much like the guided recall that Jim Baxter had told him the FBI used. He watched Allen move his head first to his left and then to his right as if he were casting about either to remember or to scent something.

"It wasn't the ground so much," Allen said, "but more like I was walking through a gray fog." He caught his breath. "Memories . . . History . . . Souls."

Toni grimaced but continued. "Did you approach the big boulder there?"

"Yes, but I couldn't touch it."

"You didn't have to. Your senses were very keen anyway. What did you pick up there?"

Allen's own face contorted, and then he opened his eyes. Gasping, he bent over the stones on the bed, fixated on them.

Ben saw how his eyes were glassy and unfocused. He'd seen that same look in trauma survivors when he'd been called out to a house fire or a car accident where there had been fatalities.

204

"Blood! Blood everywhere! Not just fresh but old . . . ancient blood."

"Breathe," Toni said, her own eyes now open.

"The scientist found old blood but it's older . . . Generations . . . Older."

"There's more. Breathe and tell me."

"There's bodies. More than what they found. More . . . Lots more . . . Native. But not local."

"Like me?" Toni asked in a very soft voice.

"No . . . Native like Dad . . . Older . . . Generations . . . They'll never find them all."

"Breathe." Then Toni put a stone in each of Allen's hands and said, "Send it all into the stones you hold. . . . All of it!"

For a few long moments, Allen gripped the stones and finally straightened.

"Ben," Toni said quietly. "Go to the bathroom counter. I put one of the plastic bags from our food in there. Bring it to me."

When Ben had retrieved the bag, she told Allen, "Put your stones in the bag and release your connection to them." He did as she instructed, and she tied up the bag. Then she instructed Ben to place it outside the door on the concrete.

Closing the door, Ben noticed Allen's stress level was considerably less. Toni still looked wound tight, but he didn't know her well enough to judge what her normal was. Ben crossed the room to the mini-fridge and retrieved one of the bottles of grape juice he had brought with him. He handed it to Allen, who drank down about half of it and collapsed against the pillows again.

"I'm good," Allen said, putting the juice bottle on the night stand. When he straightened, he grasped Toni's left wrist with his right hand.

Her eyes flashed wide, causing Ben to retake his seat and pick up his notepad. But he had nothing to write as they silently communed.

Allen released his step-mother's wrist and looked confused. "A giant head? Piles of bones? Reassembled bones walking like in an old cartoon I used to watch."

Taking a deep breath, Toni unwound her legs and stuffed her feet into the boots she'd left beside the bed.

"What was that, Toni?" Allen pressed.

She padded to the fridge and got out a bottle of juice for herself. Twisting off the cap and taking a drink, she admitted, "There's blackness up there . . . I got hit by your energy and had to pull over."

"Gosh, I'm sorry," Allen said.

"I'll bet your mom did, too."

"Oh no!"

"She's in good hands. I told you last night she's with Isaiah. We both would have known if she'd been harmed. But this. . . ." She walked over to the table, pulled out a chair, and leaned back into its comfort. "This is different. This seems to call up . . . maybe it's racial memory or triggers from childhood stories. I blocked the intensity of what you sent and what I picked up when I went up there to find you. I got your impressions, which have always been clear and unembellished." She smiled wryly. "Maybe your head never was full of spooky stories like most kids. What I picked up—." She took another drink of juice. "They were colored by old Seneca tales of *Dagwanoe"yent,* Rolling Head, and his twelve nephews, cannibals, and evil. But our tales were spooky, folk tales, usually teaching tales. They never had the gore of blood. I sensed blood up there." She shot a look at Allen. "You never told me about the case you were working on. I just picked up your distress." She looked down at her boots. "Blood is at the heart of this."

Ben grunted, realizing that Toni may have just put a few pieces of the puzzle in his own head together.

Toni glanced at Ben, suddenly looking embarrassed. "This is more than you bargained for, I'm afraid."

Ben chuckled softly. "Do you think you're the only people with ghost lore? We have *La Llorona*, the Weeping Woman, who's doomed to walk the earth searching for her dead children who drowned. She's been seen along river banks here." Shifting in his own chair, he rested his forearms on his knees, leaning in to continue. "You asked me yesterday what I know. What Allen just reported was accurate. The crime lab techs found old blood on the boulder and around it on the ground, not just recent but older, years older. They brought up cadaver dogs and targeted six areas, and Allen sensed something at the one they opened. The skeleton was at least thirty or forty years old from the decomposition of his clothing."

"When I was there, there were three areas they were examining," Toni added.

"A forensic anthropologist will be able to give us a better timeframe." Ben studied his fingers that he had just intertwined like elements in this problem. "This isn't a simple case of a family feud and one man knifing another. There's talk of a serial killer."

"Generational," Allen whispered but loud enough for them to hear, forcing both Ben and Toni to look at him.

Ben cleared his throat, returning his attention to his hands as a means to bring his thoughts together. "The current victim, the one at the center of the case Allen and the lawyers are dealing with—" Ben rested his gaze first on Toni and then on Allen. "Sandy has this information but hasn't had time to share it with you." He turned back to Toni, who seemed the most stable to handle his next disclosures. "There should have been more blood at the scene. And from what I observed, even the crime lab expected to find more on the ground than they did." He watched Toni raise an eyebrow and turn her head to study him more closely. "The autopsy showed that the victim was missing . . . his heart."

Toni sat bolt upright and so did Allen.

Mimicking their change in posture, Ben straightened in his chair. "The incision was precise and clean. There were trace fragments of obsidian."

Allen and Toni exchanged looks, as if communicating something.

"I'm going to talk with an anthropologist at UNM on Monday about ancient practices and what they mean," Ben added. "There is significance in this. Precision and meaning."

A knock at the door disturbed the flow of information. Ben was grateful. He didn't want to go down the road of speculation. "I'll add this to my notes for you," he said as he rose and opened the door.

"Oh, hi, Dr. Castiano," Caroline said, a little surprised to see him there. She craned her head around him. "I wondered if Allen and Toni wanted to go eat now." Her attention returned to him. "You're welcome to come, too."

"Thanks, but I was about to head home. My family is probably making fun, Saturday plans without me." He turned back into the room, picked up his notebook, scribbled a few things down, then tore off the sheets he'd filled and handed them to Toni. "I put my cell number at the bottom. If you have any more insights or ideas, I'd be happy to hear them." He extended his hand to Toni, "Thank you for allowing me to be a witness to this." Shaking his hand, Toni just smiled, but Ben noticed a ghost of worry in her eyes.

Chapter Fifty-Eight

"Uncle Juan!" Logan cried, running from the front of the restaurant, his arms wide, as his parents rushed behind, obviously displeased at his boyish enthusiasm.

Juan Vasquez rose from his chair at a table near a sunny window to bend down to hug the boy. He had only seen him every couple of years, when he had arranged a museum business trip in the States. His wife had refused to ever set foot north again, though she kept in touch with Dutch before she died, and Kate at Christmas. Those strong women had been Delores' midwives and brought his beautiful and healthy daughter into the world. Over the years, it had become trickier to plan his State-side business trips since Delores had demanded that he spend more time with his own young daughter who was his blood rather than with a family that was not his own.

Juan pushed Logan back to look at him. "You're growing so big, *mi hijo*," he said, realizing that he wasn't speaking the truth. Logan was small for a boy his age, not just in height but in build. His own Yvonne, almost a year older, was tall, and becoming rounded in ways that were already producing smiles from the boys in her classes. Normally, Delores wouldn't have let him travel so near his daughter's birthday. Yvonne, however, had let him know that she wanted an all-girl slumber party and that he should make himself absent. In truth, he really didn't want to be here or to take part in this rite again.

Straightening up, Juan smiled first at Marianna and stepped around Logan to kiss her cheek. "You're looking well," he said. Turning to Logan's father, Juan hesitated, unsure, as he studied the other man's face. After all these years, he still felt a little thrill when he looked at him, more bear to his otter.

Finally, Paul smiled and pulled him into a tight hug, saying, "*Hermano.*" Both of the men thumped each other on the back.

"I'm so glad you could come for Logan's rite," Paul said, looking deeply into Juan's eyes and grasping his shoulders.

Juan felt a welcoming warmth rush through him. He had made the right decision to come to support Logan.

"Uncle Juan?" Logan said in a meek voice.

Turning from Paul to the boy, he smiled. "Yes, *mi hijo.*"

"You must see my clothes for the ceremony. I've worked hard beading the designs."

Marianna interrupted. "After we eat." She said to Juan, "They're his own ideas. I don't know why he chose them."

"Perhaps they have special meaning that we cannot fathom," Juan offered. "It is his rite, after all. What protections he chooses should be ones that resonate with him."

"Perhaps," she muttered in dismissal.

Juan moved to pull out a chair for Marianna, who forced a smile as she sat. She added with a slight pout, "I suppose you and Paul will go off later to do your preparation before the fast and sweat tomorrow."

Juan searched Paul's face as he took his own chair. The other man ignored him and spoke to Logan, "You'll start your fast tomorrow. In the morning, we'll pick up the horses and all ride into the site. The men are preparing the sweat lodge for us now. You may have anything you want to eat today. And you can read or watch TV later."

Logan grinned. "Anything I want?" He picked up one of the menus already on the table and studied it intently.

"Will we be at the same place as before?" Juan asked, picking up his own menu to be polite. He'd already decided what he wanted while he waited the few minutes before they joined him.

"In the same vicinity," Paul said. "I've had more time to have my people prepare for the ceremony."

"Logan should have an easier time, since there's no one contesting his position."

Paul slammed down his menu. "It isn't intended to be easy. It's a manhood rite. He will be tested to his limits. As he should be."

"I heard one of the women say that Cesar would make an appearance," Marianna said.

"He and his mother should never have contested the rite the last time. The position is passed from male heir to male heir. I allowed my sister to let him participate or I wouldn't have heard the end of it. She should never have encouraged him. What does Cesar think he'll do? Fight a boy for a place he has no right to?"

"It would be different if Allen would stand with his brother," Marianna said.

"He won't be there?" Juan asked.

"He's off somewhere working for that lawyer he spends his summers with. I think he planned to be away. He's never had a taste for helping Logan with any preparations."

"It's that mother of his," Marianna spat out. "She's turned him from his own people."

Slowly, Logan lowered his menu. The excitement of favorite foods and dessert was gone from his face. Juan could tell the boy had lost his appetite. He himself was embarrassed that the table conversation had turned so venomous, souring his own appetite. Juan looked back at his menu and found something no boy could resist.

"Logan, they have a brownie with fudge sauce and ice cream for dessert. I think I'll have one of those. How about you?" He smiled at the boy, who stretched his lips quickly into a dutiful smile but just as quickly dropped it. Returning to the menu, Juan searched through his mind for things that Yvonne liked. She was in that pre-adolescent stage where she haughtily turned away from anything childish. He and Delores had only had the one child, but his nephews were always adventurous. Finally, he said, "They have a cheeseburger here with everything. And they have coconut shrimp. Maybe you could have a cheeseburger now and shrimp in a box for later while you watch a movie? What kind of movie do you want to watch? A Super Hero one? Or a giant monster one?"

Logan finally gave him a genuine smile. "I want to see a monster one. Allen liked to watch those with me last summer."

"I brought my tablet with me to watch movies on the plane. Maybe you can find a movie to stream while your father and I are out."

He leaned toward Marianna. "I brought headphones so you don't have to listen to the monster roars."

She also gave him a quick smile out of obligation.

As Juan returned to his menu, he wondered how many children Paul had under his roof.

Chapter Fifty-Nine

Pulling out the dipstick from its narrow compartment in the engine, Toni steadied it with a blue mechanic's rag in her free hand. She needed to add a quart of oil. It wasn't surprising, considering the age of the truck and the distance she'd traveled. After plunging the dipstick back into the slot, she opened the driver's side door and reached behind the seat for one of three quarts she had stashed there, just in case, along with a funnel. As she added the oil, Sandy walked up to the truck.

"I bet you'd rather be with your horses," Sandy said.

"I like being outside. The room was getting claustrophobic."

They both glanced at the open doors of the two motel rooms that they occupied. Leaning against the siding between the rooms, Allen and Caroline faced each other, talking quietly.

"I wonder how long it'll take them to realize they're crazy about each other," Sandy speculated.

Turning away, concentrating on cleaning her hands, Toni said, "There's an age gap between them."

Sandy looked at the other woman. "No more than you and Kate."

Toni dipped her head to the side in concession. "But we're on the sunset end of the spectrum. And Caroline is older."

"Too young to be a cougar, you think?"

A small smile creased Toni's face. "She may think the gap is too much."

"Allen's been an old man since he was 10, and you know it."

"True." Toni moved to tap the last of the oil into the funnel, replaced the lid on the container, wiped the funnel, and put it back behind the seat.

When Toni shut the truck door and walked around Sandy to the front of the vehicle, the lawyer said, "I've been thinking."

"That's a good thing for a lawyer to be doing," Toni remarked, twisting on the oil cap and then slamming down the hood of the truck. She placed the empty oil container on top.

It was Sandy's turn to smile. "Allen has accomplished what I brought him here to do. He's interviewed witnesses and did a 'feel' of the crime scene, which is turning into something bigger than an isolated stabbing. He's written up his witness reports." She looked over at Allen and Caroline. "I really hate to break that up."

"But?"

"Maybe it would be better for Allen to go home. This has been rough on him. He might need a healing. . . . I have a cousin who could help him."

Crossing her arms across her chest, Toni considered the offer. "It's always good to be on land that is home." She gazed at the landscape around her. "There are parts here that are so beautiful. And there are places that are scarred. This is foreign. Over time, a person could *make* this home."

"Like you did in Payson," Sandy said.

"I was running away. When I went back to New York, it was. . . ." She shook her head. "There are no words. But Grandmother was there and it was Kate and Allen's time to run away. When Grandmother and then Dutch both passed, I realized that home was more than a landscape."

"Will you take him home?"

Toni nodded. "And you'll stay to finish your case."

"Yes. If the DA isn't an idiot, he'll realize that this case is falling apart, despite a country sheriff who thinks it's a slam dunk." Sandy fixed her eyes on the north where, far away,

Dulce rested in the mountains. "I still don't know what's going on, but I think my client just was in the wrong place."

"And you're curious about something you don't know. Like Ben."

Sandy's attention returned to Toni. "You're damn right, I'm curious."

Toni straightened, retrieving the oil container, intending to put it and the bag of stones Ben had left outside their door into a garbage can somewhere. "Just be careful. This has a nasty feel to it."

"When do you want to leave?"

Casting one more glance at Allen and Caroline, she said, "Tomorrow morning after breakfast. That'll give the kids a little time together."

Chapter Sixty

Day 8: Sunday, early morning, near Payson, AZ

Dressed in his ritual clothing to which had been added leggings in the same white doeskin, Logan climbed out of the back seat of the car, not waiting for anyone to join him. He raced to the two horse trailers that had pulled alongside in the dirt drive at Toni's horse ranch. The boy was eager to see each one but was very curious to know which one was his.

Logan stood back as a man got out of a truck pulling one trailer and a woman came out of the other. They immediately set to work unbolting the back doors of each trailer, swinging them wide, and pulling out hidden ramps. The woman slipped into her trailer, the nearest to the boy, and sidled to the head of one of the horses. She took hold of the reins and wiggled them back and forth as a cue for the horse to back out. It was a slow process and tested Logan's patience because he wanted to see each horse's whole body. When the horse was out, the woman moved it to the side of the trailer and tied the reins to an opening in one of the windows. This process was repeated until all of the horses were out and secured.

Logan wandered, a safe distance away, as Toni had always told him, to check out each horse. They were already saddled and ready to ride. He still had no idea which was his.

The woman came over to him. "Wondering which one you'll ride?"

Logan nodded, grinning.

She brought him to a sleek, reddish brown horse. "Do you know horse breeds?" she asked.

"Only the colors," he said. "This is a sorrel, isn't it? I've seen a lot of bays here."

The woman looked around, noting the empty corral. "Here?"

"The owners are away. And we were looking for a paint for me."

"Yes, I remember." She turned her attention back to the horse. "This is a Morgan. She's perfect for you because not only will she react to your commands, even if you're a little unsure, but she's also trail experienced and will take good care you."

Logan reached the back of his hand to the horse's nose like he would have to a big dog. The animal snuffled in greeting and bent her head to look him in the eye. That increased Logan's grin. He stroked her forehead and then the side of her face. The horse gently nudged the boy and Logan took her head in both hands and pressed his cheek against the side of her face. The mare jerked her head free and then up and down.

"She likes you," the woman said.

"What's her name?"

"Sparkle. That describes her personality."

Car door slams caused the other horses to stamp, but Sparkle didn't wince. She nudged Logan again, and the boy continued to pet the big animal.

The woman turned to look at the odd group beside the car. Logan's father and Uncle Juan were dressed in muslin shirts and brown leggings, and each wore a river-smoothed shaman stone around their necks. Logan would wear the one his father had when this rite was over. He never knew what that really meant except as a sign of his place among the People. Logan thought of it as sort of a crown or scepter that a ruler would have. From what he had been told, Logan had more of the ancient blood in his veins than Allen, but he felt less worthy than his half-brother.

Logan's mother's ritual clothing was striking next to the plainness of the men's garb. She wore a bright blue, triangular poncho top, embroidered with yellow and red flowers and

218

bright strips of colored ribbon. It was edged in silver fringe. The top was paired with an ankle-length blue skirt that bore strips of silver and red. Her hair had been twisted into buns near her ears but was mostly concealed by a blue and silver beaded headband that looked more like a crown with sides that hung down each side of her face, touching her shoulders. Behind the headband, a frill of white feathers set off her face like a sunburst. Logan smiled. His mother was beautiful.

The woman holding the reins of the horse said, "Are you filming a movie out here? Or—"

Before Logan could answer, his father's raised voice broke the quiet of the morning. There was some disagreement about the paperwork that the man at the other horse trailer had stuck to a clipboard and was pointing at with a pen. Juan joined them and took the clipboard, flipping through the pages.

Logan wanted to avoid the arguments of grownups. It usually didn't end well for him if he interfered. The woman, however, began to walk his horse over to the squabble, and Logan reluctantly followed.

"We are not with a film company — independent or otherwise," his father said. "We contracted for five days for a private event. The horses will be ridden into the event and back out. And they will be well cared for in the days in between by people who know horses."

The man eyed Logan's father and Uncle Juan suspiciously when the woman touched the man's arm, obviously coming to some conclusion. "It's probably a wedding, dear, not a movie," the woman said. "They've put a lot of effort into this. It's all for the photographers. Remember last year, when we outfitted that couple and the wedding party, even the minister, for a Wild West Wedding?" She turned to her customers. "If it's a movie, we have to charge more for insurance and charge at union rates. Since this is for a private event, we will honor our initial agreement."

"We'll be back on Friday morning about ten. You can bring the trailers back to pick the horses up then."

Logan was glad all the shouting was over. He just wanted to mount up and ride. He was a little nervous, since it was a horse he'd never ridden before, but Sparkle seemed to like him.

After the papers were signed and the car locked, the woman gave Logan a leg up and got him seated comfortably in the saddle, adjusting his stirrups for him. "When you remount to ride back, you might need to stand on a chair," she said. "Now. Let's see you move your horse forward and stop."

Logan spoke softly to the horse in the language Toni had taught him and nudged the horse forward with his knees. After a few paces, he pulled on the reins and the horse stopped. Looking back at the woman, he saw her smile.

"You and Sparkle will do just fine," she said.

It didn't take long for everyone to mount up, heading toward the trees on the edge of the ranch. Logan's mom and dad set their horses into a gentle walk at the front. Logan was in the middle with Uncle Juan trailing behind. He knew that when they got near the ceremony site, his father would make him take the lead and do a fast trot in. He wasn't sure he was ready for that, or any of this. Patting Sparkle gently on the neck, he felt a new confidence.

220

Chapter Sixty-One

Allen tossed his backpack behind the passenger's seat of the truck and slammed the door. He smiled at Toni shaking hands with Sandy and Caroline on the sidewalk in front of their motel room. His step-mom had helped smooth his mother's concerns when he first applied for his PI license so he could work for the law firm. His mom had had some strange idea his work would be more cloak and dagger than it was legwork and paperwork. As he came around the hood of the pickup, Sandy stepped away from Toni and moved toward him.

"You did good work here," she said. "There were a lot of witnesses to interview and you had to deal with the Princess."

Allen couldn't suppress a wry smile.

"And going up to the site was asking a lot of you," she continued, then tossed a glance at Toni. "I should have called her in to be with you."

"Dr. Castiano didn't freak, at least," he admitted.

"I had a hunch he might be open-minded." She smiled. "Maybe some of your ability to read people has rubbed off on me."

Allen raised his head to look at the landscape around them. "It's pretty country," he said, "especially up north."

Sandy followed his gaze, finally returning to her colleague. "We did a great service to our client. I was surprised that he didn't have better representation. It's a shame we can't help more native people here."

"He's still not in the clear."

"No, but the Sheriff's case is getting shakier and shakier." Crossing her arms across her chest as if to comfort herself, she admitted, "There's something very dark going on here."

Allen nodded. "I'm glad I didn't fully open up back there."

"Well." She spoke that simple, universal word with complex meanings. Smiling, she opened her arms as an invitation for a hug and waited.

Allen nodded and stepped into her waiting arms. He was heavily shielded, but it took more effort at that moment to keep Sandy's emotions out. When he stepped back, Caroline rushed over with a plastic grocery bag in her hands.

"Make sure you stop to eat a hot meal. You do forget sometimes." She offered the plastic bag, practically shoving it into his hands. "It's for the road. There's fruit and juice and some snacks." Before he could thank her, she threw her arms around him.

Allen's shielding couldn't barricade against her broadcast of more than sisterly concern. He staggered a step as she wrenched away and fled into the motel room.

"Safe travels," Sandy said, waving, before she followed Caroline.

Shaken, Allen climbed into the pickup and fumbled with his seatbelt. He took a deep breath and centered himself before pulling out his phone and setting a route for Albuquerque and then Gallup, and finally home.

When Toni took her seat and started the engine, she backed out of the parking space and heard the female GPS voice give her directions. "Is she reliable?" Toni asked.

"What?" Allen looked confused.

Toni pointed to the phone Allen was putting on the bench seat beside them.

"Usually is. Though I've had to ignore her a few times when she'd direct me to an interstate when I knew there were side streets with less traffic."

"Any hope of that the way we're going?"

"There weren't any coming here. I drove all the way while Sandy and Caroline dealt with paperwork."

Toni flipped on the radio, dialing in *Norteno* music. "A guy where I got gas in Chama told me about this station," she explained. When they were south of Espanola, which only took a few minutes, Toni asked, "You okay?"

Allen shrugged. "Does it get easier?"

"Easier for what?"

"Not picking up stuff."

"You can't help it when people broadcast as loudly as this radio station." After a pause, she added. "Your mother was like Caroline in the beginning. She knew how to shield a bit to keep from picking up things, but her shielding was porous. She could broadcast so clearly."

Allen noticed a touch of nostalgia in Toni's last statement and smile on her lips. "But aren't there ethics involved, no matter how pleasant their broadcast is?"

"Of course, there is. You were taught not to eavesdrop by dropping your shielding just to be nosy. But you can't help it when you pick up something. And you use your skills in your PI work. What you find out isn't for your gain or that of those you work for. You sift the truth. And it's not like you're reading minds or manipulating people."

"Like Dad does."

"Your father has a gift that he uses in order to have control. He doesn't trust. It's hard to love without trust."

Allen slumped against the seat and rested the back of his forearm against his brow. "It's just so exhausting."

Toni patted her step-son's knee.

Allen didn't pick up anything except her reassurance. "I wish I was as strong as you," he said.

"That's from deep wounds, son. Greater control comes with time. Be glad you are who you are. You trust people. You can also sense danger and protect yourself. I worry—"

"Worry? About me?"

She glanced at him and smiled. "Only as a parent should. I trust your heart and your gifts." Focusing on the road again, she admitted, "I worry about Logan. Your father has groomed him for this rite that begins tomorrow."

"As he did me."

"Yes, but you had your mother's protection and your own abilities. Logan is mind-blind. Over the years, I looked for signs of a gift." She shook her head. "He's malleable."

Allen straightened in his seat. "Is he in danger?"

Toni nodded. "And we can't help him."

"You can't, but I could."

"It's a manhood rite. For most of that, he'll be on his own. And who knows what else your father has planned for him? It was bad enough what you had to endure."

Allen rubbed a spot below his collarbone where a scar reminded him of some of that ordeal. "A boy his age shouldn't go through what I did."

"No, he shouldn't. A fast and vision quest, yes. There should be water left with him."

"Maybe I should go find them tomorrow and at least show Logan my support."

"We don't know where they are."

"It's probably in the same place."

A frown creased Toni's forehead. "Let me think on it." She gave Allen another quick look. "You really aren't strong enough yet after what happened at the crime scene."

Allen felt the blood drain from his face. He grabbed the crook of Toni's arm, not muting what he was projecting. "It feels the same. Only worse. That wasn't crime. It was madness."

Toni's eyes flashed wide, picking up something. "Or belief."

Chapter Sixty-Two

Day 8: Sunday, early evening, near Payson, AZ

Logan stood outside the boulder-like structure covered with canvas, not the hides his ancestors would have used. Made of long, fresh-cut branches that had been kept pliable in water during transport, the sweat lodge was at least eight or nine feet across and five feet high in the center. The overarching dome was secured by seven horizontal circles of branches that represented the seven directions (East, West, North, South, Sky, Earth, and Creator). Logan and the men, bare-chested with only breechclouts or shorts on, had already honored the ancestors by circling the lodge, singing, drumming, or using rattles like the one the boy had in his hand. They waited now for Logan's father to signal the first of the Grandfathers, the hot stones, to be brought from a fire pit several feet away and into the lodge through the entrance that faced East.

The boy's face and chest had been painted red on one side for childhood and yellow on the other for adolescence. He would not receive the black paint of adulthood until he was sixteen, a full two years before other young men here. It was an early reckoning of maturity, but the shaman of these people was always supposed to be older than his chronological age. And wiser. Logan didn't feel older or wiser. He felt hungry and shaky on his feet. His fast had begun and would continue for three more days. He just wanted to see this sweat through tonight and then go to sleep.

Resting two large stones on a pitchfork, the firekeeper brought them through the open doorway to a small pit dug into the earth in the center of the lodge. He came out and repeated this task until he had seven large stones in the pit. A helper brought a wooden ladle and an earthen bowl of water mixed with sage and cedar inside and set it next to the fire pit. Logan's father shook his rattle and ducked inside, a signal for all to enter, Logan first.

The boy sat down in the direction of the South, where he had been instructed. Uncle Juan took his place next to Logan's father in the North, and the others, seven of them, found their own places in the circle. Logan had never met these men before, but he had been told that they would become his inner clan when he took power. He had trained solely with his father until this day.

Logan's father poured a couple of ladles of the herbed water onto the hot stones. As the sweet, fragrant steam rose, he nodded to the firekeeper, who stood at the entrance, waiting. The man pulled down the heavy tarp, plunging the lodge into darkness. Logan's father began a chant, and the men picked up the rhythm on their drums and joined their voices to the song.

Though Logan was surrounded by men who were supposed to be his new family, he felt alone and afraid. No amount of coaching and grooming had prepared him for the realities of the next few days. He couldn't think about those unknowns now. He had to get through this night.

He knew that there would be four rounds of this sweat with little breaks in between when the canvas would be thrown back so cool night air could mingle with the heat inside. The first round held prayers to the ancestors and the Creator. He needed their help, so he would pray hard. The second round would offer prayers to his people and those in this sweat. He would pray for Allen and Toni and Allen's mother, too, because they had been kind to him. The third round was for the success of this rite so that a new shaman would take his place, and the last would hold individual prayers for help. Seven more stones would be added after each round and the heat would build. As Logan began to sweat, he prayed he would survive not only this night but all that was before him.

Chapter Sixty-Three

Day 8: Sunday, early evening, near Payson, AZ

In the fading light, the truck's high beams illuminated the dark car parked at the far end of the dirt drive. Allen pulled in front of the ranch house, just shy of the steps. They had traded off driving, with Allen taking the route through Albuquerque to Gallup and Toni from there to the turn-off south to Payson. Allen had taken over the last few miles as it headed toward sunset.

"Looks like your dad left his car," Toni said. While the engine still idled, she got out and looked at the tire treads in the truck's headlights. "A couple of horse trailers, I'd guess, and hoof marks heading out beyond." She turned back to the truck. "Looks like the same place they used for your rite."

Allen shut off the lights and the engine. He grabbed his backpack and headed inside. Unlike his homecoming a few days before, the house was dark and empty. Using the house key on Toni's keyring, Allen unlocked the door but hesitated.

Toni followed quickly with her own bag. She, too, waited, listening.

Allen shook his head. "It's nothing. It just doesn't feel right without Mom being here. She's always here."

Twisting the knob and pushing the door open, Toni said, "She'll be here soon, and the house will be full of her chatter."

As Allen stepped inside following Toni, he said, "At least she doesn't nag me like Caroline."

"Well, they both want you to eat."

"Yeah, but Mom actually cooks. I'm so tired of restaurant food."

"Go see what's in the fridge, and I'll get Isaiah on the radio and tell him we're back," Toni instructed, heading toward the ranch office on the first floor.

Allen dumped his backpack on the stairs and turned on the light in the kitchen. Opening the fridge door, he found condiments and potatoes, carrots, and onions. He checked the freezer and a sheet of paper taped to a container greeted him. In his mother's distinctive half-print/half-cursive hand were instructions: "Eat this first and the cornbread. Then the pie. Tomatoes are on the counter. Love you!"

Allen smiled at her thoughtfulness. Lifting the paper, he saw two containers of what looked like chili, sitting on top of an apple pie in a glass pie plate. Beside that was a small plastic bag of cornbread wedges. He pulled out the food and set to work. He nuked the chili enough to slip it out of each container into bowls and then set about heating that until it was bubbly.

Allen looked over the tomatoes on the counter. From the state of ripening, they had obviously been picked rather green. He selected two of the ripest and sliced them onto little plates. Then he warmed the cornbread.

"Did you find any food?" Toni asked, seeing Allen busy putting the cornbread onto the tomato plates.

"Mom expected us to be hungry." Putting the pie in the microwave to warm, he instructed. "Find some placemats. I'm not going to be responsible for staining one of Aunt Delores' tablecloths."

Toni simply pulled back the embroidered cloth. "Will that do?"

Allen smiled at the well-used wooden top he remembered from his early summer days here. "Perfect," he said, and started putting out food and silverware.

Taking his first mouthful of chili, Allen grinned. "It's like she's here." He chewed for a minute and said, "But I sort of miss the green chili in New Mexico. Just not the hot kind."

Toni held up a finger. "Wait," she said, heading to the hall and rummaging in her bag. She came back with a small can of Hatch diced green chile. The label read: Mild. "Caroline handed me this when we left. She said you could probably tolerate it."

Opening the can, they spooned some into their food and continued to eat. "What did Isaiah say? Is Mom okay?" Allen asked finally.

"She's fine. He'll bring her back tomorrow morning. It really is too dark to try to do that tonight."

Allen nodded, anticipating the apple pie, whose aroma was now filling the room.

Toni stopped chewing. "He did say that he had an odd occurrence happen last night. He's had to put men on guard at night, especially."

"What was it, a wolf or coyote?"

"He wouldn't say. He did say that Rita was sending holy water with him tomorrow."

Allen thought about that. "Does she think it's something other than a predator?"

"There are predators and there are predators. Rita is one of the saintliest women I know, so any protection she offers will be appreciated." It was Toni's turn to pause and think. She looked at the clock on the wall, seeing it was well past nine o'clock. "We need to make a trip tomorrow after your Mom comes home."

"Where?"

"Old friends."

Chapter Sixty-Four

With his father, Uncle Juan, and the seven men of his inner clan following, Logan scouted the landscape a mile from the ceremony site. It was his duty to find the spot where he would stay for three days for his vision quest. He had already rejected four places, fueling his father's anger.

"What are you doing?" Paul demanded.

Uncle Juan interceded, "It's his right to find a spot that's his. He's listening to his guides and the spirits of the land. That's what you taught him."

Ignoring the discussion behind him, Logan noticed in what direction the sun was moving and where it was casting shadows. He recalled a book he had borrowed from the library, without his father knowing, about desert survival. The boy had been worried he wouldn't have the skills needed because he hadn't been raised in this landscape or by these native people — his people — who were really strangers to him. The book told him about how the heat of the day would be unbearable unless there was shelter, and the nights would get very cold. All that his father had wanted him to do was find the first level spot he could to put the prayer pole into the ground and the four stones in the four directions.

Ahead, Logan noticed a rock outcropping. He hiked to it and found it was shallow but big enough for him to sit in. The floor was dirt, and there were no crevices for snakes or scorpions to hide. He turned to look at the landscape in front of him. There was a level spot where he could put the prayer pole and the stones. He would be allowed a blanket, his leggings, prayer ribbons, and water. They would drop five gallons of water for him to last three days and part of Thursday, when the people would come for him. This would be a good place. He could see far from his vantage point, and that would give him something to do while he meditated and prayed. And the dirt floor of the overhang would be a good place to draw pictures. Logan smiled.

"This is the place," he said.

His father visibly relaxed. Logan and the party turned back to the ceremony site. There would be songs and drumming, and then all of the people would hike to his vision quest place. More songs and drumming would follow as they planted the prayer pole, a sapling with branches on it to hold the prayer ribbons, into a hole filled with tobacco. The site would be smudged, and he would find four stones to place in four directions. Not only would that honor the spirits of those directions but also the ancestors. Then he would be smudged and left alone.

As Logan walked back to the ceremony site, he looked forward to being alone for a while, away from the pressures of his father and the staring eyes of all the people. He could think and dream for a while. He worried, though, about after dark. Casting a backward glance to the overhang, Logan felt a chill in the growing heat of the morning.

Chapter Sixty-Five

Allen had slathered softened butter onto one of the biscuits he'd found in the freezer and had warmed in the microwave. He was just about to add a big dollop of his mother's apricot jam to the deliciousness when he heard the sound of horse hooves and neighs. He paused to look at Toni, who was sopping up the last of her egg with a biscuit. His step-mom stuffed the last bite of bread into her mouth, wiped her face, and got up. Allen quickly followed her outside, down the porch steps, and into the dirt yard. On the far side of the paddock, they saw horses trotting fast, with one horse leading the group.

"Looks like Sunny missed her alfalfa," Toni remarked. "Isaiah rarely gives it to the ungentled horses."

"There are more than Sunny and her saddle-mates," Allen commented, stepping up to the corral, folding his arms across the top rail as he watched the horses' approach.

Toni had already let herself into the corral and then to the paddock behind. She jogged to the far end and opened a gate that was obscured by underbrush. The horses rushed in, about a dozen more than the six they kept on the ranch. Following them were three riders.

Isaiah's black Stetson atop his mustached face was unmistakable. Allen's mother and a man with colorful neck and chin tattoos followed.

The riders came through the paddock and the corral to turn the horses to face the others. They dismounted and tied their reins to the top rails of the corral close to where Allen stood.

"You brought your horses, too?" Allen asked.

Isaiah strode to him and offered his hand to shake. "Glad you're back," he began. "We thought it would be safer for them. They're ready to transfer to the reservation, all except one that will need a day or two more care, we think."

Kate came around the horses to Allen. She waited for his move before hugging him briefly. "Will you have to go back?"

"I don't think so," Allen said.

The other man stepped away from the horses as Toni shut the corral's gate. He offered his hand to Allen. "I'm Sam," he said.

Allen gave his name, and they shook hands. He couldn't help but pick up the other man's hesitancy to be here. He wasn't sure if it was just a good read of the man's body language or something in his handshake. Allen recalled that Sam had served a long prison term for manslaughter. It seemed incongruous with the humble man, who stood shyly in front of him.

When Isaiah shook hands with Toni, he asked, "Could Sam stay in one of the guest rooms for a few days? He has some finishing to do with one of the horses."

Sam heard and stepped toward them. "No, please. I can sleep in the barn." He turned to Allen's mom. "But I would like to eat Senora Kate's cooking."

"Stay in the house," Toni insisted. "Consider it a working vacation."

"I gave most of the other men the week off," Isaiah said, "so enjoy yourself. You'll earn your keep with working the horse."

"If there's any other work you have," Sam said to Toni, "I'd be glad to help. I don't do well with being idle."

Allen offered hospitality, leading the way into the house. "There's fresh coffee inside. Have you had breakfast? Would you like a slice of pie?"

Kate rushed up the steps to walk alongside her son. "I thought that pie would be history by now."

"It's good pie, but the other food you left for us was filling."

"Sam, let me show you where your room is," Toni said, heading upstairs. "We'll make up the bed later."

"Just find the bedding. I can do for myself," Sam insisted.

Isaiah followed Kate and Allen into the kitchen and helped himself to coffee. Allen pulled out the pie from the fridge, and Kate got extra plates and silverware. Removing his breakfast plate and coffee mug to a counter, Allen asked, "You said it was safer to bring your horses here? Did something happen at the camp?"

"Damnedest thing I ever saw," Isaiah began, seeming eager to begin his tale.

Kate moved Toni's plate and mug to the sink and said, "We'll tell you when Toni comes down."

Allen decided to finish his biscuit on his feet while he waited, but first offered his chair to Isaiah.

"Thanks, but I like being on my feet after a ride."

Kate sliced pie for the two men and poured herself a cup of coffee. Taking a sip, she winced and added a splash of water from the tap.

"Too strong?" Allen commented. "My fault."

"I've gotten spoiled by Rita. She makes a lovely, civilized cup."

Toni bounded down the stairs and stopped short in the doorway, glancing at everyone standing. She went over to her former seat and sat down. It was a silent signal for all to sit. The others gathered in chairs at the table with their coffee. Kate refilled Toni's cup and set it down beside her before she took her seat.

"So, what's been happening?" Toni asked quietly.

"There's been a big cat prowling around the horses," Isaiah stated.

"A bobcat or puma?"

The big man shook his head. "A black jaguar, as far as I could tell."

"When did that happen?"

"Early Saturday morning. It was poised up on that sandstone outcropping behind the working corral. I got off a few shots, nicked it, maybe in the ear, and that might have just been a ricochet. It was dark, and it's hard to judge distance in lantern light. Didn't hurt it, obviously, since it came back last night after I got your radio call."

"You left Rita and the kids back there?" Toni asked, horrified. "Why didn't you bring them with you? We could put them up."

"I left some men with them, armed, my best shots, and I'll be back there in an hour or so. We'll still post guards tonight, but it probably won't come back, since there isn't a prey source."

Allen took a sip of his own coffee, thinking. "A black jaguar? Isn't that unusual here?"

"We've had rumors of spotted jaguars in Arizona before. And it's not uncommon to have a black offspring sometimes. They come across the Mexican border in drought years like bears come down from the mountains. This far north is odd, but perhaps there's a family here."

"I'd worry about the kids if there's a wild animal prowling about," Toni said.

Allen turned to his mother. "Do you have a sense of what this is?"

Kate, who had been studying the black contents of her cup, finally spoke up. "It frightens me." She faced everyone at the table. "It seems familiar, somehow. Like a memory or something I learned in a class long ago."

Allen shifted uncomfortably in his chair. "Is this feeling because of something I sent on Friday?"

Isaiah interjected, "Friday? Man, she picked up something pretty powerful. I've never seen anything like that before. Laid her right on the ground."

"I'm sorry," Allen said meekly.

His mother shook her head. "It just was a long time since I've had such a powerful sending. But I don't know that it was you, exactly."

"It could have been me," Toni admitted. "I got hit by something, but I don't think that was all Allen. There was his emotion. But something else was fueling it."

"What I picked up was part of a memory of long ago." She flashed a glance at Toni and looked away. "It may have colored what I felt about the big cat."

"The stone," Toni said in a whisper.

"What stone?" Allen demanded, fearful that his reaction to the boulder at the crime scene had harmed his mother.

No one spoke for a full minute as each person searched the faces of everyone at the table. Obviously uncomfortable about something that he wasn't privy to, Isaiah stood. "I need to get back to my family." He strode out to foyer and called Sam's name up the stairs. The wrangler appeared with a response in Spanish.

"I'll radio the buyer at the reservation and come back later in the week to help you transport the horses," Isaiah explained. They exchanged farewells in Spanish, and Isaiah turned back to the kitchen. "See you folks later." He quickly left the house, mounted, and headed off down another trail to the horse camp.

The silence in the kitchen lingered long after the sound of Isaiah's horse's hoofbeats had faded.

Chapter Sixty-Six

Ben knocked lightly against the heavy wooden door of an office in the Anthropology Department of UNM. A soft "Come" came from behind the thick door.

Ben entered. "Dr. Blakely?"

A small, strikingly handsome Black woman with gray, tight curls rose from her chair behind a large wooden desk. She had a shawl of red and blue kente cloth over the shoulders of her gray linen, loose-fitting dress. "Yes."

Ben couldn't hide his surprise.

"Dr. Castiano?" she countered.

When he acknowledged who he was, she smiled, an electric but warm greeting. "Please sit down."

Opposite the massive desk were two wide wicker chairs with several pillows on them in tones of red and blue. Ben sat and took in the room. There was a window on one wall and before it was a table with an illuminated manuscript open across its expanse. Ben could just make out the elaborately filigreed red T from where he sat. The walls held bookcases stuffed with books, some even sandwiched in the spaces over the tops of other books. A quick glance identified volumes of fairy tales and several different copies of the Arabian Nights. Two African masks hung over the top ends of one of the bookcases that protruded like bedposts. A goat-hide drum was tucked in front of another bookcase, along with several large brass censors like some Ben had once seen in a Greek shop in New York City. An intricately carved table with what looked like mother-of-pearl inlay on the top separated the two chairs.

"I suppose you're surprised, seeing an old Black woman in a room with romance — the detritus of travels and books gathered along the way?"

It was a rhetorical question that Ben didn't respond to. He did, indeed, feel he was in an English professor's office rather than an anthropologist's.

"Would you take Ethiopian coffee with me?"

He sensed that there was more in that offer of hospitality. "Thank you."

The woman proceeded to roughly mill a few greenish-brown beans and then mash them with an alabaster mortar and pestle. She showed him the mashed contents of the mortar and allowed him to smell its pungent aroma. "Usually, the beans are totally mashed, but I'm old."

Off to the side of her desk, wedged in the space between it and the mask-bedecked bookcase, was a ceramic pot set well above a hot plate burner via a metal rack. A loud boiling could be heard. The woman poured the beans into the hot water. "Drinking *buna* can often take many hours. I think, though, today it will be long enough for your questions." Dr. Blakely brought a napkin-covered plate from her desk and set it on the mosaicked table.

"What part of your family is from Ethiopia?" Ben asked.

She chuckled, placing three tiny cups and saucers next to the covered plate. "My family's from Savannah." She sat down on the other wicker chair. "Allow the teacher in me, if you please. There are two lessons you have just observed. Well, three. The first is all around you. Every culture is full of stories and traditions, music and dance and art. But it's the stories that keep a culture alive, because they pass the traditions down through the generations. The Bible was once an oral tradition and was only written down during the Babylonian diaspora, for fear that the stories and traditions would be lost. And that's why you're here today." She removed the napkin to reveal delicate, white petit fours on one side and dried figs and

240

dates on the other. She selected a fig and took a small bite.

Ben reached for one of the petit fours.

"My apologies," Dr. Blakely said and rose to bring two napkins to the table.

Ben reached for one and placed it on his thigh, balancing the small cake there. "You said there were three lessons. What are the other two?"

The professor smiled again. "The second is that all traditions change and adapt. I grind my beans roughly and don't mash them much by hand. It's an adaptation because of the lack of strength in my hands."

"And the third?"

"I borrowed a tradition from another culture. You assumed because of my skin color that I was of Ethiopian heritage. You are. . . ." She studied him. "Spanish, obviously. Native?"

He nodded. "Apache, according to rumor, but not enrollment."

"Ah. Your height. But you're participating in a cultural tradition not your own."

The sizzle of water on the burner drew her attention. A foamy liquid oozed out of the long spout. The professor turned off the burner, picked up the clay pot, and found a colorful straw coaster that looked like it had been made in Mexico. She put the coaster down on the table and put the pot on top of it. "This is called a *jebena*. I did buy it in Ethiopia when I went there for a conference. There's something about the brew in a ceramic pot that modern coffeemakers can't surpass."

She sat again. "So, what are the questions that bring you to my office today?"

Looking over the food and smelling the strong aromatic coffee, Ben said, "I'm afraid it's not proper table conversation."

Dr. Blakely chuckled. "You don't know anthropologists very well. I was once at a conference in Michigan. I was having dinner with four physical anthropologists. One of them worked as a state forensic anthropologist out of his office at Ohio State University. He and his colleagues were having a very graphic discussion about the time sequence of decomposition of remains while we were all carving into steaks and having Pasta Bolognese. So, please proceed with your questions."

Taking a deep breath, Ben began, "This current case brought me back to a conference I attended in New Orleans a few years ago for law enforcement, mainly the FBI. Its speakers were practitioners from non-traditional beliefs like Wicca, Voudon, Hoodoo, Pennsylvania hex magic, *curanderismo*, and even Satanism. It was eye-opening, because it wasn't what the movies describe."

"It never is," Dr. Blakely said, crossing her legs and resting her hands in her lap. "But those are viable beliefs."

"It was an effort to separate legitimate practices and really sick serial killings."

The professor nodded.

"I borrowed notes and materials from an FBI friend who keeps everything. As I read, I wondered."

"About a current case?"

"Yes."

"Tell me about it." She paused. "As much as you can without breaching any confidentiality." The professor picked up the *jebena* and poured a bit into the third cup. She examined it closely. "Not quite yet." She leaned back in her seat. "And your current case?"

"Well, I examined a body up north. There just wasn't enough blood at the scene."

"Was the body moved?"

"I thought so at first, until I examined this boulder he'd been propped against. It had blood on it."

Dr. Blakely raised an eyebrow but didn't interrupt.

"When the ME put the body through the MRI, the man had no. . . ."

"No what?"

"Heart."

The professor scrunched her face up as if trying to remember something. "There have been burials in historic times of people who chose to have their hearts buried in a place other than where the rest of the bodies were interred. It was common in medieval times among both nobles and commoners. As I recall, Thomas Hardy was cremated, but his heart was buried someplace else next to his wife . . . No, first wife."

Ben stared at her. It wasn't the kind of information he expected from an anthropologist.

She smiled again but with some embarrassment. "I have a photographic memory. I remember . . . everything." This time she poured the bit from the third cup into its saucer and put fresh coffee from the *jebena* into the used cup. This time, she poured each of them generous amounts in the other cups. "Do you take cream or sugar?"

Ben shook his head and thanked her. He sipped the hot liquid carefully. It was rich and concentrated with a fruity undertone. He smiled.

"Anything else about your case?"

"Yes," he continued. "The ME found traces of obsidian in the wound. The crime lab director went up to the crime scene again, and we walked the land, looking for the murder weapon. The wound was done with scalpel-like precision. We didn't find anything."

"You probably won't. An obsidian blade? It would have been a ritual blade, highly prized or revered. It wouldn't be cast off on the ground. Anything else?"

"Well, yes. Dr. Ward from the crime lab found a lot of older blood on the boulder and around it on the ground. Years old, he thought. He also had brought up cadaver dogs. They made six hits, and he uncovered one when I was there and it was at least thirty or forty years old. And five more possible sites of remains."

She nodded, and then abruptly rose from her chair and approached the bookcase next to her. The professor ran her finger across the titles until she found the one she sought. She pulled it out, sat down, and searched the index. When she had found the page, she handed it to Ben.

He looked at a photograph of an ancient painting from the Mayan Codex. It was of a ritual sacrifice, and the victim's heart was being removed.

Dr. Blakely reached for the book, searched the index again, and turned to another page. She scanned it and summarized. "A priest, who traveled with the Spanish, documented ritual sacrifices of enemy warriors, as many as twelve to twenty a day. The Aztec and the Maya both removed hearts. But the Maya valued blood more than the heart itself. Different belief systems. To the Aztec, human sacrifice was not only to appease their gods but to show their power over a subjugated people. The Maya just sacrificed because they felt that, if they didn't, the world would stop."

"Mayans? Aztecs? In North America? Now?"

Dr. Blakely shrugged. "Who is to say? People from Mesoamerica traded with native peoples in areas of what is now the United States — here in New Mexico, Arizona, Georgia, and Florida. It was all open land then, full of resources. I can point you to a professor in the Archaeology Department who could guide you to more reading about that exchange of trade." Putting the book down on the floor beside her feet, the professor picked up her coffee cup and one of the petit fours. "As for today? Remember the last two lessons you learned here. People adopt and adapt traditions."

Ben turned to his own coffee and reached for another petit four. "I don't know how comfortable I am with that."

Leaning back in her wicker chair, Dr. Blakely said, "It is the exquisite beauty of diversity and adaptability."

Chapter Sixty-Seven

The old truck seemed to find every rut and pothole on the dirt track, despite Toni's careful avoidance. She blamed it on her distraction. A quick look at Allen sitting sullenly in the passenger seat didn't improve her concentration. That long silence in the kitchen had continued from Kate and especially from Allen. Sam had avoided the awkwardness and went out to unsaddle the one horse that Isaiah had left him, seeming to be more comfortable among those beasts than he was with people. Toni could relate.

Now she sought some answers from a *curandera*, a Mexican folk healer, who might be able to help Allen. It was clear to Toni that the boy was not bouncing back as quickly from his psychic experience as he had once been able to. She herself was still a bit frayed but felt that ranch routine and her beloved horses would be her best medicine. For Allen, she felt at a loss to help him, and this morning's conversation had added more tension and a guilt he shouldn't have to bear.

As Toni pulled the truck onto the asphalt of the county road, she wrestled now with revealing a truth that was not hers to share. Kate was in no emotional place to tell the boy, and it was something no mother should ever have to explain. But he had to know what the stone was that Kate had spoken of. Turning onto a dirt side road on the left, Toni downshifted as she approached the Texas crossing below the hill above where Chuck Tiananmen's trading post and his wife's *Yerberia* had been built. Toni eased on the brakes and pulled to the side of the road, well short of the now dry wash.

Allen stirred as if to question why they were stopping.

Letting the old truck idle, Toni put it in park and waited.

"Toni?" Allen inquired softly.

His step-mom turned in her seat toward him. "There's something I need to tell you."

"About what?"

She inhaled deeply and began. "This isn't my story to tell. It's your mother's." Draping an arm over the steering wheel, almost as an act to anchor herself, Toni continued. "She told me about it. In bits at first. Then over the years in more detail after we were together. I think it may have been a factor in why she was comfortable with me being one of the other genders."

"You mean she was gay and didn't know it? I met a couple of people in college like that, guys and girls."

"That may have been a factor." Toni looked down, struggling to find a few words that would explain without leaving more wounds to suffer or ignite new anger. "Allen," she said, focusing on his eyes, "the night you were conceived was not what you might have thought." She looked away. "As if children ever think of their parents together that way."

"What are you saying?"

"It was part of a—" Her throat closed. She couldn't tell him all of it, but he had to know what his mother had meant this morning. "It was a ceremony. On a stone."

"What?"

"Whatever you think of your father," she rushed to explain, "he did save her life that night. He changed the rite from sacrifice to fertility."

Allen leaned back, staring at the ceiling. "On a sacrificial stone." Then he jerked his head toward Toni.

"Not the one near Dulce that you saw. It was another, in Arizona. Your mother is a contact clairvoyant," Toni continued. "She was able to detect whispers from objects she held. As an archaeology student, she sometimes used that ability to get feelings about a group of people. It wasn't fully developed." The woman took a deep breath. "Her entire body was in full contact with the sacrificial stone. It awakened her abilities,

246

which grew stronger, but she had little training." Again Toni paused. "Your abilities come from both your mother and father, but the stone may have amplified yours. Luckily, you had Grandmother's training."

Allen nodded as if that revelation made sense to him. Quietly, he asked, "Are you sure he is my father? The People could've. . . ."

"Yes, he is. That's certain." Toni relaxed a little. The worst was told as far as she could reveal to him. "I think he wanted to create a super child, a *wunderkind*, who possessed a combination of his abilities and your mother's that were just emerging and growing more powerful. You were more than he ever expected."

"And I walked away from what he offered, from what he had created." He paused. "Now, there's Logan."

"Yes, Logan." Toni turned away.

"Who's an ordinary boy."

After a few moments of silence, Allen asked, "What are we doing here? Where are we going?"

"I—," Toni tried to answer but suddenly felt that her intention was so much sand. She raised both hands in a helpless gesture. "I was going to take you to a *curandera*, a good woman I know, for a healing. I was worried about how that experience up in Dulce affected you." She sighed. "Maybe I was seeking a healing for myself, as well." Then she admitted. "I've failed you, son. I'm out of my depth." There was a frightening catch in her throat and a quiver in her voice that threatened to betray the fear she felt.

Allen shifted in his seat. "Toni . . . Dad."

The word startled her, forcing her to look at him again.

"You've been a dad to me for years. Not a step-mom. Not my mom's partner. But Dad. You and Great-Gran, and Mom, too, always did what was best for me without ever thinking about yourselves. You've shown me more about how to be an honorable man than my father did, trying to make me into the next shaman, who was supposed to lead the People. We are strong. You and I. We may be fried a little by all that's been going on, but we're strong." He reached over and grasped Toni's wrist for a few seconds, opening fully to her, allowing her to see his fragility but also his strength and the truth of his words. Releasing her, he added, "It's Logan who needs our help. But I don't know how."

Not having any idea how to do that either, Toni just nodded, backed up the truck, and swung into a three-point turn. She shifted and steered the truck home, realizing that she needed her grandmother now more than she ever had.

Chapter Sixty-Eight

Buzzing from the rich Ethiopian coffee and the disturbing information Dr. Blakely had revealed, Ben Castiano forced himself to keep checking his speedometer to make sure he didn't creep over the limit on I-25. It was easy to speed when he was thinking. He'd get on a train of thought and suddenly be cognizant of his surroundings and then look down to see he was going 90. He was grateful his instincts seemed to click in when he was in those zoned-out moments.

Today, as he headed back to his home office, he sifted through the new information. It all made sense but still didn't exactly rule out the old man that they'd found at the scene of the crime. Once, when Ben was in Chicago, he went out for a beer with some local homicide detectives. He'd learned that a lot of what they did was what scientists did. That appealed to him. The detectives said that they'd build a case based on a theory of the crime. It often began with circumstantial evidence, like finding the old man beside the body. When evidence didn't fit, the detectives would rethink their original theory and draw up a new one. They'd keep doing that until all the evidence fit, especially when working a cold case. As forensic science improved, answers often came faster but not necessarily easier.

In Ben's current case, the old man could have been working with a group. In his state of inebriation when he was found, that theory didn't seem plausible. He'd have had to find the victim and lead him to the boulder. But would the victim have gone with the old man? In another scenario, he could have given the victim's name to accomplices, and it was just a bad coincidence that the old man found the victim there. Then, again the old man could have had no clue about any group or ritual.

Ben's mind began to churn through why a group would still participate in human sacrifice. What gods would the members be trying to please? Keeping the sun in the sky or aligning with the god of war didn't seem plausible in modern times. Whose power would they be wanting to elevate that would involve someone seeing the ceremony and giving the individual the glory then and there? Or was it the power derived from the ritual killing and the blood that was more important?

The only people with power that Ben knew were politicians. And he doubted any one of them would resort to such a dramatic and messy means to gain office. He figured one or two might enlist *Santa Muerte* to mete out vengeance, but that always came at a cost. Most would just seek the support of Our Lady of Guadalupe and the protection of St. Michael — and a good PR man.

Still, what do you do with a man's heart and the rest of the blood?

Suddenly, he had a thought that turned his stomach. Punching his phone on, he told it to dial Dr. Morales. When she answered and he identified himself, he said, "I've got a strange question?"

"About your case?"

"Yes."

"Nothing will ever surprise me anymore after this," she said. "Dr. Ward called about using my bone man. What else has happened?"

"Well, this is just a theoretical question, a what if."

"Shoot."

"What would happen if someone ate that heart or drank that HIV-positive blood that's missing?"

"Hmm," she remarked, not seeming to be fazed by the question. "I wondered about that, myself. I called around,

HANDFUL of DIRT

including the blood bank at UNM, someone in hematology, and a friend of mine in Vice. Don't ask," she added quickly. "Despite old vampire movies and goth young people who think drinking blood is a neat idea, the human stomach just can't handle it. A little bit, like when you cut your finger and stick it in your mouth — You can tolerate that. But anything over a tablespoon would make you throw up. And Dr. Ward didn't see any evidence of vomit at the scene. Did you?"

"No, except for the young sheriff's deputy, who I had to keep clear off the crime scene."

"Then there might have been some blood drinking there — a sip. But—"

"But?"

"If someone did drink HIV-positive blood, they could become infected. Oh, and speaking of the stomach, I did some more research on those strange stomach contents."

Ben heard papers rustling on the other end of the phone line as he had another thought. "What if someone cooked the heart like we do a beef heart?"

"You ever eat a beef heart?"

"Actually, I did once. And a tongue. It was very tasty."

"Stay away from the brain. Mad Cow isn't totally eradicated." More shuffling was heard. "Here it is. I scribbled it on a piece of paper. That fermented milky substance could be *pulque* or *iztac octli*. It was made from the agave plant."

"Like tequila."

"Yes, but from a different variety. It was a sacred drink used by Mesoamerican people. The priests drank it and gave it to their sacrifices."

"That makes sense, then. Our victim would have had to be drunk or sedated to endure what he did without more trauma found on the body."

"I got this from a call with an archaeologist at UNM. He also said that victims were often painted."

"What color?" Ben asked, knowing the answer.

251

"Mayan blue with almost the same composition as what we found."

Putting all this together, Ben said, "Dr. Blakely showed me pictures where the Maya and Aztec both sacrificed their enemies by having priests cut their hearts out. The Maya collected blood."

"So, we have a victim painted in Mayan blue with his heart removed and not much blood at the scene, right?"

"Yup."

"And there are more bodies and blood on the ground up there. Sounds like ritual to me. And more than one person."

"Even if the victim and the accused were enemies, this seems bigger and more organized," Ben observed.

"Sounds like that to me, too. Are you going to talk to the lawyer? We don't have to. It's up to the DA to prove a case."

"But we'd be called to testify, and I don't know how they could muzzle Dr. Ward, do you?" Ben asked.

Dr. Morales laughed. "Just try. He's like a hound dog on scent. I'm sure he sees several articles in prominent and varied journals in his future."

"You should write it up before he does," Ben suggested.

"Don't tempt me. But we can't do anything until this goes to trial or it gets tossed."

Still thinking of implications, Ben said, "Thanks for the help. I have a stop to make before I get back to my office."

"Be thankful you haven't had another call or two up in your area."

"Shh," he said. "You'll jinx it. It's like a beat cop when someone says it's a quiet night. Then all hell breaks loose."

Chapter Sixty-Nine

The wild smell of horsehide, hay, and manure soothed Toni as she walked among the horses in the paddock. The newcomers kept to the trees on the far side. It was rare for them to be in the shade and near that much vegetation, though they could see it every day from their working corral at the horse camp. Sunny and her other mates crowded around Toni. A couple snuffled her hat or her shirt. Two stood politely near her, while Sunny, the oldest, and another mare nudged the others aside to butt Toni's chest. Opening her arms wide, Toni encircled each horse's head in an arm, pulling them to her cheeks.

The bonds had been strongly forged over the past four years after she and Kate had moved back, at Dutch's request, to help with the ranch. Toni missed Dutch, too. Never one for more than a word or a couple of sentences, Dutch always seemed to offer a practical turn to any crisis. Thankfully, there had been few since they had returned.

Behind her, she heard Sam's gentle commands as he worked the green horse through the polishing phases of understanding a rider's instructions. The mare was skittish, more so than the others, making Toni wonder if the young mustang had experienced an animal attack before being rounded up, or the incident with the black jaguar had affected her more deeply than the others.

The thought of the big cat with its connection to Mesoamerican legends brought Toni back to her current worry. Was there anything she could do for Logan? Should she even try? Logan was no kin of hers nor of Kate's, but Allen was determined to find a way to help his half-brother. Toni wondered what Grandmother would advise. She thought back to her childhood days with the woman, who seemed ancient even then, and her lessons with Allen. She always taught in stories, but different from the parables that Jesus used, where a moral was either given or it was evident through the narrative. Grandmother's stories were a means to meditate to find one's own answers. Toni searched through all of the old tales that she could remember. Nothing seemed to apply. Even her clan's Turtle tales were about how clever the green water turtle was, especially in races around her pond with Bear and Beaver. To Toni, it seemed the turtle had cheated — cleverly, yes — but the turtle never abided by the rules that were agreed upon. Turtle seemed more like trickster Coyote among the Plains native nations. And what this all had to do with the impressions Toni and Allen had picked up and what Kate had experienced or the criminal case Allen had been involved with was beyond comprehension.

Hearing a quiet laugh behind her, Toni craned her head away from the horses to look at what Sam was doing in the corral. He was grinning as he bent down from the saddle to put his own cheek against the horse's neck and pat the other side. "Let's do it again, my beauty," he said.

Toni noticed that the reins had been looped around the saddle horn, freeing Sam's hands. He placed them on either side of his hips in the saddle and clicked his tongue. The horse moved forward and then started making wide turns first to the right and then to the left and once totally doing a 360. Toni watched closely and found that the horse was following commands that came from Sam's knees or his stirruped boots. These were subtle changes that the horse noticed and moved with, exactly where Sam wanted her to go. Toni marveled at the precision, especially in a horse that had appeared so skittish.

Separating herself from her mares, Toni walked closer to the gate of the corral. Her movement caught Sam's attention, and he urged the horse to the corral fencing where Toni stood.

"That was impressive," Toni said.

"I think she would make a good cutting horse," Sam said. "She's not comfortable around people so much."

"Then she wouldn't make a good riding horse. Though a single rider, who took her on trails daily, might be all right."

"That's hard to guarantee," Sam said. "But if she's trained as a cutting horse, she could work for her living. I'll just need to work her with some cattle."

"It was clever of you to find something more suited to her personality."

"Not so much," Sam said. "I just thought outside of the box."

Toni nodded, opening the gate and stepping inside the corral. "Good work," she said. "I'll go see how lunch is coming." She continued through the gate near the ranch house. Sam's words lingered in her mind. Maybe that was what Turtle did. It wasn't a matter of following the rules, thereby thinking linearly, but thinking a different way. For the first time since her childhood, Toni realized that that was the lesson in Turtle's stories, not cleverness, not cheating. But thinking differently.

Chapter Seventy

Logan stared up at the thick, bark-clad pole that had been sunk deep into the ground. It was bigger than the prayer pole that had just been planted where he had selected his prayer spot. Though tall as a two-story building, this pole cast no shadow yet since the Solstice sun was high overhead. Nailed a foot from the top, long ropes hung limply, waiting.

Logan would face it like his brother, Allen, had, but only after his personal ordeal in the desert was over. It had been done to Allen first. Logan wondered how his brother had endured the ritual piercing and then gone on to fast alone.

Logan was weary already, having walked several miles that morning. He was hungry and thirsty, but the hunger was soon becoming just a familiar gnawing, no longer an audible growl. His supply of water waited for him in the overhang, covered by his blanket and leggings. There would be one more smudging, a puff of smoke from a sacred pipe, and much singing and dancing again. He would dance all the way to his spot by the prayer pole, where he would pray for three days.

Logan was happy about one thing today. He looked down at the white doeskin sheath that was now tied to his breechclout on his right side. It held a shiny new knife with a heavy cedar handle. It was a sacred knife, but also a practical one that he was earning in this manhood rite. He was eager to handle it and get used to its feel. His mother had embroidered the snake on the sheath, and his father had selected the knife. It would be a good knife to take fishing when he went with Allen or to use on a craft project or to fix something at home. He smiled, unaware that the drumming had started and then stopped.

A gasp among those gathered around him drew his attention away from the pole and his thoughts. He turned to see the crowd behind him back away, moving closer to the pole, exposing a rocky outcrop dotted with scrub to his view. Standing on a flat space was a black-feathered figure and an equally black big cat. It looked like a panther to Logan. The cat's yellow eyes shone as it snarled at the people below, revealing very large, sharp teeth.

As Logan studied the first figure, he saw that it was a man with a large, black feathered headdress and cape. The man spread the feathered cloak aside as he stretched forth both arms and both legs in an X shape with only a red-trimmed white breechclout showing between. Black snake tattoos crawled up his powerful legs, and owls, the harbingers of death, peered from his thighs. But it was the large spotted jaguar that mirrored the black one at his side that made the figure all the more menacing. In one of his hands was a gold bejeweled cup.

The figure chanted in a strange tongue, singing words Logan had never heard. Then in English, the deep, powerful voice cried out: "I am the strength of the world. I am the strength of life. I am the one who comes forth. I am jaguar. I am snake. I am bear. I am coyote. I am all that is. I am Huitzilopochtli's chosen. I am night and I am sun. I cannot be stopped. I am your rightful leader."

The figure then brought the cup to his mouth and drank deeply from it, choking as its dark red contents spilled down the sides of his chin and over his chest. Still he drank. Still he choked. Triumphantly, he held the cup aloft for several seconds. His shoulders heaved as he coughed once, then twice. He swirled the black cape around him like an old Dracula actor and stumbled along the rock outcropping, with the big cat following.

The people around Logan had been stunned to silence as he was. Now, they began to murmur in wonder and then in outrage as someone thought they recognized the man. They did not watch the figure leave as Logan did. He saw the man stop by a scraggly bush, clutch its thin branches, and bend behind it. The arching of the man's back, up and down, was a sign Logan knew. He'd done the same thing last summer after Manuel and Alexander had twisted him too many times in an old tire swing. They had laughed at him. Logan didn't feel like laughing at the man behind the scrub bush. He was nothing to be afraid of, but the big cat now lapping up what the man had just spewed on the ground was.

Chapter Seventy-One

Day 9: Monday, early afternoon, north of Abiquiu, NM

Ben winced as he sat outside the church at the monastery of Christ in the Desert. The Benedictine order kept the monastic rule and sang their prayers at specific hours. When he had heard them several years ago before he had met his wife, he had felt as if he'd stepped into medieval times. The church vibrated with beautiful tones and the strength of contra-tenors hitting the highest notes. He had almost been tempted to take the cowl back then when he had come, struggling with a vocation decision, knowing that whatever he decided would displease someone. He'd been back periodically when he needed a bit of extra peace. Today, during None, two o'clock, the order had apparently welcomed a new batch of novices, and they were exceptionally tone deaf.

Looking out onto the farmland where the monks eked out enough to feed the order, Ben marveled at the hard but simple life that these men lived. They grew their own food and raised their own livestock. Work and Prayer. It was a good life. Though it tempted him in stressful times, Ben would never choose it today. His life was full of valuable work that often felt as holy as the monks' when he could bring closure for a family. Ben also had the love of a good woman and the delighted chaos of children, who blessed his life. He had made the right decision.

As the brothers and a few retreat guests filed out of the open church doors, Ben was roused from his peaceful meditations. He noticed the abbot slip outside and squint at the bright sunlight, finally resting his gaze on Ben. A smile broke through the monk's grizzly beard and he stepped toward Ben with his hand outstretched.

"Good to see you, my friend," the abbot said, taking Ben's hand into both of his. "Have you come with another life question?"

"Not exactly, Father Abbot."

"I'm always Brother to you, Ben. That's where we began and will remain." Removing his hand, he said gently. "Walk with me." They followed the walkways around the monastery buildings, past the gift shop, to find a wooden bench along a side wall that created shade. The temperature felt at least ten degrees cooler there. As they sat, both facing the meager attempt at a floral border in front of them, the abbot said, "In your own time."

Ben smiled. "Nothing has changed."

"Should it?"

"No, I suppose that's why I keep coming back here."

"Are you happy?"

"Yes." Ben marveled at the flowering plants that had been coaxed to bloom here in the desert. "Life is good."

"Then it's a work question?"

Ben nodded. "I'm not sure why I need to even ask for advice. I probably already know the answer."

"But you need to talk it through."

"Yes."

Looking down at his hands where he had entwined his fingers, Ben began. "I have a case that, I think, has ritual sacrifice at its core. I don't normally share information with anyone except the ME's office and the crime lab people, but I just found more information from an anthropologist at UNM and—" He stopped, unsure how to explain what he'd witnessed on Saturday at the Sunset Motel in Espanola.

"And?" the abbot prompted.

"I saw two people who had been deeply affected by the crime scene."

"What they had seen there?"

"Yes. Well, no. What they had felt there. They both seem to be—"

"To be what?"

"Sensitive."

"Sensitive," the abbot repeated.

"Sensitive, like my *tia,* who knew who had died."

"Ah."

"Ah?" Ben turned to the abbot. "It was real."

"I'm not saying it wasn't," Father Abbot said. "All of the old testament prophets had visitations and messages and feelings. We can't discount the paranormal. Our belief is based on things we can't explain, but we trust." He paused. "So, what's your dilemma?"

"The new information. I wonder if I should share it with the accused man's lawyer or if it'll just stir the pot of speculation."

The abbot was silent for some minutes while Ben sifted through what he had just revealed.

"There are three things to consider," Father Abbot said. "First, is the information true or speculation? Second, can you verify the information in some way? And three, if the information is verifiable, do you feel in your conscience that the lawyer needs to know this information? In short, is it true? Is it necessary? Is it kind?"

Ben grunted out a little laugh. "That's the rubric for resisting the urge to gossip."

Father Abbot smiled. "Yes. But it applies here. What does your Hippocratic Oath say?"

"First, do no harm." Ben nodded. "And that covers silence as well."

"Let me ask you. Would you want to know this information if you were the lawyer?"

Ben nodded. "Yes. I would."

"I would suggest trying to verify the information and then pass on what you know. Full knowledge is often better than partial knowledge. It's up to the lawyer whether to use the information or not."

"Thank you, Brother. I'll make a few calls when I get back into cell range."

The abbot stood. "Walk for a bit before you go. Seek the peace here." He extended his hand again. "And come more often, Ben."

Chapter Seventy-Two

Day 9 Monday, early evening, near Payson, AZ

The night wasn't as restful as Allen would have liked. He gave up, made some coffee, and carried the mug far down the big front porch, well away from the horses. They'd never had more than ten horses in the paddock since he could remember, often just the six they had before Isaiah had brought those from the horse camp. He leaned on the far railing, gazing into the darkness in the direction Toni had speculated that Logan and his parents had traveled and Allen himself had gone eleven years before. There was just the sliver of a waning moon in the sky, not providing much light at all for Logan's first night of his vision quest. Allen hoped that the boy had been spared the rigors of what he had endured. He had been bigger, sturdier, and people often forgot he was as young as he was. His step-brother, on the other hand, was a creative, sensitive soul in a child's body. That backcountry was isolated. If anything happened to the boy, Allen wondered how they could get emergency help in there, much less call for it, unless his father had thought of having a battery-operated ham radio with them.

Hearing a slight creak on the floorboards behind him and feeling another presence, Allen sensed his mother before she came closer and spoke to him.

"It's good to have you home," she said, leaning against the railing beside him but not touching him.

"It feels different," he admitted, taking a little sip of his coffee. "It felt empty last night, and now there's just too much energy everywhere."

"Sam does bring different energy."

"He has quiet energy," Allen said, "but there are things connected to him. Still."

"Still?" Kate moved her body away from the railing to look at him.

"He fights personal demons. There's truth in the saying 'having a monkey on your back.'"

"What do you mean?"

"Addiction attracts . . . things."

"He never said he had problems with alcohol or drugs."

Allen turned his head toward her. "Would you?"

Kate gave her head a slight tilt in concession.

"He keeps himself pulled in tight. Like I do around most people. It was easy to recognize."

"But you don't have an addiction."

"No," Allen said, "but, like him, I have to constantly be aware of myself so I don't pick up or broadcast something."

Facing the darkness again, Kate said, "I never knew it was that bad. I only pick up a major sending, though I can feel what you're feeling."

"That's just being a mom," Allen said, smiling.

"I still broadcast," Kate admitted. "Or Toni says I do. Most people can't pick it up. We're both partially open to each other, more so since we moved back here and there aren't people around."

Taking another drink from his mug, Allen considered how to ask his next question. "Logan isn't like us, is he?"

Kate took in a long breath and released it. "No, I don't think so. He's a lot like Manuel and Alexander, except that they're wild little boys raised in the country."

"He's never really learned to play. I doubt he's ever yelled like boisterous kids do."

"I've never heard him. He'd watch Manuel and Alexander play tag, but he'd never join them."

"Do you think Logan could pick up a sending or send one out like I did last Friday?"

"I don't think that was you," Kate said. "I think that message was hijacked on your emotion, but it didn't come from you. It was odd."

"Toni said she picked up an old Seneca legend. But I don't know if I sent it to her. I didn't consciously send to anyone — not like I did to you when I was in danger at my testing years ago. But would Logan be able to pick up something if I tried to reach him?"

"I don't know, Allen. It may take intense emotion to send or pick up. But you could try."

"Try what?" Toni said behind them, startling both of them.

Kate turned and swatted her wife on the chest. "Stop sneaking up on people."

Allen was embarrassed he hadn't sensed Toni's approach. "You're getting lighter on your feet," he said.

"Or you're slipping, old man," his step-mom teased. "But you may be on to something. We could try to contact Logan, something light and friendly, so as not to scare the boy."

"Let's try," Allen said eagerly.

"We can't do it here," Toni said. "Let's go to the paddock. We can use all that horse energy."

Puzzled, Allen followed Kate and Toni down to the drive, through the corral, and into the paddock. The horses were clumped in bunches. The new horses were still near the far trees and the ranch horses were closer to the corral gate, where they had learned over many years that sweet feed came from. The three humans spread themselves along the corral fence but within touching distance, with Kate between Toni and Allen. The ranch horses were curious, but let the humans alone tonight.

Toni quietly guided them. "Just relax against the fence and take in some deep breaths. . . . It's a beautiful night. The horses are happy. They're even happy to see us." After a few minutes, Toni took Kate's hand, and her wife automatically reached for Allen's without direction. "Our boots are rooted in the ground here. We're safe. We're content together."

Allen suddenly felt his mother's love rush into him and from her, he even felt Toni's. He automatically sent that love circulating back to them.

"Think now of Logan when you saw him the happiest," Toni instructed. "Fishing. Or eating. Or petting the horses. We each have a happy memory. Think of that happiness and then send him love, our deep caring as family."

Allen remembered the first time Logan had caught a fish. It was a tiny sunfish, just barely legal size and wouldn't make more than a bite or two when cooked, but the boy had been so happy he had been able to do something on his own. He had grinned up at Allen, exhibited the first boyish pride Allen had ever seen him possess.

After a few minutes, Toni calmly said, "Tell Logan goodnight. Then ground."

They all dropped hands and bent down to touch the grassy paddock, sending any excess energy into the earth.

Suddenly, Allen felt hungry, as if picking up Logan's emotion or just the habit of eating as part of further grounding.

Kate said, "Pie's gone. I can scare up some toast and apricot jam."

As Kate rushed ahead, Allen lingered with Toni as she secured all of the gates. "Do you think it worked?" Allen asked.

"Even if he didn't pick up anything," Toni said, "there's no harm in sending the child some love." In a rare moment, she put her arm around Allen's shoulders and guided him inside.

He felt her open sending of love to him. Smiling, Allen slipped his arm around her, finally feeling at home and beginning to ground.

Chapter Seventy-Three

Night did not creep up on Logan where he lay huddled, wrapped in his blanket on the dirt floor of the overhang. Darkness had come crashing as if someone had pulled down a giant window shade across the sky. The temperature had dropped when the sun had set, and Logan felt the cold creep into his body on the ground. Though the sky was filled with stars, the moon had not yet risen, and it was not going to be full, just a sliver.

He was very tired and hungry. The water had helped by keeping something in his stomach. From the book he had read about desert survival, he knew that he shouldn't drink too much at a time. Logan had counted the gallon jugs and figured how much he could use per day. It was more than he thought he could drink, until he started in on the first jug about midafternoon when he'd returned to his vision quest site for the final blessing.

After everyone left, Logan had sat for a while in front of the prayer tree and prayed over the ribbons that he had been given. These he also counted and divided into the number of days he would be there. It would give him something to do each day besides sit.

He had also found four stones to mark the directions around the prayer tree. His overhang luckily faced the East where the sun would rise. It would wake him and warm him in the morning. He had placed his stones and asked for the blessings of the stone people and the spirits of those directions.

As the sun set behind the hill where the overhang protruded, Logan had taken refuge in its protection and hoped he had no animal visitors in the night. A skittering noise told him that there were critters out there. Logan hoped that was Brother Lizard and his companions. He could use their company. But he didn't want to deal with a snake or any other bigger critter like that black jaguar the man had at the ceremony. Suddenly, Logan felt very alone and very afraid. Despite how tired he was, his eyes were wide open, scanning the dark shadows outside, ever searching for danger.

Tears filled his eyes and slid down his cheeks. He missed his own bed. He missed the protection of his own room. He missed food, especially Allen's mom's pies. He began to think of all of the kinds she made. Then he thought of the horses on the ranch, how they smelled, the feel of their velvet noses, the quiet noises they made as they chewed on hay and alfalfa. Logan smiled, remembering the fun he had with his brother, Allen, especially fishing in a creek and catching his very first sunfish. Allen's mom had breaded it in a mix of cornmeal and flour and egg and then served it proudly to him with lemon slices and her olive tartar sauce. It wasn't much to eat, but it was well-earned food.

Feeling his body begin to warm under the blanket, Logan smiled. Here, in this place, he was in charge. No one told him what to do. No one watched him. No one judged whether he was doing something right or wrong, except maybe the spirits of the land here. Logan respected them and asked for their help tonight and for the next few days. He figured he was sort of like a modern-day Robinson Crusoe in that adventure book his class had read last year. He had no Friday to help him, but Logan could make this place his own. He thought about gathering more stones to make sort of a wall in front of the overhang. It would make him feel protected like the door of his own room. He thought about gathering some scrub branches to make a warmer bed.

As his mind bounced from idea to idea, creating, building, his eyes closed and he slept.

Chapter Seventy-Four

"How long are you gonna keep my deputies up there?" Sheriff Mendoza demanded from the phone, wishing he could have a smoke indoors. Chewing on a fat stogie right now would soothe him, even if he couldn't light it up. He started calculating overtime for the two men on alternating shifts and weighing whether mileage was cheaper than lodging and meals for them.

"You got a crime wave down there?" Dr. Ward asked, chuckling.

"We do have a whole county to police."

"Well, we got bodies up here, and we need to keep the site secure."

"Bodies?" He almost choked. "Bodies. Plural. How many?"

"The dogs found six so far."

"What do you mean so far?"

"The dog handler only went down a few thousand yards on the non-rez side of the creek up there. But not far."

"You can't touch rez land. You know that," Mendoza warned.

"We might need to, if we find more farther away. There could be more on the other side."

"Oh, geez." He wondered what kind of bedevilment he had opened up when he arrested that old man. "You think he's a serial killer? That old man been killing for decades?"

"I doubt one man did all of these from the tentative ages of the burials. At least, that's what the forensic anthropologist is guessing."

"I thought scientists didn't guess."

"Scientists guess all the time, Sheriff. That's what hypotheses are," Dr. Ward replied. "I sent you and the DA all the results of what we found up there so far and from trace evidence on the first victim. Whatever was done to him wasn't done by one man, and there seems to be a ritual element to it."

"So, we got a Satanic cult up there?"

Dr. Ward hesitated. "Could be," he said finally. "Or something older. I don't know this land or the people here."

"You think it's some native thing?"

"No locals. Something else."

"How far back does this graveyard go?"

"It'll take time for tests to prove conclusively."

Mendoza saw that Dr. Ward was withholding. "Give. How old?"

"Maybe a couple hundred years, if not more. And there seems to be a time pattern, but only tests will prove that."

"What do you mean, time pattern?"

Again, Dr. Ward paused. "It seems to be happening periodically, maybe cyclically, every few years."

Mendoza saw his watertight case against Harley Manwell just disintegrate into so much sand. He needed to call the DA. But first he needed to trim his own costs. He probably was already paying to house an innocent man. "Can't you get some private security or some of your people to stay at the site? Or foist it off on the FBI or something?"

"It's not my job to figure out jurisdiction. Call your boss or the State Police."

"I'm the boss," Mendoza muttered. "I'm an elected official. You'll get security. But I need my deputies back here." Slamming the phone onto its cradle, Sheriff Mendoza realized that the best thing for him was to get rid of this case as quickly as he could. Hand it off to somebody else with the budget to thoroughly investigate it. Reaching into a drawer, he pulled out a directory of area law enforcement agencies and found the number of the local FBI office. He was determined to toss this hot potato into somebody else's lap. Then he'd call the DA. Retiring from public office was looking better and better.

Chapter Seventy-Five

The day was growing warmer, as expected. After tying his second day of prayer flags, Logan started working on his wall. He had scoured the area around his vision quest site, carrying football-sized stones to the overhang. He wasn't sure it would be very sturdy without something to stick them together with, but he figured gravity might work in his favor. Logan placed larger stones snug together on the bottom layer wedged against the left-hand edge of the overhang. It angled out enough so that he could sit against the back wall and stretch his feet out if he wanted. Layer by layer, the wall grew until it was about three feet tall, enough to keep the early morning sun out of his eyes and allow him to sleep a little longer if he chose to do so. This morning's sun had disturbed him, but its warmth was welcome. Logan figured that the stone wall might absorb the day's heat and keep him warmer at night.

Stopping to rest and drink some water, the boy began to plan for his comfort in the overhang. He'd already emptied one water jug. He planned to wrap it in his vest at night and use it for a pillow. It would be better than sleeping on his arm. His next quest was to use his new knife to cut some small branches from the scrub scattered around. There wasn't much, but it would occupy his time. He'd then lay that down on the floor of the overhang for a softer and warmer bed.

As he sat planning, he saw movement near his wall. Patiently, he waited until he saw the alert brown head of a lizard peek around the stones he had placed. It twisted its head to one side and then the other as if looking for something. It waited as Logan did, watching. Then, suddenly, it skittered away. Logan was happy Brother Lizard had come to see him. It made him feel welcome in this place.

As the boy got to his feet, he realized that he was very tired and beginning to feel weaker. He decided to only cut a couple of branches. It would be enough for today. Tomorrow he would cut more for his bed.

Logan surveyed the landscape and spotted a small bush not far from his encampment. He tramped over to it. On inspection, he found it was covered in thorns. He couldn't sleep on that, but thought that a couple of its branches might make a good protective covering for the small opening that the wall had created. He tried to grab a branch so that he could use his knife, but he kept sticking himself with the thorns. Finally, he folded the front of his breechclout into a double layer and used it to hold the branch while he cut. Even the thin branch and a sharp knife took longer than he expected. Logan persevered, cutting four of the branches. With the cut ends wrapped in his breechclout, he dragged them back and angled them over the wall and the opening.

Totally fatigued now, Logan decided to postpone more work until tomorrow. He drank some more water and watched the afternoon sky. He saw what looked like a hawk far in the distance. That was a good sign. Hawk brought messages. News. Maybe the news would be that his days would pass quickly here.

The faint cry of an animal in the distance disturbed Logan's thoughts. He searched the sky, looking for buzzards, carrion-eaters, to see where an animal had been injured or killed. The late afternoon sky was cloudless and as blue as those he'd seen almost every day in Arizona. He looked at where his knife was, cleaned and safely secured in its sheath. He really didn't know how to use it for anything except making things. Suddenly, he wanted the security of the overhang. Putting his hands on each side of him in order to climb to his feet, he felt rocks bruise his hands. He had looked all day for larger stones for his wall. Beside him on the ground, though, were smaller stones, hand-sized and tinier. He remembered one day at Allen's ranch, watching Manuel and Alexander having a play battle where they'd thrown stones at each other's legs. They thought it was great fun until Manuel had reached down to pick up more ammunition and got hit in the forehead with a rock. Their father had quickly put an end to their shenanigans.

Logan selected a few of the bigger stones, placing them in his turned-up breechclout. He shuffled back to his overhang and dumped out the stones in the entrance gap. They would be at hand if there was need. But he hoped he wouldn't have to resort to warfare of any kind out here.

Chapter Seventy-Six

"A week!" Sandy complained to Caroline after ending a call to the hospital. "I can't believe it took them a week to do an HIV test. Don't they have those thirty-minute ones? They said they were backed up. And then they sent the results to the Sheriff's office, along with the law enforcement test results." She stuffed a large yellow notepad into her briefcase. "Guess we need to get over there and do a wellness check on our client, anyway."

Gathering up handbags and briefcases, the lawyers left their motel room. When on their way to the Sheriff's office, Sandy's phone rang. Punching it on, she said, "Sandy Lopez."

"Hi, Sandy. This is Ben Castiano. Have you heard from our young friend?"

"Hi, Ben. Actually, I haven't checked yet. I figured he needed time with his family. We were planning on calling him later."

"Good idea. I'm calling to share some . . . speculation I've gathered from my research."

"Will it help my client?"

"Possibly. I don't know. I got a call from Dr. Ward from the crime lab. He's sharing a lot more than I've ever seen him. But then again, we've never had a case like this one before."

"What did he have to say?"

"He found six shallow graves up there, and a forensic anthropologist has looked at them. In fact, she's arranging to have the remains, bones mostly, brought back to OMI. She's made tentative estimates of length of time in the ground. Some are archaeological."

"Archaeological? Ancient remains?"

"There is archaeology and there is archaeology. This would run into historical archaeology, over a hundred years. The criterion is 'not in living memory.'"

"How many did you say?"

"The dogs scented six. But Dr. Ward thinks there may be many more. He said the forensic anthropologist said they were all males of various ages and speculates that the ages of the burials are cyclical, every twenty or thirty years or so. But the freshest seems to be about forty years ago."

"That's odd. It can't be a serial murderer, then."

"No, but I think it's something equally sinister."

"Like what?"

There was a long silence before Ben spoke again. "I think it may be a ritual."

"Like in Satanic?"

"I wondered about that myself and researched it. It could be evil but not particularly related to Satanism."

"Then what?" Sandy pressed.

"I went to see an anthropologist at UNM, who was a specialist in folklore, myth, and ritual. Remember that the victim was missing his heart and much of his blood. The body could have been moved, but I don't think it was. The blood may have been collected, and the heart removed for a ritual purpose."

"That's done in a ritual?"

"Yes," Ben said. "The professor showed me drawings about Mesoamerican priests doing that to their enemies. The Maya valued blood more than the heart."

"So, there's an active Mesoamerican cult up there?"

"I have no clue," Ben admitted. "It's clear from examination of the crime scene and the autopsy and trace evidence that your client couldn't have done that alone. It always required at least three men, sometimes five, even when the victim had been drugged. The ME found a fermented drink called *pulque* in our victim's stomach contents. That's classic, from what I've been told."

Sandy let out a breath. "My client is very Christian, very moral. I doubt he would participate in something like that, no matter how much he hated the man. He'd be more likely to strangle him, act out of passion, than do something as coldblooded as that."

"That's what I've been thinking. Ritual isn't for revenge. It's for a purpose, usually to gain favor of some god or other or to have power. I think we may be dealing more with power here."

"Well, this certainly colors our case. How will the Sheriff ever find who's responsible?"

"He'd be a better man than me if he could," Ben admitted. "But I think this may become one of those open, cold cases like they had in Albuquerque a few years ago."

"We're heading to the Sheriff's office right now. They sent our client's blood results there. Thanks for keeping us in the loop."

"Glad to help. I'll keep you posted if I hear anything else."

Ending the call, Sandy glanced over at Caroline, who looked totally bewildered. "Our duty is to our client," she said. "No matter how curious this case has turned, as soon as our client is in the clear, we're heading home. And when we get back to the hotel, call Allen."

Chapter Seventy-Seven

Day 10: Tuesday, early evening, near Payson, AZ

"Allen?" Caroline's voice over the phone sounded tentative.

She had been swinging from ignoring him to chiding him to mothering him, lately. Allen wasn't sure which he preferred. He supposed having her make some kind of contact was better than silence.

"Caroline, how are you?" Allen said, stepping outside his room, walking down the hall, and onto the open back porch. He needed the space to breathe.

"More importantly, how are you?"

"Oh, you know me. I bounce back."

"You had Sandy pretty worried about you."

Allen smiled. Sandy was concerned, sure. But Caroline had been clucking over him for days. In a way, not having her energy around him had been a relief. Allen marveled at his parents' ability to be in each other's psychic fields daily and only have to barrier when company came. The whole household now was shielded because Sam was under their roof, but it would only be temporary.

"How's the case coming along?" Allen asked, stretching out on one of two chaise lounges on the porch.

"It's been really odd," she admitted. "We've found out all sorts of things from Dr. Castiano. And we finally got our client's blood results back."

"What blood results?"

"Oh, you weren't here when we got the information. The victim was HIV positive, so we insisted that they test our client. And he's negative. It took them over a week to get the results, and they sent them to the Sheriff's office."

"That'll relieve his family about one thing, at least. What other news did Dr. Castiano bring?"

"He seems to think there's a cult up there recreating Mesoamerican blood sacrifice, and they've been doing it for over a hundred years."

Allen bolted upright to sit on the side of the lounge.

"How many years?"

"About every twenty years or so, but the last one was about forty years ago. Maybe they couldn't find the body for the gap years. Dr. Castiano thinks it's some way to appease the gods or gain power. They took the victim's heart, and he figures they collected most of the blood."

Allen's head swam, and he found it hard to breathe. He bent his head down between his knees and tried to take in a deep breath. Concentrating, he managed one deep breath and let it out slowly. Then another and a third. It must have taken some time, because Caroline was nattering over the phone he still had at his ear.

"Allen? Allen, did the call drop? Allen, are you all right? Allen?"

"I'm okay," he managed to say as he slowly raised his head. "Caroline, let me call you tomorrow. Good night."

He tapped off the call and sat for a minute before he went inside in search of Toni. It wasn't that late, but the kitchen was dark, and no one was on the front porch or seemed to be near the horses. Allen didn't want to disturb his parents if they were in their room, but he needed to intrude. Retracing his steps upstairs, he paused at his parents' door. He heard muffled voices and movement in the room. He knocked and waited. Then he knocked once more and opened the door slightly.

"I need to talk," he said, as Toni opened the door wider to let him in. She was bootless, still jeans-clad and wearing the white, sleeveless undershirts she always liked.

Allen saw that his mother was in her nightgown, sitting at an old-fashioned vanity, brushing her hair. He remembered

284

that the vanity had once belonged to Dutch, the only feminine thing the ranch owner possessed. His mom had always admired it. The old woman made sure that his mother and Toni had moved it into their bedroom before she died, and his mother had painted it white. As she turned to look at Allen, he noticed how delicate she looked, as if these past few days had touched her more than she had revealed.

"What's on your mind?" Toni asked, and closed the door as Kate crossed to her side.

Allen strode to the cedar chest at the foot of his parents' bed and sat down. "I just got a call from Caroline." He looked up at them both, feeling helpless.

"Is she all right?" his mother asked.

"She's fine, but I asked her about the case. There's more information."

Toni squatted near him like she used to do when he was a boy and wanted to be on the same level as he was when she had difficult things to tell him. She never liked to tower over him. "What did she say?"

"She said Dr. Castiano thought what happened up near Dulce was a ritual sacrifice. It's been going on for over a hundred years, every twenty years or so. The victim in this case had his heart removed and his blood collected. Dr. Castiano thought it had some connection to Mesoamerican practices." Allen transferred his attention from Toni to his mother. "You don't think Father's family would . . . or he. . . ."

Kate sat down on the chest near him. "I don't think he would do anything like that. But his people have an ancestry that. . . ." She looked away, clearly uncomfortable with the information. "The night you were conceived," she began.

Toni reached over and took Kate's hand. "I told him about the change in ceremony intention. It wasn't mine to tell, but he needed to know."

"The People actually did blood sacrifice?" Allen asked.

"I can't say for certain. But as the old women prepared me for the ritual, they seemed eager for it. I wasn't one of them, so my life had no value except for the purposes they chose."

"But this isn't some ancient people!" Allen was horrified. The images of the graves up at the crime scene came flooding back and more. Then the room darkened, as blood drained from his head. In that gloom were images. A bird-cloaked figure stood on the steps of an ancient pyramid. Its headdress of long feathers spread out like a dark crown. A black obsidian knife, its shape clearly outlined in the moonlight. And a bejeweled cup raised high.

Once more, Allen felt blood rushing back into his bent head and the presence of love beside him, each touching a shoulder and a wrist. His vision finally cleared, and he raised his head to face the reality of the room.

"We saw it, too," Toni said.

"Then someone has done this, really done this?" Allen asked, still in shock.

"Yes, probably for power," Kate said.

"Who?" Allen pressed.

"I don't think your father would do this for Logan."

"Logan!" Allen searched his parents' faces. "He has no idea what he's involved with. I had no idea. We have to tell somebody. We have to tell Sandy. It could affect the case."

Toni frowned. "We need to think about this. We don't want to bring the full force of the law down onto an entire native group for what could be the actions of just a few. The People may not even know about old practices. Besides, what happened at the crime scene was a whole state away. We can't say that all that was done there was done here by your father's people."

"But it could be."

"Yes, but it's highly unlikely. There could be a connection. But it's not for us to decide."

"We have to do something."

Toni thought for a moment. "I'll call Sandy tomorrow." She looked over at Kate. "With your permission." Her wife nodded. "I'll tell her what we know. If we have any more energy left tonight, let's send Logan some love, OK?"

They sat quietly for a few minutes, centered themselves with breathing exercises, and then did a gentle sending.

Chapter Seventy-Eight

The county sheriff's office had the look of busyness, though the officers seemed to be doing the regular things they had always done at their desks whenever Sandy and Caroline had been there. Today, though, there was an added tension in the main room, as if some kind of inspection was being conducted. As soon as the front door closed, a deputy jumped up from his desk and rushed to the counter.

"The sheriff's expecting you," he said. "Go right in."

Sandy raised an eyebrow at Caroline before turning to walk the few feet to Sheriff Mendoza's closed door. She knocked but didn't wait for a response. Inside, two men, dressed in well-tailored suits, stood at the foot of the massive desk. Both turned serious faces to the lawyers.

Not rising from his worn office chair, Mendoza gestured from the men to the women. "These are Manwell's lawyers. Sandra Lopez and Caroline . . . Coyote."

The nearest man to the door was the elder, very tall with streaks of gray in his hair. He stretched out a hand to Sandy, and, in deep tones that sounded like God Himself but with the slight hint of college-educated South, he introduced himself, "Special Agent Harold Shoopman." He glanced over his shoulder. "And Special Agent Thomas Bower."

Sandy shook his hand and reached around him to the agent behind to shake his, also. Caroline followed suit, but added, "Caroline *Wolfe*," emphasizing her last name.

"Special Agent?" Sandy clarified. "FBI?"

"Yes ma'am," Agent Shoopman said.

"Are you new here?"

"No, ma'am. I've been here ten years. I asked for a place with a better climate, after twenty years in North Dakota."

"This is a change, then. Was North Dakota far from your home town?"

Agent Shoopman gave her a self-deprecating smile. "It was. I was sent there as a punishment."

Sandy's eyes opened wide in shock.

"Give him time, and he'll tell you his whole life story," Agent Bower said, shifting his weight onto the balls of his feet and fiddling with the button of his jacket.

Giving the other agent a brief glance like a disapproving school teacher, Shoopman smiled at Sandy again. "Maybe sometime over coffee."

Sheriff Mendoza loudly cleared his throat. "They want to interview your client."

"We thought you'd like to sit in with us," Shoopman added.

"What do you expect to learn from my client?" Sandy asked.

Again, that charming smile. "We hope he'll help us with our inquiry."

"Your inquiry." It was a statement that held a question. Sandy's mind quickly sized up the FBI agent: educated, Southern poise, charm, and at least thirty years of field experience. In some ways, Shoopman was as calculating and manipulative as she'd come to understand Paul Rodriguez was over the past decade when she had worked out alimony, custody, and visitation rights with him. Instinctively, she stuck her tongue in her cheek and waited.

Gesturing toward the door, Agent Shoopman offered, "It's a courtesy we're extending to protect your client's rights."

As they crossed past the counter and down the side corridor to the detention area and interview rooms, Sandy mentally sifted through the pile of information she had received from OMI, the crime lab, and Dr. Castiano. She also weighed charges that the FBI would be interested in: murder on native lands, conspiracy to commit murder, serial murder, ritual crime. What her client could contribute to an inquiry about those was probably very little. The present crime was not on native soil, and his only motive was a decades-long grievance. When Sandy entered the interrogation room where her client waited, she was confident that the present case had suddenly outgrown her client, the only available suspect.

Taking her seat from among the extra chairs in front of the table across from where Harley Manwell sat, Sandy told her client, "Mr. Manwell, these men are from the FBI. I want you to tell them what happened after you left your great-great-granddaughter's christening party. They'll ask you some questions. Please answer as truthfully as you can. If you have any doubts, please ask me for clarification. Remember, I'm on your side."

"*Mi bonita, si.* I will."

Sandy suppressed a smile at her client's endearment and his subsequent launch into the virtues of Alphonso's fine, top-shelf tequila.

Before he got to the crime scene, Agent Bower interrupted, "We've read the transcript of his statement."

Sandy allowed her smile to show. "I thought you should hear it from him," she explained.

Shoopman waved his hand in dismissal and leaned back in the metal chair to listen as Manwell completed his tale. Finally, he clarified, "So, it is your assertion that you didn't recognize the man you stumbled upon and passed out over?"

"No. Had I known it was that *puto*, I would have fought him then and there!" The old man put up his fists in fighting position.

"Was anyone else around? Did you see anyone else?"

"No. Just me and the stars and that *puto*."

"Do you know of anyone practicing old spiritual ways?"

"You mean like burying St. Joseph upside down to sell your house quickly?"

Shoopman smiled. "No. I'm not talking about Catholic practices. Old native ways."

"You need a dance or a healing?" Manwell asked. "You need a *diyin*?"

The agent turned to Sandy for clarification.

"Holy man," she translated. "Shaman."

Shoopman shook his head. "More like the opposite. A bad person. Someone using power for his own gain."

"What do you need *'ilkashn* for?" Manwell was not only suspicious but wary, now. "I got no need for evil."

"Would you seek out such a person to harm that. . . ." he smiled and then added, "*puto*?"

Manwell shook his head violently. "Never!"

Shoopman wasn't finished. "Did you ask for help to get back at Mr. Valencia?"

"Si. I pray every day to St. Jude and St. Michael. He got their justice, finally."

Sandy looked down, pressing her lips tightly together to keep from laughing out loud.

The agent, however, was not daunted. "Have you heard of people in the area doing ritual by cutting out someone's heart?"

"What?" Manwell was horrified. "Who do you think we are? Savages?"

At that, Sandy turned to the FBI agents and said, "I think we're done here." She turned to her client. "Mr. Manwell, I'll talk to you tomorrow."

Chapter Seventy-Nine

Day 11: Wednesday, late afternoon, near Payson, AZ

Logan had risen well after dawn on his last full day of his vision quest. The rock wall had kept the sun from stirring him awake. The previous day's sun had warmed the stones, so that he slept more comfortably. The newly laid bed of tree branches would add to his comfort, though the exertions over the past three days had fatigued him.

Feeling safer now that he had made a respectable camp, Logan wondered if it would anger his father and the People because he had sought comfort for himself. He expected a reprimand, so he planned to dismantle everything before his father, Uncle Juan, and his seven helpers found him at noon the next day. He would scatter the stones and the branches and try to leave no trace. The boy had enjoyed planning and constructing his quarters, feeling a strange kinship with his architect father for the first time. His mother was also an architect, though she had stopped working after he was born.

Logan did his prayers and tied them to the prayer tree. He also checked his water supply, which was down to just one gallon. His efforts had made him extra thirsty. He calculated that he had enough for the rest of today and tomorrow.

Settling down with his back to the outcropping that supported the rock overhang, Logan watched the sky. It was still that cloudless blue. He wondered what other boys had experienced on their vision quests. What had his father felt and done? He had not had a vision yet. In fact, the only one of the spirit people he had seen was Brother Lizard, when he first built his wall. Since Logan had no tasks or plans to occupy his mind now, he thought he should probably just sit and chant and hope for a vision to come. He had not brought a rattle with him. No one had said that he should, though he had had one in the sweat lodge. The boy felt a need to keep time with his chanting, and there was nothing at hand. As Logan put his hands on the ground to settle into a better position to chant, his right hand fell on the small stack of palm-sized stones he had accumulated. He found one that fit well in his hand. He tested it by beating on the ground in time with a chant. Its hollow thud would work. Mother Earth was his drum.

Settling back, Logan closed his eyes, thumped the ground, and began a low chant. He prayed he would have a vision, something to prove that he was worthy to be the next shaman, something to prove his father's efforts to train him hadn't been for nothing. As he chanted, he relaxed into rhythm and words, letting his mind slip away, drifting farther from this isolated place in the wilderness.

Chapter Eighty

Toni paced the dirt driveway as she waited for the call to connect. "Finally," she muttered. "Sandy, it's Toni. I wanted to talk to you earlier, but I've had my hands full with transporting horses. Tribal members have been here all day with horse trailers."

"You know you can call any time. What's up?"

"I. . . ." Now, that she had the lawyer on the phone, Toni wondered if her revelations would make things worse.

"Out with it. You've never been one to hold back."

"I just wonder if what I have to tell you will bring trouble. You are an officer of the court, after all."

"Look, you and Kate are my clients. Anything you tell me is confidential. First, have you or anyone in your family committed a crime?"

"No!" She was shocked Sandy would ask.

"Do you plan on committing a crime?"

"No! Why are you asking me this?"

"Then my obligation as an officer of the court has nothing to do with anything you tell me. If you have knowledge or suspicions of a crime done by someone else, it becomes hearsay. Now, give."

Still in a quandary, Toni squatted on the ground in the middle of the drive as if making herself small would make things easier. "Well, it's some information we found out last night that sort of put some perspective on what Kate and Allen and I have been picking up. Kate told me that Paul's people had ties with Mesoamerica."

"Lots of our nations did. We traded with them all over here."

"Yes, I know and Kate told me a long time ago even into other parts of the South. There may have even been trade as far north as Ohio and Minnesota. But Paul's people are supposed to be *descended from* some group in Mesoamerica."

"And?"

"Well. . . ." Toni was uncomfortable discussing something that was not hers to share. "Kate said that Paul's people had a history of blood sacrifice."

"Are you saying Paul participates in that?"

"Now? I don't know, but . . . Allen and I both think that maybe some other group is doing that, over where your client is."

Sandy was silent.

"So, you think it's possible?"

"I think it's probably the only explanation, Toni."

"I just don't want to bring scrutiny to a native people for something that they aren't doing. The government has interfered with us far too much."

"I agree," Sandy said. "I think, though, that my case here is winding up. The FBI has been brought in and they're sniffing around about ritual murder. My client is such a staunch Catholic that he wouldn't dream of even passing his age-old enemy to somebody who'd do what was done to him. I've got a call in to the DA, and I hope Caroline and I will both be back in our own beds very soon."

Toni managed a smile. "Allen will be happy to have you both back."

"Well, at least Caroline. I want to give the boy a rest before he has to go out using his talents for me again."

"I thank you for that."

After goodbyes, Toni finally straightened. Instinctively, she turned in the direction she had determined that Logan had gone a few days before. She wished him well and turned to the ranch house where a good supper and the love of good woman awaited.

296

Chapter Eighty-One

A gray mist filled the boy's vision. Peeking through the top of it as if from a ship's mast, he saw the sun dance pole strain as four dancers moved backwards, leaning to stretch the rawhide they were tethered on. Then, as one, they danced forward, endlessly repeating the prayer dance of sacrifice. One figure, hair traced with gray, staggered, losing the rhythm the drums set. He had long since ceased singing. The physical strain on the older man's body, soft from comfortable living, matched the agony on his face. He raised a hand to his chest, just under the bone pieces that had been inserted beneath each collarbone to hold the long strips of rawhide. As the dancer struggled to lean backwards, he slumped to his knees before falling face-first to the well-packed earth.

The dancing didn't stop as two men flanked the fallen dancer. One man raised an anguished face to the people watching. It was Uncle Juan. He shouted something over and over. Finally, an old woman appeared and turned the fallen man over onto his back. She bent an ear to the dancer's mouth and placed a hand on his chest. She gestured to the people around her, giving some kind of order. Two other men appeared and cut the rawhide cords, then all four men lifted the man to a *portal* that had been erected for the comfort of the elders. Chairs were moved to make room for the dancer.

A younger woman appeared and stooped over the man on the ground. It was Logan's mother, and the fallen man was his father. "He can't die yet." She stood and then grabbed Juan's upper arms. "The doctor said a few more years. Not now. I can't raise the boy!" Then she started screaming.

Logan jerked alert, his head hitting the stones behind him. Keeping his eyes shut against the pain, he rubbed his bruised head, realizing it had just been a dream or a vision. Then he heard the scream again, but it wasn't his mother. Logan opened his eyes to horror. About thirty feet from him, the black jaguar slowly paced closer, releasing a rumbling snarl. Opening its mouth wider, revealing sharp fangs, moist with saliva, it emitted a sharper cry.

Chapter Eighty-Two

Day 11: Wednesday, late afternoon, near Payson, AZ

Allen raced down the front porch steps to the barn where Toni was mending tack. Now that the extra horses were safely with their new owners, there was time for regular chores. Sam had been glad to saddle his own horse and head off to the horse camp after an early supper.

Grabbing the edge of the open barn door, Allen skidded into the barn where Toni, sitting on a stool next to her work bench, took advantage of the last of the light. She raised her head as Allen said, out of breath, "Something's wrong!"

Dropping the reins in her hand onto the bench, Toni was on her feet in a shot. "Kate?"

"No. Logan, I think."

"I didn't sense anything," Toni said.

"You might not. I got sheer terror."

"Let's find your mom." Toni closed the barn door and locked it.

Both of them rushed to the kitchen where Kate had let out the dishwater and was wiping her hands on a towel. Before she could ask about their hurry, Toni pulled her to the table, where they all sat.

"It's Logan, I think," Allen explained, holding out his hand for his mother to hold and one to Toni.

When all three had created a circle of hands, they closed their eyes and centered themselves with their breathing. Allen sent out a strong call to Logan, but there was nothing except a wall of fear. He kept trying to break through.

"Toni, help me. Please!" Allen pleaded, squeezing his step-mother's hand. "Send your energy as a weapon, as you helped me years ago."

"No." Toni released Allen's hand. "It was a fluke before. You had that ability. It was latent. You could handle it. Logan can't."

"Okay," Allen conceded, knowing Logan had little spiritual ability. "But help me reach him."

Grimly, Toni took Allen's hand again and closed her eyes. A surge of energy flowed through Allen's hand and up his arm. It coursed through his body. Again, he sent out a call to Logan. It hit the boy's fear but still couldn't shatter it.

"Your fear is feeding Logan's," Kate said. "I feel it."

Allen changed tactics. He took a deep breath and focused the energy on clear thinking. He remembered times when he had been challenged and used the fear to spur his actions. Now, he channeled all of their energy into using the adrenalin of fear as fuel to combat whatever Logan was facing. All three focused.

Chapter Eighty-Three

Pressing his back against the rock outcropping, Logan dared not move. His eyes darted, looking for help or a weapon. His mind was flooded with ideas — too many to sort through.

The black jaguar edged closer, keeping its feral eyes fixed on the boy. One of its ears twitched while what was left of the other tried to move but only spasmed. The animal paced ever closer, bringing terror with each step.

Slowly, Logan removed his hand from his head and eased his whole arm down his body to his side.

The animal inched closer. Its musky odor emanated from its glossy fur.

Logan slipped his knife from its sheath and placed it on the ground beside him. Then he stretched his right hand along the ground, finally feeling one of the palm-sized stones underneath. His fingers closed around the rock.

Just as the animal crouched to leap, Logan shouted, waving his other arm, and released the rock in his hand. It grazed the animal, only stalling the leap that was relaunched immediately. Logan pelted the animal with rocks in midair, which changed the animal's trajectory so that it landed near the boy but not on him. That diversion forced a back claw to rake across the boy's left thigh. As the animal tried to scramble to its feet, Logan found the knife, stabbing wildly at the jaguar's neck, but not doing much damage. He shouted as he stood and kicked the beast's spine. The big cat finally got upright, and Logan threw more rocks at the animal's head, not allowing it to even think about attack. He picked up one of the football-sized rocks from his wall and hurled it with the strength of terror. It struck the animal in the ribs. Hard.

A loud, shrill whistle caused the animal to stop and snarl louder. The whistle came again, and the black jaguar bounded off in the direction the sound had come from.

Shaken, Logan stumbled backwards, leaning against the outcropping. His thigh was bleeding. He didn't need the blood to attract other creatures. Reaching inside the overhang, he saw he had only a half-gallon of water left. He really needed to wash the blood away. Taking the jug, his blanket, and his bloody knife, he limped far away from his camp and carefully washed his wound. It was about eight inches long and a clean slice, but not deep. He cleaned his knife on the ground, then used it to cut a strip from the blanket. He wrapped that around his thigh and then hobbled back to the shelter. Pulling the thorny branches well over the opening, he took a long drink from the jug and then wrapped himself in his blanket. Though exhausted, it was a long time before his eyes would shut in sleep.

Chapter Eighty-Four

Sandy and Caroline rose from their chairs, both extending their hands to their client, Harley Davidson Manwell, in the sterile interview room. "It's been a pleasure serving you, sir," Sandy said.

The old man tried to stand, but the weight of his shackles made it difficult.

He grasped Sandy's hand in both of his. "Gracias, *mi bonitas.*"

The old man then took Caroline's hand and repeated, "Gracias."

"Your family is on its way with a change of clothes. You should be home to your wife's cooking very soon."

"If you need anything — anything," the old man said, "I will do it or make sure it is done."

Sandy smiled, knowing that the gesture was well-meant but hollow. Then something struck her. "Do you have any relatives in the south?"

"You mean Mescalaros?"

The lawyer nodded.

"*Si. Primos.*"

Smiling again, the lawyer said, "We may be in touch."

In the corridor, the younger lawyer began, "What—."

"I'm surprised the DA folded so quickly," Sandy said, cutting her question off. "I guess the FBI realized it had a bigger case than an old grudge."

Once outside in the car, Sandy pulled out of the parking lot and headed toward Santa Fe. She reached for the iced soda in her cup holder. "I'll be glad to sleep in my own bed tonight," she said before taking a long drink.

"Me, too," Caroline said, "And eat some of my auntie's roast mutton."

"Chile too hot for you?" Sandy teased.

"Chile is fine in small quantities. I just want back to things I know for a while."

Sandy grinned.

"What?" Caroline demanded.

"And that includes a certain PI we both know?"

"He's just a boy."

"He's over twenty-one, and he's emotionally been an old man all his life."

Caroline finally smiled.

After a mile or so of silence, Sandy said, "I've been thinking about something."

"More matchmaking?" Caroline chided.

"No. Business."

"What's on your mind?"

"We only have so many land title disputes, domestic violence, and divorce cases. The reservation paperwork is well under control. Even Toni is able to create Bills of Sale for the horses now."

"Are you saying you want to dissolve our partnership?" There was panic in Caroline's voice.

"No, not at all," Sandy clarified quickly. "I've been thinking about setting up a satellite office to serve native people."

"Where? Here?"

"We've made some good contacts here."

Caroline frowned looking out the passenger-side window. "You want me to start over?"

"You're young, Caroline," Sandy said. "You're itching to make a name for yourself. It's either in your own practice, linked to mine, or we lose you to Washington or some other big city." She paused, then added. "I don't think Allen would want to live in a big city."

"Allen?" Caroline swung on her partner. "What does he have to do with my legal career?"

"Well, I'm not going to open another office without having my best PI on the payroll. You'll need him. Besides, he won't stay here if you go, and you know that."

"You're making a life for us, and we haven't even dated." Caroline was near tears.

Sandy realized that though she had read the relationship correctly as she had seen it blossom over the years, it was far more complicated. The age gap, pride, the uncertainty on Caroline's part, fear of rejection, and lack of normality in any part of it were all factors.

"Look, it will take time. You'll need to qualify to practice in New Mexico, and so will Allen as a PI and as a teacher. He'll need time to find another teaching position. There'll need to be a legal needs assessment for the area."

Finally, Caroline said what was really troubling her. "He won't want to come back here. Not with what's up there near Dulce."

"There are other Apaches in New Mexico."

"Others?"

"The Mescalero in the South."

"But isn't that desert? We're mountain bred."

"I checked. The Mescalero reservation is in the mountains. Lots of trees and streams. There's a small town nearby, Ruidoso, where you could draw local cases besides native ones. It gets lots of snow in the winter, too. It'd be just like home in Payson."

Caroline finally laughed. "You have this all figured out, don't you? Now, all we have to do is go back to school, jump through all sorts of licensing hoops, and get Allen to propose."

Sandy focused on the road but grinned. "Easy peasy."

Chapter Eighty-Five

Logan pulled the blanket tighter around him as his body shook with chills. The boy had fallen asleep almost as soon as his body took refuge under the overhang. He had slept soundly at first and later fitfully. Images of yellow eyes in black fur and sharp, sharp teeth haunted his dreams. Drumming filled Logan's head. He wondered if it were from his vision or dream of his father at the sun dance pole or the headache he had acquired during the night.

"Logan! Logan!" Calls of his name were just dreams as were shrill whistles. An image of a black cat's alertness came to him. Drums louder and closer. Then voices. More voices calling his name.

Groaning, the boy sat up. His thigh hurt. Folding back the blanket over his leg, Logan saw that the scrap of fabric he had tied over his wound was moist. Taking his knife, he cut through the knots where he had tied the makeshift dressing. The boy shifted the foot of that leg flat on the ground so that he could unwind the wrapping. The wound looked angry and raw but was not bleeding. As his fingers explored the skin around the wound, it felt hot. A wave of chills struck him, and he gathered the blanket around him tightly. Logan wanted to get out into the sun to warm himself. Before he could reach to remove the thorn branch gate over the entrance, it was torn away. He screamed as strange faces crowded around and hands reached for him. The boy threw off his blanket and lashed out, not realizing he still had the knife in his hand. Someone cried out and firm hands wrested the knife away. Still fighting, the boy was pulled from the overhang. Someone wrapped him tightly in his blanket, pinning his arms. Several voices shouted in a jumble of noise. One soothing voice with a heavy Spanish accent spoke quietly in his ear. The boy felt himself being lifted up into someone's arms like a baby.

He protested. "I'm not a baby. I'm a man, now. I had a vision. I fought a giant cat and survived. I'm not a baby."

The Spanish-accented voice soothed, dropping English and into a language it was obviously more comfortable with. The words were soothing. Something seemed familiar. A smell. It was a good smell. A safe smell. It was like the smell of aftershave that Uncle Juan wore. The drone of words, the warmth of the blanket in the sun, and the familiarity of Uncle Juan's scent made Logan feel safe. He stopped protesting and drifted off to sleep.

Chapter Eighty-Six

Day 13: Thursday, just past noon, near Payson, AZ

The siren startled the horses in the paddock, forcing them to the far side, near the cover of the trees. Toni paused in her mucking out of the corral where the extra horses had been. Setting her pitchfork against the railing, she let herself out to greet the driver of the ambulance and the fire rescue vehicle that had sped into the drive.

"We got a call about an emergency, a possible heart attack," the ambulance driver said.

"No one here is ill." Then a guess filled her mind. She swung around the ambulance and rushed up the steps yelling for Allen. Catching him just coming out the door, she said, "Get details from the ambulance driver about their call. I'll go check with Isaiah."

Toni rushed into the office and switched on the ham radio. After sending out her identification code and that of Isaiah, she finally got him on the receiving end. "There's an ambulance here looking for someone who's ill. Can you check out the chatter on the Indian grapevine ASAP?"

"Will do. It'll take a couple of minutes."

Toni stuck her head out of the office. Seeing Kate in the foyer, she called her over. "Go get any details from Allen and the ambulance driver."

Kate fled outside but soon came rushing back. "They're looking for an older man who had a heart attack. They said he might be in a remote area."

The crackle of the ham receiver drew Toni back to the microphone. "Go ahead."

"An operator relayed a message to fire and ambulance about a middle-aged man in distress," Isaiah said.

"Where did they think it was?"

"Well, it sounded like somewhere between your place and the camp. Pretty isolated."

"Could it have been at the ceremony grounds where Logan and his parents are?"

"Actually, it sounded like that."

"Thanks. Over and out."

Toni rushed passed Kate back outside to the ambulance. The two extra paramedics from the fire rescue vehicle were crowded around the ambulance driver's door, along with Allen. "I think it may be in the back country," Toni explained to them. Turning to Allen, she asked, "Do you think you could find the ceremony grounds?"

"I was ten," Allen said, helplessly. "I don't know."

"Well, I can help track. There should still be traces of where they went on Sunday."

Turning to the first responders, Toni explained. "It could be at a private ceremony way out in the bush. There are native healers there. But if someone needs an ambulance, it'd be hard to pack them out."

"We'd need to fly them out by helicopter," one of the fire paramedics said. "But it'll take time to arrange. How long to get to the site?"

Again, Toni deferred to Allen. "How far?"

"It seemed like a long time when I was a kid. But maybe a half hour to an hour. That is, if we can find the trail," Allen explained.

Toni scrutinized the four men. "Any of you sit a horse?"

The man in the passenger side of the ambulance said he rode. One of the fire paramedics said, "I'm a member of the Sheriff's Mounted Posse."

"Perfect. Then you know about search and rescue and that's just what we have here. I'll go cut out four horses and bring them to the corral. Allen, you and the men get the tack. We'll start saddling as soon as the horses get into the corral."

310

She looked at the other two men. "Gather what the men will need and somebody call for the helicopter. Is there any way you have to communicate in the back country? There's no cell service."

The other fire paramedic said, "We keep a satellite phone in the truck when we get called out to ranches. They can be pretty remote. The phone should be charged, and we always have our radios."

"Good. Then make the call to put the helicopter on standby. And make sure the one of you coming with us has communication equipment."

It took about twenty minutes for all of the tasks to be completed. The two paramedics swung themselves easily into their saddles after they had packed their saddlebags with medical supplies and portable equipment. Toni and Allen mounted and headed past the end of the dirt drive into the trees where Toni had seen sign of horses on Sunday.

Chapter Eighty-Seven

Logan stirred from his sleep. Uncle Juan was arguing with another man. "He cannot walk. Do you not understand?"

"But he must show his strength. He's a man now. He's our new leader."

"He is injured."

Logan wriggled in Uncle Juan's arms. "Let me down," he said and was gently placed on the ground while Uncle Juan continued to argue. Nearby, the sound of drums and singing drifted to his ears. Struggling to unwrap himself from his blankets, Logan finally was free and then tried to stand. His thigh hurt, and he had to use both hands to push himself upright. It hurt to put his full weight on the injured leg. He managed a step or two but could do no more. The other six men of his inner clan surrounded him.

"Why are they arguing?" Logan asked.

"Testosterone," one of the men replied in a snarky tone.

A man knelt on one knee in front of the boy. "They're debating whether you should walk in on your own power. Your uncle is protective. The other follows tradition."

"Is it important that I walk in by myself?"

"Yes," the man before him said. "It will show your strength. You're a man now. You're our new spiritual leader." He smiled. "You said you fought a great cat." He looked at the wound on Logan's thigh. "Claw or fang?"

"Claw," Allen said. "It was the black jaguar."

"The one we saw with Cesar?"

"That was my cousin?" Then he nodded. "I think the cat had the better of me, but I fought him until a whistle drew him away."

The man smiled again. "Perhaps you require a new name now. Jaguar Warrior."

Logan smiled. "What's your name?"

"I'm called Wes."

"Am I permitted to elevate one of my inner clan?"

Wes looked up at the men surrounding them both. The snarky-voiced one said, "Yes, as your Clan Leader."

"But that implies power over," another said. "It isn't always so."

"None of us should have power over another," someone else said.

"Advisor might be better," another man said.

The boy searched the faces of all of the men. "I will need your advice and wisdom," Logan said, and then looked down at the kindness he saw in Wes' eyes. "But you will be my Clan Brother." Shifting his weight painfully onto both of his legs, he said, "I will walk in on my own. But, Clan Brother, stand near, in case I need to steady myself."

Taking a deep breath, Logan proceeded into the camp. He winced every time he put weight on his leg, but it held him. It was just an injury to the skin and some bruising, though it might be infected. It wasn't a sprain or a break. For that, he was grateful. Step by step, he marched with his inner clan into the ceremony grounds. Dancing and drumming continued, but no piercers were in sight. He searched for his father, only now surprised that he had not come to collect him to process into the ceremony. Logan surmised that his father had lingered to prepare a welcome for him since he was supposed to endure the piercing, also.

The dancers were no longer moving close to the pole and back out. They gathered as in a women's round dance in a circle around the sun dance pole as a single dancer, clad in a black feathered cloak and a huge long-plumed headdress, moved in time with the drummers. He was singing in a language that Logan didn't recognize and his dance was foreign. Against the sun dance pole, the black jaguar perched regally, watching. Occasionally its pink tongue licked blood from his black furred mouth.

Two steps behind the boy instead of by his side, Wes shouted out, "Ho, your spiritual leader approaches."

Both the drummers and dancers stopped immediately, turning to the voice, backing away to open the circle. The lone dancer continued to dance and sing but trailed off when he realized the drums had ceased. As the figure straightened, the big cat stepped to its side, running its head under the figure's dangling right hand. Almost reluctantly, the figure scratched the jaguar's ears.

Striding forward toward the boy, the figure smirked. "So, you survived." He looked down at the boy's thigh, which had started to bleed again. The big cat licked its jaws. "How did you like playing with my kitty?"

"Go home, Cesar," Logan said loudly. "There is no place for you here."

"But this is my home. I am the rightful leader." He spread both arms wide. "I have done all that should be done to ensure my place. It was done for your father. But he couldn't bring himself to sacrifice his new bride nor sacrifice for his first son nor for you. All has been done as our forebears and their extended clan groups had done so long ago. We are everywhere now in this land, and we have not forgotten the old ways." He laughed. "You have no Sundance scars. You haven't suffered. You just bear a tiny kitty scratch."

Wes stepped to Logan's side and so did another of his clansmen. The other five men spread out behind the boy, giving him protection. They stood legs spread, knees slightly bent, with their right hands on their daggers at their sides. Uncle Juan was in back somewhere.

Cesar grinned. "So, it will be seven of you who stand with a boy. Do you all plan to fight me? I can take you all. I am powerful. Nothing can stop me." He flung off the feathered cloak and pranced in a circle to reveal the huge snake scar on his back. Its ugly scabs rippled like snake skin as Cesar flexed his shoulder muscles.

Juan stepped around the clansmen and stood beside Wes.

"Ah, our kinsman from the far South. You take his side as you did for that usurper ten years ago."

A couple of older men shuffled to stand in back of the clansmen around Logan. A few women followed. Some younger ones shuffled from one foot to another.

Cesar's laugh now was maniacal as he pulled his knife and dropped into a combat crouch. The action caused the big cat to dig its claws into the packed dirt and lower its body to spring.

Chapter Eighty-Eight

Toni had managed to find the trail into the woods fairly easily. The paramedics had proven to be experienced riders, and the fire paramedic, Quincy, helped them look for more horse sign. With that and Allen's vague recollections to keep them pointed in the right direction, they made good time picking their way through the woods. When they emerged from the trees, the trail became more pronounced as another, more worn trail merged with it. It looked as if several horses had traveled back and forth over several days. The landscape had become a bit rockier with large sandstone outcroppings, and huge granite boulders punctuating the open range. They all urged their horses into a trot. Ahead, the trail appeared as a pass through two rocky bluffs that hid whatever was on the other side. They passed through at a clip and then pulled to a halt as the ceremonial grounds came into view.

Before them, a lone, scarred and tattooed figure, with a plumed headdress and an obsidian-bladed ceremonial knife, crouched beside a black panther that appeared poised to spring. The figure faced Logan and eight men who had gathered around him. One looked like Juan Vasquez, Paul's made-brother. Behind them were old men and a few old women.

Suddenly, a young woman came rushing out from a *portal* toward Toni and her party. "Come quick! He's dying!"

The paramedics dismounted and gathered their equipment, following the woman at a jog. Toni swung her right leg up over the saddle horn and slid to the ground, grabbing the reins of the paramedics' horses. Allen took his time getting off his horse, clearly trying to read the situation. Toni could see him hesitate between following the paramedics and heading toward his brother. Finally, deciding, Allen walked slowly toward Logan.

The disturbance had distracted the lone figure and the big cat. The man straightened, watching the commotion at the *portal*. The black animal leaned close to the man's legs as if checking his reaction to see if there was danger from another front.

Toni watched Logan turn toward the woman's frantic emotions with worry on his own face. Realizing then that it was Marianna who had come screaming about Paul, Toni searched for a bit of scrub, secured the horses reins, and headed toward the *portal* to check the situation. She knew that she couldn't help there but needed to see for herself. From the experienced efficiency of the paramedics' actions, checking vitals, putting in an IV line, and administering oxygen from a small portable unit, Toni was sure that Paul was not dead yet and was in good hands. As soon as they stabilized the patient, Quincy stepped away, more into the clearing, pulled out his radio first and then the satellite phone. He passed Toni when the call was done and said, "The chopper's on its way. It'll be here in ten, fifteen minutes."

Giving the man a slap on his back, Toni then headed toward Allen who was now between the figure with the big cat and Logan.

"—nothing to prove here, Cesar," Allen was saying.

Toni stood beside Juan and let her step-son handle this situation. She wasn't a part of these people. She didn't even have the status that Juan had of being brought into the nation as Paul's brother through ceremony. She was just a mother — and an adoptive one, just another woman among these people, who didn't understand the many genders of the Seneca or even the Apache, on whose land this ceremonial ground abutted.

"I see you have your whole family here now, Logan-boy," Cesar said. "The witch people. Your witch brother and his witch stepmother, an unnatural abomination. At least, you are like me, cousin. We don't use witch tricks to win like your brother did." He turned on Allen. "Why don't you fight me like a man now. For the right to rule." He laughed. "But you didn't want this, did you, coward cousin?"

"I don't want it now, either," Allen said. "But it's Logan's right. He's earned it through his sacrifice in his vision quest and by his blood. He has as much blood of the People as you do and more than I have. I won't fight you."

Cesar waved the knife around, tossing it from hand to hand. "Then who will fight me? Will no one? Then I claim my right as shaman."

"You made a sham of your right when we were boys," Allen said. "You tried to fight me then for your right. You walked away from this, too, and my father continued to lead the People. He's an old man, and it's time for his rightful son to take his place. He's earned it."

"NO! It's my right!" He made a sudden lunge, not toward Allen, but toward Logan, the real threat to his dream of power. The black jaguar, seeming to sense its master's target, leaped toward the boy.

The clansmen pushed the boy behind them as Logan pulled out his new knife. They tackled Cesar en mass, forcing him to the ground. At the same time, the black jaguar leapt over the pile of men and landed on Logan, who had fallen back with the knife held in both hands protecting his bare torso. Wes and another clansman were on the cat immediately, pulling it off the boy. It was nearly dead, the knife driven to the hilt deep into its chest by the animal's own weight.

Mala, Cesar's mother, rushed out from the back of the crowd of people and began beating on the clansmen with her fists. "Let go of my boy! He's the rightful shaman!" One of the men separated from the tackle pile and pushed Mala away as she pounded his chest. He managed to restrain her arms by grabbing them at the wrists.

Toni and Juan helped Logan to his feet. He was shaking, partly from fright and partly from the angry wound on his thigh. Toni waved at Quincy, who stood gaping at the activity that had just unfolded. The man jogged over and looked at the boy. Quincy felt over limbs to see if bones were broken and then took a hard look at the wound. "We'll clean that up and give you some antibiotics. Was it tooth or claw?"

"Claw," Wes said, coming over to check on the boy.

"That's good. We don't have to worry about rabies or other diseases transmitted by the cat's mouth."

"Can I get some food now?" Logan said. "And can I sit down somewhere?"

Wes laughed. "We have a throne for you."

"A what?"

"Well, we call it a throne. It's just a chair draped in blankets. The children have been decorating it with flowers. And the women have been making a feast for you."

"Has he been fasting?" Quincy asked.

"Yes, for over three days," Wes answered.

"Start with broth first. A bit at a time. Then bread and protein. Otherwise, it won't stay down. Put the young lad on his throne, and I'll bring supplies over to treat him."

Allen joined the group. "Want to lean on me, little brother?" he asked Logan and then asked Wes, "Where's that throne?"

The three of them hobbled off toward a space under another *portal* that had been bedecked with garlands of flowers like giant daisy chains.

Quincy pulled Toni away from the commotion of the clansmen, who were still restraining Cesar. "I don't know what was going on here, other than a ceremony," he said, taking another look at how the tattooed man was fighting his restrainers. Turning back to Toni, he said, "I have been deputized." Quincy pulled the satellite phone from one of the many pockets in his pants. "I can have that big guy picked up.

It looked as if he tried to attack the boy, and with that animal, too."

"That decision will have to be Logan's now."

"That traumatized boy?"

Toni tilted her head in concession. "I'm not one of the People. I have no say."

"You're not from this tribe?"

Toni shook her head. "My people are the Seneca."

"From New York? How'd you ever end up here?"

"It's a long story, my friend."

Quincy smiled. "Maybe I can buy you a drink sometime. You really helped us to get out here."

Toni grinned, showing about two inches between thumb and forefinger. "Maybe a wee Jameson."

The beat of rotors sounded in the distance, making Toni glance up to scan the skies for the emergency evacuation helicopter. The day wasn't over yet, but at least for a brief while she could breathe a little easier.

Chapter Eighty-Nine

After tidying up the kitchen, Kate came out onto the porch with a bushel of green beans that someone from the tribe had brought on top of the payment for the cutting horse he'd bought yesterday. She went back in and found a white enamel basin and a huge Dutch oven. Kate needed to keep busy while she waited for Toni and Allen to return. Settling comfortably on the porch, she started breaking beans, a rhythmic task that she always found meditative and calming. The strings and ends went into the basin in her lap and the broken beans into the pot on the porch floor between her feet.

The start of the ambulance's engine drew her attention. The vehicle pulled further along the dirt drive and then turned around, slowly moving back the way it had come. The red fire rescue truck also turned around but pulled up in front of the barn. The driver got out and walked up to the porch. "Ma'am," the young man began. "The helicopter is transporting the patient and one of the paramedics, so the ambulance was released. If you don't mind, I'll be staying until Quincy, the other EMT, comes back. There's more need for an ambulance than for me at the moment."

"Would you like some coffee?" Kate asked.

"Thanks, ma'am, that would be welcome. Could I use your bathroom?"

"Up the stairs and to the right. Would you like a piece of pie to go with your coffee?"

His young face lit up. "Yes, ma'am. Thanks."

It didn't take long to slice pie and bring out coffee. Kate set it on a log that had been converted to an end table on the other side of the bentwood settee on which she settled back into her bean breaking.

The EMT came out and sat down cautiously beside Kate. "My granny used to do that."

"Did you help her?"

"Naw, that was my sisters' jobs. I had three sisters, two older and one younger. They all learned to snap beans. I gathered eggs."

"I remember doing that, too."

"It wasn't the easiest job. The hens wouldn't budge. They often wanted to brood. My grandad would just come in and rob the nests right under the birds. I tried doing that, but the biddies would peck me on the forehead. When I'd grown enough, they'd just squawk and try to peck my hand."

"They could've put out an eye," Kate remarked. "My grandpa used to shoo them out of the hen house before I'd gather eggs after one tried to peck me."

"Guess your granddad gave you latitude because you were a girl."

Kate laughed. "Maybe so." Her thoughts turned to her current worry. "Did they say how the patient was doing when they helicopter transported him? Was it a heart attack?"

The EMT quickly finished chewing the pie he had just put into his mouth and swallowed. "Yeah. It looked like a heart attack. They got him stabilized, and he was fit to transport. His wife went with him. Quincy said that there was also some sort of fight with a guy and a big cat, a panther or something. He's a mounted deputy, so he arrested the guy and was waiting for a law enforcement chopper to come take the guy away. Quincy thought he needed a psych eval. He said the guy and his mother were ranting. Maybe the guy's mother needs one, too."

It made sense to Kate who the players in that drama probably were. She wondered if the heart attack patient was

324

Paul. No matter how things had turned out, no matter how manipulative Paul had been, she didn't want harm to come to him. She sighed and continued to break beans. The young EMT had retreated to his vehicle, saying he was going to take a nap.

By the time Kate had finished the last bean in the bushel, she heard the two horses in the paddock snuffle and then move toward the railing of the corral. It was probably feeding time. She knew where the hay was kept and the sweet alfalfa. Kate would tend to that after she put the beans away. Once the porch was cleared and the beans were on the stove starting to cook, Kate stepped out onto the porch, intending on doing the evening feed. The horses were neighing loudly, indicating that this wasn't just hunger. Then she heard other horses coming out of the trees. Toni and Allen each led a saddled horse. So did Quincy. Two other men rode behind. She squinted her eyes. One was Juan Vasquez, and the other was unknown to her but definitely native. And following the lot was Logan, looking weary.

The caravan stopped in front of the corral and dismounted. The unknown native man helped Logan down. The boy was limping and bore a long bandage on his left thigh. They turned toward the house, and Kate met them. "Are you all right?" she asked Logan.

"I'm fine. I just want to go home, but I don't know when I can," he said.

"You know you can stay here as long as you like," Kate said. "You're family." She turned to the stranger.

"That's Wes," Logan said. "He's my Clan Brother."

"Forgive my intrusion. But I needed to make sure he was all right," he said.

"I'm Kate," she said, offering her hand. "Allen's mother and Toni's wife." She opened slightly to read this stranger, who had bonded himself to the boy. All she read was kindness.

"You're welcome to stay. We have room." She turned to Logan. "Have you eaten?"

"I'm stuffed," he said. "I just want a shower. I feel icky."

Kate laughed. "A boy asking for a bath. That's a first. Go up to the bathroom. I'll bring you some clothes. I'm sure Allen has a t-shirt at least. I don't know about pants."

"They're in the trunk of the car," Logan said. "Uncle Juan has the keys."

Kate led the boy and Wes up to the bathroom and found a t-shirt for him. Then she went downstairs to find Juan Vasquez. He was sorting through a set of keys at the back of Paul's car. "I understand Logan has clothes in the trunk," Kate said.

He looked up, startled, and then smiled. Extending an arm, Juan pulled her into a brief hug and kissed her cheek. "It is done, at last. I don't ever want to participate in this again."

"I understand."

Returning to sorting through the keys, he added, "It is all chaos and drama. I'd rather be home with my daughter's giggling little friends, who think I'm stuffy and silly."

"Of course, you would. How are Roberta and Yvonne?"

Finally finding the right key, Juan inserted it into the trunk's lock and raised the lid. He pulled out a backpack that looked as if it belonged to a boy. "I think this is his," he said.

"You can stay. We have a houseful already."

"No, I want to go home. I'll stay in Payson overnight and then drive the rental car I have there to the airport tomorrow. I was supposed to fly out then, anyway. Marianna said she'd call from the hospital later."

"It was Paul who had the heart attack, wasn't it?"

"Yes, they said it looked like a mild one, but even that sometimes means a bypass." He looked concerned at Kate. "I'll call you when I know anything."

"Thanks. And give Roberta and Yvonne my love when you see them."

Kate took the backpack into the house and dropped

it off at the bathroom door after knocking and reporting its whereabouts. When she came outside again, Juan had turned the car around and driven off. Quincy, Allen, and Toni had put the horses in the corral after unsaddling them. Toni was separating the ranch's horses from the rented ones to be ready when their owners came to pick them up. Allen, Quincy, and the other EMT hauled the last of the saddles and tack to the barn.

Kate walked over to the corral fence and put her arms over the top rail, resting her chin on them. When Toni had closed the corral gate and tossed over hay and a handful of alfalfa into the paddock, she offered some feed to the four rented horses in the corral. Kate enjoyed watching her wife with the animals. Toni was so much at ease with them and often treated them like big pet dogs rather than working horses. She smiled.

Toni finally came out of the corral and joined Kate. "What's got you grinning?"

"You," she said, turning to her wife.

"Oh? You miss me?"

"Always."

Toni kissed her. Kate put a finger on her wife's lips. "But we have a houseful tonight. Logan will crash early I'm sure. And he'll need a new dressing for whatever happened to his leg. Wes is in the bathroom with him. He's OK, isn't he? I didn't pick up anything bad."

"No, he's fine. He's bonded to Logan. Apparently, there's an inner circle of men, seven of them, who help the young shaman."

"Allen never had that."

"I'm glad Logan won't be doing this alone, no matter what happens to Paul."

"The EMT said that it was a mild heart attack."

"This time. It isn't the first one, apparently."

Hearing footfalls approach, they separated. Allen and Quincy joined them. Kate noticed that the other EMT had returned to the fire rescue vehicle. Kate turned to Quincy. "Logan is having a shower. You might want to redress whatever you did on his leg."

"That's a good idea. The wound needs a good wash."

"Allen, would you take him up to the bathroom? Wes is up there with Logan now."

Allen gave his mother a kiss on the cheek and then took Quincy into the ranch house.

Kate turned to Toni, "Is it over?"

"Is anything ever?"

Kate punched her wife's shoulder. "You're such a fatalist."

Chapter Ninety

Allen lugged the last of the saddles from the rental horses to the two waiting trailers that had turned around facing the way they'd come. Toni had already helped the horse owners load their horses. As the male owner locked the last trailer gate after putting in the saddle, his wife turned to Toni and extended her hand, which Toni shook.

"The horses look in fine shape, and so do yours," she said, jerking her head toward the paddock where Toni's six mares grazed.

"I gave them all a handful of alfalfa last night. I thought they might appreciate a treat," Toni said.

"I'm surprised those people didn't rent from you. You've got fine stock."

Toni shrugged. "We weren't available."

Toni and Allen backed away as the trailers pulled out. When they had passed the barn, Logan hobbled down the porch steps, dressed in jeans, a Mandalorian t-shirt, and tennies. Wes, now in a pair of Allen's old jeans and a NY t-shirt, stood on the porch, watching.

Allen wondered if his father realized that there would be an additional member of his household now that Logan had taken his rightful place as spiritual leader. Wes had fully embraced his role as Clan Brother. It had not been an option for him when he had been tested. There was no Inner Clan. Allen wondered whose idea that had been or from what book his father had taken that idea. He had always pulled rites from a mishmash of sources. It was a good idea for the boy. Maybe his father had now sensed his own mortality.

Logan took Allen's hand. "I need to talk to you," he said.

"Sure, pal. What's up?"

The boy looked at Toni and then looked down.

"Let's go to the horses," Allen suggested and took the boy through the corral gate. Both of them climbed the fence and straddled the top of the far railing facing each other. They had a great view of the horses. "So, what's on your mind?" Allen prompted.

Logan hesitated a long time before he said, "I had a vision."

Allen quietly waited for more.

"Did you?" Logan asked.

"Yes, Great-Grandmother came to me. I didn't even know who she was, and she brought spirits with her. She told me I was going to be okay and that I should go to her and learn. And I did."

"But you left? You didn't become the new shaman."

"It wasn't my path."

"And teaching school and helping the lawyer lady is?"

Allen smiled. "For me, it is."

Logan looked away. "I don't have . . . gifts like you."

"You have your own gifts. You like to make things."

The boy offered a small smile. "Like our dad."

Allen smiled, too. "Yes, like our dad. I think I have my mom's ability to teach. She enjoys it a lot. She told me last night that she's going to be homeschooling Manuel and Alexander in the fall."

Logan looked away from the horses toward the ranch house where Toni stood talking with Wes. "Toni is a good teacher, too."

"Yes, she is." Allen waited, sensing that there was more the boy wanted to say. "What was your vision about?"

Logan cast his eyes down but moved his head back toward Allen. "I saw Dad's heart attack. He did the Sundance. In my vision, he died and Mom — well, she didn't want me." He raised his eyes to Allen's, fully confessing. "I don't know how to be shaman. I don't know how to lead the People. I can't do this by myself. You have to help me, Allen." He was becoming agitated, flailing his arm, swaying on the railing.

Allen grabbed the boy's arms and steadied him. "You aren't alone, Logan." Allen moved his head so that he could see the boy's eyes clearly. "You have your Inner Clan. I didn't have that. And you have Wes, your Clan Brother. He's older than I am. He knows the ways of the People. I don't. I am Seneca now. I've been adopted into the Turtle Clan as Toni's son. Wes will treat you as part of his family. He's already very protective of you, but he's not smothering."

"Dad won't like that."

Allen laughed, releasing the boy's arms. "I suppose he won't. But, actually, he has no say over your training now. You're the new leader. You have your Inner Clan and Wes."

"I don't want to be like Cesar. Where did he get all of that dark stuff from?"

Allen sighed. "The People have old roots, but that doesn't mean you have to embrace dark ways. You can honor your ancestors, but this is the twenty-first century. You have to bring the best parts of the past into the future." He smiled again. "It was a wise thing for you to do when you passed judgment on Cesar. He did attack you with two lethal weapons, the knife and the big cat. He endangered everyone."

"He isn't one of us. He's something else. So, I asked the police to take him away and for him to be forever banished. He'll have to find his own place somewhere else."

Allen beamed. "See, you are a natural leader."

"It just made sense."

"And you don't need special gifts to lead from wisdom and kindness."

For the first time in a very long time, Allen saw Logan relax and really smile. His small shoulders handled a large burden, but he would grow into his role.

The noise of another vehicle coming up the drive drew both of their attentions away. It was Sandy Lopez's black town car. Allen climbed down off the fence and helped Logan down. The boy raced for the porch as best he could and climbed the steps as the car stopped, and Sandy and Caroline got out.

Allen suddenly felt a churning in his insides. Logan had been nervous about his future, and Allen realized he was, too. Caroline had put on a sky-blue Western dress with a ruffle at the hem. She wore big, red beads, hand-painted with little desert designs, around her neck, and had red, tooled boots on her feet. Her hair had been taken down from its fussy French twist and flowed around her shoulders. As he closed the corral gate and locked it, Caroline sauntered over to him.

"There's a big dance later at the Odd Fellows Hall," she said. "I hear there's a *Norteno* band from Albuquerque playing. It's some big name. The Chris Arellano Band. Ever heard of them?"

"N-no," Allen stuttered. "I mean. Yes, he's a favorite. You know how to *ranchera*?"

Caroline's laugh made him light-headed.

"Is chile hot?" Then she reached up, pulled his face toward hers, and kissed him. "Well, are you going to take me dancing or not?"

THE END

About the Author

Janie Franz comes from a long line of liars and storytellers with roots deep in east Tennessee and honed by the frigid winters of the Northern Plains and the ever-changing landscape of the high desert and mountains of New Mexico. She is an author, a professional speaker, and reviewer. Previously, she ran her own online music publication (Refrain Magazine) and was an agent/publicist for a groove/funk band, a radio announcer, and a yoga/relaxation instructor. Readers' comments welcome at brigidswell@gmail.com

Made in the USA
Coppell, TX
31 March 2022

75789257R00193